THE THIEF'S COUNTESS
BORDER SERIES
Published by ALTIORA PRESS

Printed in the USA.

Cover Design and Interior Format
© The Killion Group Inc

BORDER SERIES

CECELIA MECCA

GET A FREE BORDER SERIES PREQUEL NOVELLA

Thirty years before The Thief's Countess, an arranged marriage set the stage for temporary peace along the Anglo-Scottish border. Learn the story behind Richard and Hugh's friendship in The Ward's Bride.

The best part of writing is building a relationship with readers. The CM Insider is filled with new release information, special offers and other news. Get The Ward's Bride, a free prequel novella to The Thief's Countess, by signing up for the CM Insider at ceceliamecca.com/Insider.

To Mike who has always believed in me.

CHAPTER I

Northumbria, England
1271

"THIEVING BASTARDS." SIR GEOFFREY WARYN wasn't talking to anyone in particular, but his uncle wouldn't let the comment pass.

"Should I remind you this raid was your idea?" Sir Hugh Waryn shouted, riding next to him. "Besides, neither of us should comment on thievery."

Ignoring that last remark, Geoffrey urged his horse to a gallop. He needed to undo what he'd done, and that meant finding the others before the daylight faded. They couldn't be far ahead, but the forest was dense enough to restrict his view.

"There," he whispered. The trees had opened to a small clearing, and there they were, the small gang of reivers Geoffrey and his uncle had aligned themselves with a few weeks earlier. The crisp autumn air filled his lungs as he deliberately slowed his breathing, preparing for the worst.

He should have trusted his instincts and his uncle's counsel. Even among thieves, these men had no honor. The raid had gone well until the lord's young son had made an appearance. Then, before Geoffrey realized what Elliot and his cousins were planning, they'd sped away with the boy in tow.

Stealing cattle was one thing. Geoffrey and his uncle needed resources, badly. Stealing a lad was quite another.

The last thing he wanted was a fight with these men, but he

would not let them kidnap the boy.

Geoffrey easily passed all four mounted reivers, including the one who held the young boy, and angled his horse in front of the front rider. His uncle skirted a massive oak to remain at his side.

"Give him up, Elliot," Geoffrey shouted to the startled man in the lead.

The leader abruptly stopped, leapt from his horse, and grabbed the lance at his side.

Damn. Elliot isn't going to make this easy. Well, neither will I.

A leering grin spread across his former ally's face. "If you want him, take him."

Swinging his own lance into place, Geoffrey decided to make a quick demonstration of the leader as the other men began to dismount from every side. Towering above his opponent, Geoffrey swung his lance, laying the man flat on the ground with two deft strokes. He tossed the lance aside, slipped his dirk from its leather sheath, and held the knife to Elliot's neck. The leader's eyes darted to the other riders, one of whom had dragged the bound and gagged hostage with him toward the fight.

"Don't be stupid. You know exactly how this will end." He had no desire to spill the blood of a fellow Englishman.

But he would.

"Drop your weapons." His tone made it clear that it was not a request.

Geoffrey had a bit of a reputation with his lance, and he wasn't surprised when they tossed their weapons to the ground. "I have no desire to call the Elliot family an enemy, but you go too far."

"Sir Geoffrey." Elliot's eyes darted desperately from him to the hostage. "Think of the ransom."

Geoffrey sheathed his dirk and walked swiftly over to the child. He said nothing as he pulled the boy out of his kidnapper's grasp and lifted him onto his own destrier.

Only then did he turn back to his opponent, who was rubbing his back and attempting to stand. "Elliot, think of your honor."

A ransom that would feed them for months wasn't worth terrifying an innocent young lad. The captive was no more than ten and one, and his eyes were wide and full of tears. Geoffrey's stomach roiled.

Had it really come to this?

"THANK YOU, MILORD."

Geoffrey didn't correct him.

"I'm sorry you were so mishandled, boy." After a short ride, he and Hugh dropped the boy off a safe distance from the search party that had been sent out for him.

Without speaking, Geoffrey followed his uncle's lead as they rode away from the sight of the botched raid. Their mounts expertly navigated increasingly uneven terrain as they headed south into the Cheviot Hills. A steep incline and rocky descent finally gave way to a narrow valley surrounded by mountains on both sides. When they reached flat ground, they exchanged a nod, then dismounted to give their horses a much needed rest.

And resumed the argument that had begun before that evening's doomed attempt to steal a few heads of cattle to feed his siblings and sell to retain mercenaries for their campaign.

"I won't do it." Hugh was the last person Geoffrey wanted to contradict, but the stakes were too high. They'd been building momentum, gathering promises from men to fight along with resources, and this wasn't the time to stop. Five years earlier, Scottish raiders had stolen Geoffrey's home, his inheritance. Everything he and his family owned. And he would not rest until his parents were avenged. "I'm not a nursemaid to be ordered about by Caiser's steward."

When his uncle had received word the day before that his assistance was required at Kenshire Castle, the seat of the Earldom of Kenshire, Hugh had shocked Geoffrey by instantly agreeing to the request. He immediately sent word to Geoffrey's siblings that their return would be delayed.

"What of Lettie and Simon? They need the spoils of this raid."

His mother's aunt and her husband cared for Geoffrey's brothers and sister. They took them in when Bristol was lost, but the small manor could hardly sustain itself even without extra mouths to feed.

"Taken care of. The messenger has been properly compensated to deliver the coin we've earned."

Kneeling beside the stream that crisscrossed the valley, Geoffrey cupped his hands against the current. It would be hours before they next stopped to rest.

When he stood, he turned his eyes to the sky, praying for patience, before he finally met and matched his uncle's stare. He couldn't imagine any mission more important than the one they'd spent the last five years preparing for. This was a distraction they didn't need.

"It's no concern of ours if the lady—"

"Sara," said Hugh.

"Fine, Lady Sara. It's not our—"

Once again his uncle cut him off.

"Actually, it is our concern. As I've said before, Lord Kenshire was a friend." Hugh broke eye contact and turned away, his normally proud shoulders slumping slightly as he spoke. The earl had apparently died after a long illness three weeks earlier, and the man's steward had immediately sent for Hugh. It had taken some time for Kenshire's men to find them, but now that the message had been received, his uncle could not be swayed from his decision to attend to the new countess and help her secure her claim.

"When we were young knights, Lady Sara's father and I met at the very first Day of Truce. In truth, I saved his life. Before he was addressed as 'Your Grace,' —" Geoffrey's uncle turned to him again, his stance daring another interruption, "—we were as close as brothers. Later, our paths took us to separate places. I will help his family now."

Geoffrey tossed the stone he was holding. Just like that, his protests no longer mattered. "But what of the men we've gathered? Nothing—" he stressed the word with as much force as he dared, "—is more important than taking back Bristol." They'd spent years gaining support and promises of aid when it was needed. But rather than build on the momentum they had gathered, his uncle would have him head south, *away* from Bristol.

"I know you're impatient," Hugh said, "but Lady Sara's claim is tenuous. Sir Randolf Fitzwarren believes his claim to Kenshire is strong, and he may have the support he needs to bring an army to Kenshire."

"Fitzwarren? That traitor is Caiser's relative?"

"A distant relation, yes. And desperate for power." Hugh narrowed his eyes. "Lady Sara needs us. I made a promise to her father, and I intend to keep it."

"I'm surprised the earl recognized a man who fought against the king."

"He didn't."

And now he tried to claim Kenshire in the earl's absence. Geoffrey had heard enough. "Then it seems we have no choice. Someday I'll have the full story." He grabbed his horse's saddle to prepare for a ride into the devil's lair. "For now we leave on your command."

He saw his uncle's smirk out of the corner of his eye. What did he have to smile about? Hugh must know their actions would likely be detrimental to them both.

"You win, Uncle," he said, grudgingly resigned to their task. "Let's go start a war."

LADY SARA CAISER WAS RUNNING out of ways to avoid her staff.

She had skipped the morning meal as well as her daily meeting with castle officials, opting for a short ride to the village instead. Discussing castle accounts wasn't her favorite part of the day, but it was still preferable to answering questions about their "guests." Today she'd managed to avoid both thus far. Her good cheer must have shown, because when she walked into the spacious kitchen, Cook said, "It's good to see milady smilin' again."

A flurry of activity greeted Sara. The kitchen staff was scurrying all about, large black cauldrons hung over an open fire and the smell of roasting venison made her mouth water. She reached for a loaf of bread, expecting to get her hand slapped. She wasn't disappointed.

"Breakin' apart a fine loaf before it's cut. Hmph." Cook wiped her hands on her well-worn apron.

Winking at a nearby kitchen maid, Sara reached for the bread again. Making herself sound as pitiful as possible, she said, "I missed breakfast." She tore off the prize and popped it into her mouth.

"Mayhap you should eat with the rest of the household then," the woman replied.

"Perhaps. But how would I avoid Peter then?" She flashed Cook her biggest smile and averted a lecture by making a hasty retreat.

Sara left the kitchen and made her way to Kenshire Castle's main keep. Every step felt heavier than the one before as she approached the ancient stone walls marking the entrance of her home. There was no use in trying to hide from the inevitable. Lifting her blasted skirts so she could climb the stairs, she made her way to the very place she'd been avoiding. The room attached to the lord's chamber was where her father conducted business. Usually it was a spot that lent comfort to her, but not today.

The only person currently occupying Sara's solar didn't waste any time with pleasantries. Her anxious lady's maid began talking as soon as she opened the heavy oak door. "Our guests are expected tonight, milady."

"Tonight?" If her unusually sharp tone startled Faye, her maid didn't react. The middle-aged woman served as a surrogate mother, friend and, at times like these, a much-needed calming influence. She was well-accustomed to Sara's moods.

Faye guided her to a cushioned stool and began brushing the unruly hair the young countess had inherited from her mother.

"I don't care how renowned these men's 'skills' are. I simply refuse." A knock at the door meant she would quickly be outnumbered. Faye stopped her ministrations to allow the entrance of Sara's steward.

"Lady Sara." Peter made his way toward through the solar. "The kitchen has been informed of the altered supper plans. The guests' rooms are being readied as well."

Of course he'd already seen to the preparations. Peter was stocky for his advanced age, and his full grey beard, gruff manner, and proper dress intimidated those who didn't know him. To Sara, he was like the grandfather she'd never had.

Peter seemed to be gauging her response.

She took a deep breath, determined to remain calm. "About our guests," she started, not wanting to take out her displeasure on a man who was only following orders. Her father's orders, no less. "I'd like to speak to you about them."

"Lady Sara, we discussed this. At length. There is no other option."

As they stared at each other, Peter's bushy eyebrows rose. She'd seen that familiar look more often since her father passed away. Sara would not doubt herself this time.

"Peter, we don't need those men. They're reivers. Lawless thugs who murder and steal for sport and take advantage of the uncertainty at the border. The thought of being protected by them is … unacceptable." Once, an English marshal whose manor lay just across the border from Scotland had stopped to seek shelter at Kenshire. Sara still remembered his stories of brutal Scottish and English reivers who cared not for the origins of their victims. Master horsemen despite the mountainous terrain, they spent their days rustling livestock, stealing household goods, and even taking prisoners for ransom. She shuddered at the memory, bringing herself back to the present.

But when she looked to Faye for support, her lady's maid tilted her head to the side, which could only mean one thing. "Lady Sara, you know as well as I do that Sir Randolf will not stop until he has his hands on Kenshire."

"But he has no claim!" It infuriated her that a distant cousin could think the earldom was his for the taking simply because she was a woman. Her father had trained her from early childhood to take care of the earldom. He'd left her in charge many times, and she'd proven herself a competent leader before.

So why did he doubt me in the end? Why send for those men? Why betroth me to the Earl of Archbald?

She tried to push the thoughts from her mind.

"Through misadventures, numerous rejected marriage proposals … my lord gave you more freedom than proper," scolded Faye.

Peter and Faye were only trying to help, but that didn't mean she had to agree with *how* they were trying. Her head hurt from trying to imagine ways she might stop the reivers' arrival. And her impending marriage of convenience, for that matter.

"My lady." Faye resumed her ministrations with the brush. "We've been through this before. I have no authority to give you orders save appealing to you to consider your father's wishes. But murderers for sport? I hardly think the late Lord Kenshire would have had dealings with such men."

"And if I may," continued Peter, "marriage to Lord Lyonsford isn't a fate worse than death as you'd have us believe."

"Not unless one has no desire to marry an elderly gentleman." She couldn't keep the mockery out of her voice. "His 'vast lands' and 'favored countenance' aside." It was an old argument, but not one that had been settled to anyone's satisfaction.

Neither Peter nor Faye replied. Sara gathered her freshly brushed hair to one side, giving Faye a tight smile of thanks.

"My lady," Peter sighed, "please don't look at us that way. At your age, as an earl's daughter, 'tis a wonder you've not been wed three times over."

Faye nodded. "Lady Sara, earl's daughters simply don't marry for love. But that doesn't mean you won't share affections with Lord Lyonsford."

"And as for our visitors," Peter added, "you must remain Countess of Kenshire until your wedding day."

What was the point of arguing? Everyone in the room knew how it would end. She would be married to the Earl of Archbald, and these border thieves her father had summoned would come to protect her in the meantime.

She was in charge of an entire household—a village!—but not herself.

Sara closed her eyes, not wanting to look at their expectant faces. She was the Countess of Kenshire, but Faye and Peter had a talent for making her feel like a wayward child. Her father would never have let anyone sway him from his decisions.

But he was the one who had wished for both of these things—the engagement and the reivers—and now he was gone.

She stood, smoothing the front of her deep green overcoat, picking imaginary stray threads off its silver lining. "When do they arrive?"

Both Peter and Faye looked more than a little relieved.

"Anytime now, my lady," Peter beamed.

"Then thank you for preparing the kitchen. Let's be about our day."

She made a quick decision as she watched Peter and Faye exit the room. Sara made her way through the door that adjoined the bedchamber. From the ornate trunk in the corner, which had belonged to her mother, she selected a soft white cloak with a fur-lined collar.

Wrapped up in the cloak, she crept quietly to the great hall and then exited through a side door adjacent to the hall. Though she felt a tad guilty about escaping preparations for the second time that day, she knew her advisors would ensure all was ready for her unwanted guests.

The cloak protected Sara from the crisp air that always accompanied the change in seasons. She was grateful for it as she made her way down a path known only to a few. The "sea path," her father had called it. A gateway to the North Sea.

Eventually she found herself walking through tall grass, her feet sinking deeper into the gritty sand with each step.

How did he do it?

When he was alive, her father had been both reticent and giving, uncompromising and yielding. Somehow he'd demanded respect without asking for it, and he'd always made the right decision. Or so it had seemed.

How?

She straightened her back, resisting the tingle in her cheeks. She would not cry. Her duty was to the hard-working people who lived and worked on the unforgiving coast of Northern England. They needed her to do everything in her power to retain her title. There were so many dangers for her in Northumbria—at least until she had a husband. The border. The Scots. Sir Randolf Fitzwarren, that vile usurper who tried to steal Kenshire from under her.

For her people, she'd accept Lord Lyonsford. For them, she'd allow the reivers to stay at the keep.

But that didn't mean she had to like it.

CHAPTER 2

AFTER CHANGING INTO A BRIGHT crimson surcoat adorned with as many gems as she could tolerate, which wasn't many, Sara slowly approached the second floor stairway. The guests had arrived—Faye had come upstairs to tell her so. She willed herself to remain calm, but she already longed for her typical attire. The low-hanging sleeves of the surcoat were undeniably stylish, but they were hardly practical for anything more than folding her hands in front of her. With the announcement her "guests" had arrived, Sara willed herself to remain calm.

This is what Father wanted.

Sara caught her first distant glimpse of Hugh and Geoffrey Waryn as she descended the stairs leading to the great hall. Her eyes were immediately drawn to the nephew. Luckily, she reached the bottom before getting a better look at the man. She would surely have tripped and thoroughly embarrassed herself had she seen him any earlier.

Sir Geoffrey was easily the most handsome man she'd ever laid eyes on. With jet-black hair, broad shoulders, and a more imposing height than any other man in the room, he commanded attention. Sir Geoffrey's square, hard-set jaw—clean-shaven, unlike most of his peers—and obvious confidence lent him an air of superiority at odds with his station.

Pretending composure she didn't feel, Sara slowly approached the men. She lifted her head, ignoring her warm cheeks, and clenched her fingers to steady her hands. Clear blue eyes of steel locked with her own, boldly and without reserve. As Sir Geoffrey continued to stare, her chest tightened in a peculiar way.

Not daring to hold his gaze any longer, she took in the nearly equally imposing figure of his uncle. Age had not diminished his erect posture. In many ways, the uncle was an older version of the nephew.

Thank the heavens she wasn't yet expected to speak. Sara was sure her voice would betray the odd sensations assaulting her.

Before Peter could introduce the men as decorum dictated, Sir Geoffrey stepped forward to close the gap between them and knelt before her. Bringing her hand to his lips, he gently kissed it. She'd been greeted this way many times before, though never by a man she'd just met.

Somehow, the greeting felt different, more intimate than any other.

She held back a rebuke and warned off Peter with a glance.

"Lady Sara, my uncle and I are pleased to make your acquaintance." She separated her weakened legs ever so slightly to get a better foothold. Sir Geoffrey's finger caressed her palm as he brought his lips to it, but the feeling was so fleeting she wondered if she'd imagined it.

Gesturing for him to stand, she stepped backward, hoping distance would help dampen her reaction to him. Letting out her breath, Sara accepted a greeting from Sir Hugh, who also knelt before her but did not kiss her hand.

Finally trusting her voice, which thankfully sounded strong, she welcomed both men. "Good day, gentleman. Come, I've had rooms prepared."

So much for sounding calm.

"I'm sure you'd like time to rest and refresh before the meal."

"Thank you, my lady," Sir Hugh said. "We'll gladly take you up on your offer. Geoffrey and I made great haste traveling here."

Sara kept her gaze fixed on Sir Hugh, not daring to look at the nephew.

"Please accept our condolences on your father's passing. He was a good friend and a better man."

"Thank you, Sir Hugh."

Not a hint of nervousness. Mayhap she'd get through this greeting after all.

"I'd like to offer my condolences as well, my lady." His voice was deep and strong.

Sara turned to accept Geoffrey's offer, studying the contrast between his black hair and ice blue eyes. "Thank you."

Dangerous.

It was not as though Kenshire's retinue lacked for handsome men. Her dear friend William, though she thought of the knight as a brother, was unusually good-looking.

But even he didn't compare to this … thief. He was perfect.

Allowing Faye to show them to the private rooms that had been prepared for them above the great hall, Sara watched as they disappeared from view. Peter had insisted on the courtesy despite their station. The reivers were here, he'd admonished, to protect her. That fact earned his respect despite her reluctance. Peter and Faye accepted them because her father had decreed it. She was not so convinced.

Sara would not allow Sir Geoffrey's handsome face to distract her from the fact that he was the last person in the world who should be protecting Kenshire.

How exactly did her father come to trust Hugh Waryn? She'd met him a few times as a girl but couldn't recollect anything to shed light on the important station he now occupied. Sara refused to doubt her abilities to hold Kenshire.

A short time later, Sara was wearing a new outfit—equally unsuited to actual movement—and sitting in her usual place on the dais. She watched as her guests were seated at one of the trestle tables beneath her. From the good cheer of their dinner companions, it seemed she was the only one with reservations about hosting the reivers. Trying hard to avoid Sir Geoffrey's gaze—moments earlier Sara had caught him staring unabashedly at her—she shifted her attention to the room around her. Much to her satisfaction, the great hall displayed a woman's touch everywhere, from the lilac-scented rushes on the floor to the intricately woven wall tapestries that kept out the coastal chill.

It currently boasted the welcoming scents of venison and freshly baked bread.

Unfortunately, her attention kept returning to Sir Geoffrey. The man was insolent, his manners exactly what she'd expect of an out-of-favor knight who made a living by stealing from others. *Kissing my hand before being introduced?*

To be fair, he and his uncle appeared almost civilized at the moment. She just couldn't reconcile her father's hardened sense of morals with his decision to invite these men to their home. Reivers roamed the land, taking from others and terrorizing innocents.

"Lady Sara," asked John, the cupbearer. "More wine?"

Not one to overindulge, she was quite surprised to see she'd drained her glass.

"I didn't realized there was a hole in this goblet." She nodded to indicate she'd have another serving.

"My lady, you must have accidentally switched goblets with Maude." John nodded toward the young wife of an older knight who was known for her propensity for wine.

She laughed, grateful to concentrate on something other than her non-existent appetite.

DOZENS OF MEN AND A handful of women were dining in the great hall, which was designed to hold a large retinue. But the ordinary sounds of the meal couldn't quite dull Lady Sara's laughter. It felt as if she were close enough to be sitting on his lap.

A dangerous thought.

When Geoffrey looked up to the dais, his hostess's transformation amazed him. Gone was the serious, dark-haired young woman with the weight of the world on her shoulders, replaced by a dazzling, carefree maiden. Simple but elegant, her pale yellow overcoat seemed to match her mood. Only the low-hanging sleeves offered a clue to her elevated station. Her deep-set eyes crinkled ever so slightly with the laugh, indicating the expression was a common one for her. The urge to touch her high, elegant cheekbones, to caress the delicate skin of her cheek was so strong, it took him aback.

He was still reeling from the way he'd lost control earlier, but he understood why it had happened.

The first moment he saw her, two thoughts had bloomed in his head. The first … Lady Sara was extraordinarily beautiful, every feature perfectly formed, but despite her confident manner, Geoffrey was positive the lady wasn't aware of her effect on those around her.

Second, he had longed for the opportunity to touch her. Never one to second-guess his instincts, that's exactly what he'd done, despite knowing that decorum dictated his uncle make the first move. That simple touch had almost been powerful enough for him to forget his resentment at having to travel to Kenshire in the first place.

Almost.

Once, when he was a lad of ten and eight, Geoffrey had allowed himself to fall in love. The young maid was more beautiful and graceful than her station demanded. Though his father insisted as the eldest brother that he marry for political advantage, Geoffrey began to envision a life with the merchant's daughter. And he would have been prepared to do just that. But the sacking of their village had ended their love—it had ended life as he knew it.

Life was cruel, and love weakened a man. While he had lain with his share of women since then, none had diverted his attention from his mission to reclaim his home. And none had demanded his attention as firmly as the gently bred woman before him, who was even now meeting his gaze. The lady was out of bounds. Betrothed. Noble. The very one they were here to protect.

She was nonetheless enticing, her full lips made to be kissed. Small but well proportioned, her dark features were out of place in this cold, harsh northern climate. Her large brown eyes held his gaze until Geoffrey reluctantly pulled away.

"Geoffrey?'

"Uncle?"

"I asked if you are staying for the entertainment."

Geoffrey was rarely taken off guard. "Your pardon."

"Lad," his uncle said, glancing from him to the dais and then back, "if I were a young buck like you, I'd be having the same thoughts. The pretty maid I knew has grown into a beautiful woman."

Geoffrey knew that tone. And the accompanying stern look. "Your concern is misplaced."

"The music," Hugh repeated, pointing to a lutist setting up nearby.

"Aye, I'll stay. Why do you ask?'

"I need to speak to the steward and want you to keep a close eye. I know Lady Sara is well-guarded, but it can't hurt to be extra cautious."

"How close an eye are you suggesting I keep, Uncle?" He lifted his lips in a small grin.

"Ha!" Hugh clasped him on the back and stood from the bench. "If I didn't know you so well, I'd stay myself to watch you both. I'll trust you to keep watch on her for the remainder of the evening."

"Uncle." He grasped Hugh's arm to prevent him from leaving and leaned close. "We don't belong here. Sitting in this hall. Drinking, listening to music—"

"You're uncomfortable."

"Indeed, I am. We're outsiders here. You can see for yourself that the castle and its lady are well-protected. We should be gathering men, not listening to the lute."

A near-mirror image of him, though more advanced in years and equipped with a bit more padding, Hugh stood his ground. "Go, if you will. My duty is here."

"And my duty is with you." Geoffrey released his hold.

"Be at ease. These last years have been difficult, Geoffrey, and you're as deserving of good food and music as any man in this hall."

Geoffrey watched his uncle amble away and then asked for another mug of ale. If they weren't leaving, he may as well take advantage of the quality of Kenshire's brew.

"Is it true you're a reiver?" the young knight next to him asked, motioning for the serving maid.

"Aye." Ale in hand, Geoffrey tried his best to take Hugh's advice and enjoy the evening.

"I knew a man, a mercenary, who lived so close to the border he could spit into Scotland."

"Is he still alive?"

"Nay. He joined with a local family when his pa's entire livestock was stolen. Last I heard, his whole village had been burnt to the ground."

"Sounds familiar."

But the boy's affinity for his fallen companion must not have run deep. He'd apparently already lost interest in their discussion and was flirting with the girl as she filled his mug.

Glancing up at the dais, Geoffrey noticed the countess was making her way down from it. Without thinking, he rose and followed her from the hall.

"My lady." Either she didn't hear him or pretended not to. Sara continued to climb the stairs leading to the upper chambers.

He wasn't used to being ignored.

SARA'S HEART RACED. WHILE SHE loved the lute, she couldn't bear to be on display tonight, nor could she bring herself to care about appearing rude by leaving before her guests. Everything had changed at once—her father, the engagement to Lord Lyonsford, the reivers—and it was all simply too much. And housing retainers meant a castle brimming to capacity. While she was grateful for the extra men, she longed for a more peaceful, quiet keep.

"Lady Sara." Approaching from behind, Sir Geoffrey called to her as she walked onto the gallery above the great hall.

Sara stopped and turned with as much decorum as she could

muster given her wildly beating heart. "Sir Geoffrey, how can I be of assistance?" she managed to say.

He seemed to weigh his answer carefully before speaking. "I was asked to watch you, my lady," he finally said. "'Tis why my uncle and I have come to Kenshire."

His intent gaze unnerved her. Sara turned toward the banister, listening as the lutist began to play beneath them, watching her father's people … nay, her people. "I apologize for retiring early, sir, but it's been a long few days." She was proud her voice betrayed not a hint of the nervousness she felt.

"I understand, my lady. But my uncle swore an oath to your father that we mean to uphold. I'd like to talk to you about our role while we wait for Lord Lyonsford to arrive."

Sara winced at the mention of her betrothed. "Perhaps in the morn after mass would be a better time?" Although her words spoke of dismissal, she made no move to leave.

"I'll speak plainly, my lady. We rode here in haste. Your steward asked my uncle to spare no time in traveling to Kenshire Castle to protect you from Sir Randolf. As his eldest nephew, I've accompanied him to do just that. For better or worse."

Sara could only imagine what he meant by that. Her defenses up, she turned from the railing to face him head on. "While I appreciate your loyalty to my father, let me be plain as well. This castle and I are well-defended against any potential threat."

As they squared off, Sara started to rue that second cup of wine. She felt unsteady, off-kilter. But when Geoffrey continued to stare at her rather than politely deferring to her dismissal as any trained knight ought to do, she began to wonder if it was the wine's doing at all. The man before her was stubborn and insolent. And breathtaking. And also a bit of a mystery. He was well-dressed for a reiver, the bright white of his linen shirt unusual for a man on the run, and his manner resembled that of a highborn lord rather than a lawless thief.

Something about him made her feel reckless.

"Do you intend to follow me into my bedchamber to fulfill this vow?"

His expression instantly changed, and she regretted the hastily uttered words. She could hear her father's voice. *Sara, you spend too much time in the stables listening to the lads' wagging tongues.*

"Nay, milady." His darkened eyes and slowly spoken words sent a strange shiver through her. "But I would like to discuss our quarters."

Sara, normally quick-witted, had no retort.

"Is that your lady's maid searching frantically for you?"

She followed his gaze to the festivities below.

"Aye, I left without word." Sara grinned, wondering if Faye would resort to looking under the trestle tables for her.

"Why did you leave so early?" he asked.

She'd be well within her rights if she refused to offer an explanation, but she decided to give him one anyway. One that skirted the truth while not embracing it.

Leaning slightly on the balustrade overlooking the hall, she gestured to the activity below. "These people, Sir Geoffrey, many of whom who have been in our family's service for years, counted on my father for their well-being." Sara warmed to her topic. "The hundreds of knights sworn to service and those beyond these walls who've lived here for generations now rely on me."

She paused, noticing Faye had temporarily given up her search in favor of speaking to John, the cupbearer, and chanced a glance at Sir Geoffrey. He stood straight, his jaw set, waiting for her to continue. Sara temporarily lost her train of thought.

Perhaps a dose of the truth was warranted after all. "I cannot afford any distractions." This man was most certainly a distraction. "My duty is to be on guard, ensuring all is ready for Lord Lyonsford's arrival." She would be surprised if her cheeks weren't at least slightly pink.

"Which is exactly why I need to be moved closer to your personal quarters," Sir Geoffrey said. "My uncle is in your father's debt. As an extension of that debt, I'll give my life, if necessary, to protect you."

Just as she was starting to think him noble, he added, "But

make no mistake, I'm not happy about it."

"Be that as it may, Sir Geoffrey, perhaps it's best you move on and allow Kenshire to defend itself."

For the second time that day, Sir Geoffrey grabbed her hand and forced her to face him. She should have pulled her hand back immediately—propriety dictated it—but she did not.

"We are here to stay," he insisted. "Unfortunately my uncle has asked I guard your person as he assists with the gatehouse fortification."

This was the closest she'd been to him. Closer than she'd planned to allow herself. He had a battle-hardened face, the evidence in a faint mark extending from his cheek to his lower jawbone, a scar she hadn't noticed before. His hand, calloused and strong but also warm and protective, held hers tightly.

"In that case—" Sara finally pulled her hand free. "We'll make the best of a situation neither of us desires."

His eyes darkened once again, or perhaps the way they narrowed only made the light blue color appear shadowed. He might not desire the situation, but she could tell he did desire her. Sara nearly forgot herself as they continued to stand closer than was proper. She should be appalled, even nervous, but was neither.

"Aye." His voice was low, reverberating.

"I'll ask for your things to be moved to a chamber closer to my own."

"The empty one across the hall."

Startled, it was Sara's turn to narrow her eyes at him.

"I'd ask how you know the chamber is empty, but I have a feeling you're privy to more information than I would like."

Why did he look guilty?

"You've already made arrangements to sleep there." It was stated as a fact rather than a question—she didn't expect a response, nor did she receive one. Disliking the turn of their conversation, she nodded her head and quickly walked away. She'd speak to Peter, the traitor, in the morning. The high-handedness of men never ceased to amaze her.

But Peter's misguided loyalties would have to wait. For now, other thoughts occupied her mind.

CHAPTER 3

SARA PULLED THE BLANKETS CLOSER when she awoke in her pitch-black chamber. Grief welled up inside her, filling her eyes with tears.

She'd dreamed about her father again, about the conversation they'd had the evening before he left this world.

Lord Kenshire had been desperate to make her to understand the precarious position his illness had put her in.

"I raised you with more freedom than I should have," he'd said. "Sara, the man you're betrothed to is an honorable one. It's rumored his first marriage was a love match, and he treated his wife well. He'll do the same with you, and then Randolf will have no claim on Kenshire."

"But Father…"

"Nay, save your arguments. I know them well. You have a claim, but a tenuous one. We're lucky the king has agreed to the match instead of arranging for you to be a ward of the crown. In the eyes of the law, though not my own, you're a mere woman. Randolf has the ear of the Earl of Covington. We need his support."

"Papa, please—"

"I will ask the same of you." His eyes had looked so tired. It had clearly been a struggle to keep them open. "Please."

It had been impossible to resist him. She'd known all too well that her beloved father was dying. The physician had warned her it could be any day.

"Aye, Father, I'll obey." She'd laid down her head so her

father could stroke her hair. It was then she'd realized tears were streaming down his face.

It was the first time Sara had ever seen her father cry.

Before the next sunset, Lord Kenshire was gone and Sara's life thrown into turmoil. She'd never known her mother, the woman who died giving birth to her, but her father…

Peter had sent for Lord Lyonsford immediately, but a messenger had informed them weeks later that the earl was out of the country on crusade. In the meantime, Sir Hugh Waryn and his nephew would arrive to "see to her safety."

Her eyes heavy, Sara attempted to fall back to sleep, but thoughts of a strong hand grasping her own kept her awake. That simple touch had held so much sensual promise.

She couldn't sleep.

Though it was much earlier than when Sara normally rose from her bed, she climbed out of the covers. The air was crisp and cool. The fire had died hours earlier since Faye didn't sleep in her bedchamber. The arrangement was unusual for a lady of Sara's station but wasn't unheard of at Kenshire. Privacy, coveted in any castle, was a luxury her parents had insisted on, which had prompted the construction of additional rooms.

Her thoughts heavy, Sara dressed herself simply since Faye wasn't due for some time.

Rather than leave the room, she made her way to the small glass window and stood watching the sky as it began to lighten. Sara always vowed to wake in time to see the sun rise, but rarely managed to do so despite the fact that most of the other castle inhabitants were up and ready to start their daily routine by the time the sun peeked its head above the horizon. She was grateful for the moment of peace this morning, but as she watched the waves crash on the nearby shore, she felt as powerless as the grains of sand being pulled out to sea. For once she wished she could be the wave, a powerful force to be reckoned with, rather than a speck on the beach waiting to be swept away.

Her unconventional father was to blame for these thoughts. He had often warned her to understand that her independence may be seen as a threat to others.

Reluctantly turning from the window after a time, she walked to the door, opened it, and

nearly screamed.

"What in God's name are you doing?"

Sir Geoffrey rose from the floor and gave her a slight bow, his expression inscrutable. "Waiting for you."

"And why, may I ask, are you waiting for me outside my bedchamber?" More than a touch shrill, Sara's voice sounded matronly even to her own ears. To think, he had been sitting out here, so close, while she thought about his strong hands...

"That should be obvious, milady, given my role here at Kenshire."

"Your role is to help protect Kenshire."

"Aye, but we both know treachery can take down a castle even this well-fortified," Geoffrey said with a yawn.

"Are you accusing my people of something?"

"Nay, not accusing. Just stating a fact."

She took a deep breath, attempting to compose herself. She was a countess, not some silly shrew, tongue-tied when the conversation turned tenuous.

"Be that as it may, sir..."

Geoffrey's hard stare gave way to a small grin.

That smile made her fumble her words. Sara could have kicked the man for making her feel so foolish.

"As I was saying, Sir Geoffrey, guards do not simply station themselves outside my door. You'll find a man at the top of the stairs, plenty close to protect me should something happen. This just won't do."

Rather than reply, Geoffrey leaned back against the stone wall and crossed his arms.

They stared at each other. But before either could break the charged silence, Sara's maid came rushing around the corner. "My lady, I heard your voice and ... oh!"

Spying Geoffrey, Faye stopped in her tracks. She looked from Sara to her protector, hesitant to interrupt a private conversation. "Your pardon, Lady Sara." Faye turned and began to shuffle away.

"Nay, Faye, return to me. We're finished here. Sir Geoffrey and I were merely discussing the terms of his *protection*." She glanced at the man in question, trying to read his face. It was inscrutable.

"I'll fetch Anna to attend to your chamber, my lady." Faye walked away quickly, prompting Sara to glare across the hall at her protector.

"You frightened my maid." This time it was she who folded her arms accusingly.

"You give me too much credit."

Why is he smiling?

"It wasn't a compliment."

"It sounded like one."

"So, frightening maids is an accomplishment to a man of your station?" She hadn't meant to sound quite so angry.

Ignoring her question, he asked one of his own. "Why are you still unmarried?"

"Pardon?" Her tone was as impolite as his question had been.

"Most maids of your age at twenty and two are already mothers."

His impertinence was maddening. "As if the reason for my state of matrimony is any of your concern! I have nothing more to discuss with you. Now, if you'll excuse me, I must be off to morning mass."

"I don't take mass each morning," the reiver said. Oddly, he appeared to be enjoying their verbal sparring, and his tone was anything but deferential.

Sara was finished attempting any modicum of politeness.

"I'm not sure why that should concern me." Walking away, she felt rather than heard him follow. "And I can't say I'm surprised."

"Where you go, I go. But I'd prefer to dispense with daily mass if you don't mind."

Sara whirled around, prepared to tell Sir Geoffrey her opinion on that particular request. She could not remember ever hosting a more rude and forthright guest at Kenshire Castle.

Well, that might not be exactly true.

They'd had their fair share of men willing to step outside the bounds of propriety to secure the hand of the fairest maid in Northumbria. Most ladies refused to reside along the tumultuous border, so Sara could only assume she'd earned the ridiculous title by default.

"Then feel free not to follow me, sir!" Her breath quickened as she imagined Sir Geoffrey at her heels all day. The thought, and her reaction to it, only angered her more. "If you're here to play lady's maid, so be it. But if you think I'll alter my routine simply because you're a heathen, you're sorely mistaken."

After she made this impassioned speech, she heard a gasp behind her and whirled around to find Peter.

"My lady?"

She refused to be embarrassed by her behavior. Peter hadn't heard the reiver's previous comments.

"Good morrow, Peter. I was just excusing myself to mass."

EXCUSING? MORE LIKE MARCHING.

Nodding to Peter, Geoffrey strode after the countess and prepared to wait for her outside the small chapel. He was looking around with a critical eye, taking in the sights and sounds of Kenshire's inner bailey, when his uncle approached him.

Looking into Hugh's face, so similar to his own, Geoffrey decided to humor the older man. "Impressive, is it not?"

"Not many days past you cursed me for bringing us here. Your mood seems much improved," Hugh said. There was a twinkle in his eyes. At least someone had been able to get some sleep. Thoughts of a dark-haired countess had interrupted his own.

The men sat in companionable silence as Geoffrey contemplated their role at Kenshire and waited for the lady of the manor to emerge. Sometime later, he broke the silence. "Uncle, mark my words, this won't end well. I've asked around, and while

Sir Randolf's claim on Kenshire isn't strong, he's the only male relative. If the rumors bear any truth, he's firmly in league with the Earl of Covington. He'll be coming. She's in more danger than she thinks."

"Aye," Hugh said with a nod. "Her father knew it as well. With Covington's support, he could very well take Kenshire by force. But we'll do everything in our power to keep Lady Sara safe until Lord Lyonsford arrives. A marriage with a man that powerful is no small thing."

"But it will only protect her if the marriage takes place before Sir Randolf arrives. Why is she still unwed?" He hadn't meant to ask that question. Some urge, perhaps to avoid his uncle's scrutiny, drove him to his feet, and he began to pace.

He watched as Hugh stared at the impressive structure that was the main keep of Kenshire Castle. Its position on a rocky plateau high above the Northumbrian coastline made for a spectacular sight from every angle.

Forgetting his question for the moment—Hugh either didn't know or wasn't inclined to answer—Geoffrey inquired about their temporary home.

"Peter told me a little about the earldom and this estate. It's been in Sara's family since King Henry II bestowed it on her great-grandfather after they suppressed a revolt in Wales."

"All true," Hugh replied, looking back to him. "I was just a lad when the secondary keep was constructed. Richard and I had never seen anything like glass windows or a chimney," he said. "His father, the second Earl of Kenshire, was a most impressive man, very accustomed to being in command. He was appalled by the idea of windows, even small ones." Smiling, Hugh continued, "But if he was impressive, his wife was even more so. She knew proper defenses could mean life or death in a castle situated so close to the border, but the windows were non-negotiable."

So Sara wasn't the only Caiser woman with strong opinions.

"You speak of my grandmother?"

Geoffrey turned in the direction of the voice and saw Sara

walking toward them as graceful as a queen.

"Aye, Lady Sara, I was telling Geoffrey about your grandfather's renovations to the keep."

She looked curiously at Hugh. "You were here when it was built?"

"I was," he answered, looking pleased with the memory.

Lady Sara smiled. She obviously found Hugh's company more pleasant than his own. He watched the two as they spoke of times long since past. Their talk couldn't help but remind him of his own history. His grandfather's feudal barony was no earldom, but it had been earned in battle. It was honorable, but unlike Kenshire, which had obviously flourished through the years, Bristol Manor was now in the hands of his enemy.

Meanwhile, he sat here playing lady's maid, as the countess had so neatly pointed out. Scowling, he caught a question which piqued his interest.

"Sir Hugh, you speak intimately of my family, but we've only met on a few occasions."

"A long, boring story," he smiled gently, moving toward her. Geoffrey was all too familiar with that soft yet firm tone, "My lady, we're here to protect you. I know you feel you don't need protection, and Kenshire is indeed impressive. If attacked by Sir Randolf, I've no doubt your men would be victorious. Your father and grandfather saw to that. But my nephew and I are here at your father's request. He saved my life, and I'll not leave until you're safe."

Geoffrey considered intervening but knew his uncle wouldn't appreciate it.

Better to remain silent when you have nothing of value to add.

His father's advice.

Both he and Sara waited patiently for Hugh to continue. He studied the hard lines etched into his uncle's face, which were a stark contrast to Lady Sara's smooth complexion. She may have momentarily forgotten Geoffrey's presence, but he had not taken his eyes off her.

"I should have made myself clearer yesterday when we arrived,"

Hugh said. "Sir Randolf may come to lay claim to Kenshire not only with a retinue of his own men, but also with the backing of someone more powerful."

Geoffrey broke his silence. Lady Sara needed to fully grasp the threat Randolf posed. Hugh was being too delicate.

"If he brings support of his claim from the Earl of Covington," Geoffrey interrupted as Hugh and Sara shifted their attention to him, "you'll be fighting a political battle as well. One which could see Sir Randolf as the next Earl of Kenshire. And you in his service, at best."

Sara straightened her back as though she meant to take on Randolf and an army herself. If she had forgotten his presence earlier, she remembered it now. Lady Sara stared at him as though he was the one trying to wrest the earldom from her.

"I will never—" She paused and narrowed those big brown eyes. "Allow that to happen."

He believed her.

CHAPTER 4

THE INFURIATING MAN ACTUALLY INTENDED to follow her everywhere she went. Sara walked from the chapel back to the keep with a mixture of excitement and foreboding, determined to go about her day as normally as possible.

However, the situation she had found herself in was anything but normal, and she wasn't stubborn enough to believe otherwise.

Perhaps she should simply accept the reivers' presence. After all, their goal was the same as hers. To keep Kenshire. Once she was married, she knew it was unlikely she and her southern husband would spend much time in the borderlands. But at least her people would be safe. It was the only thing that truly mattered.

Still, the thought of marrying that man…

Growing up, Sara had always known she would one day marry for advantage. The Caiser family was one of the most powerful in Northern England. She was the fourth generation to inherit the earldom, her great-grandfather having secured the title from England's king.

But knowing and doing were vastly different.

Sara made her way through the hall to the kitchen, where preparations for the morning meal were already underway. When she stopped abruptly to readjust an off-center trestle table in the great hall, she was nearly knocked to the ground from behind. Before Sara could topple into the table, someone caught her. *Him*.

"Really … if you weren't walking so closely—" Sara fully

intended to give her protector an earful, but the words caught in her throat as he pulled her upright.

Geoffrey kept his hand firmly in place around her wrist.

"I…" Sara had no idea what she'd been about to say. She could only think of his firm grasp on her.

"Yes?"

Sara was appalled not only by how often this man had touched her, but by her own reluctance to pull away, as if she had not been bred a gentlewoman but instead a wanton, letting a perfect stranger grope her at every turn. Seconds ticked by—it felt more like hours—as she looked into his eyes. She couldn't remember ever seeing a more brilliant shade of blue.

The spell was broken a moment later. The minstrel who had played so expertly the evening before had entered the hall.

"My lady, a word?"

Sara forced a smile as she turned toward the bright colors of the musician's garb. A prior obligation allowed him only a few days respite at Kenshire—more the pity. She had a particular fondness for the lute, and she and her father had always agreed that music brought a welcome cheeriness to the long winters in the north.

"Pardon me." Geoffrey attempted to take his leave, but the minstrel stopped him.

"Sir, if you will. A word with you both would be greatly appreciated."

Sara gave him a curious glance. *What could he possibly want with Sir Geoffrey?*

"I'm writing a ballad about a woman named Phillida who doesn't return the attentions of a man—a knight of the realm." The man's high-pitched voice and quick speech gave away his nervousness.

Sara caught the raised eyebrows of her companion.

"As the song is about a lady and a young knight, I thought mayhap you could lend some insight?" the minstrel pressed.

Although she adored the traveling minstrels who made their way through Kenshire, the man's question reminded Sara of why her father refused to retain permanent musicians. Their code of conduct, he'd often said, differed from what most considered polite conversation. She, however, enjoyed their creativity and was happy to help.

"What seems to be giving you trouble, sir?"

Ignoring the great bulk of a man beside her, who was barely hiding his contemptuous gaze, Sara smiled kindly at the bald, plump minstrel.

"Well, my lady, the woman of my story tells her knight, 'Maids must kiss no men' when he attempts to steal one from her. But it seems I'm stuck on the next verse."

Sir Geoffrey made a grunting noise neither she nor the musician could ignore.

"I should ask *you* then," the man said to Sir Geoffrey, "do you think my knight should acquiesce and admire from afar or press his suit?"

Sara's father would be mortified by this open talk of courting and kisses.

"Do you often need advice to compose your ballads?" Sir Geoffrey scoffed.

The minstrel looked embarrassed, and Sara could have kicked the barbarian for having asked such a question.

"What Sir Geoffrey means to say is that while he may be a knight, the intricacies of courtly love clearly elude him."

The knight in question stared at her then, slowly uncrossing his arms but continuing to raise thick black eyebrows at them both.

"Perhaps you should be about your business, Sir Geoffrey," she added. "We can manage without your assistance."

His voice like a caress, the reiver gave his opinion regardless of her dismissal. "Courtly love or nay, your knight should find another fair maid for his attentions."

The minstrel tilted his head, inviting an explanation. Sir Geoffrey did not give one.

Sara knew she shouldn't ask, but sometimes her tongue was not connected to her sense of reason. "Why do you say so, Sir

Geoffrey?" she asked, the words seeming to tumble out of their own volition.

"Why should he pursue her if she has no interest?"

At least he had the decency to look sincere. Her experience with love was limited to minstrels' ballads, but Sara refused to believe he could be so callous. Surely love was worth fighting for. She believed it, even though her own loveless marriage awaited on the horizon.

"Because he cares for her?" she pressed.

"Nay, Lady Sara. He desires her. And he can just as easily desire another."

Spoken like a man without morals. Sara suddenly realized they were alone.

"Where is the minstrel?"

"He must have found his answer." His sardonic reply revealed a barely discernible dimple.

"Well, I'll be curious to hear his tale this eve."

And for the second time in the space of one afternoon, Sara found herself looking into the most mesmerizing set of eyes God had ever gifted to any man.

She felt exposed. Flushed.

"I can tell you how it ends, if you like," he said, still staring into her eyes.

"Clearly you have experience in such matters." She really should stop talking.

"You believe so?"

The conversation needed to end, but damned if she'd be the one to end it.

"I didn't mean it like that. What I meant was that..."

"I know what you meant."

Sara could feel her own heartbeat. Gently bred but not naïve, she sensed the connection between them. But it was one that needed to be cut short. "Excuse me," she said.

At the same time Geoffrey said, "I'm sorry for nearly knocking you down."

This man who lived outside the law had no business making

her feel anything other than wary. And yet, as they stood inches apart, Sara had the most ridiculous impulse to move closer. Which, of course, she did not. Blinking her eyes, hoping to shut out such thoughts, Sara said, "Thank you for your gallant rescue."

Her words were more lighthearted than she felt.

"My lady," Geoffrey reproved, his voice deep and strong, "I'm far from gallant. You'd do well to remember that."

With those terse words, he turned from her and walked toward the exit of the hall. She watched his retreat, attributing her unmaidenly appreciation of his perfectly formed backside to her inability to think straight. Looking down, Sara was appalled to see her hands trembling slightly. So *this* was attraction, the kind non-noble ladies were allowed to pursue.

Fierce and unbridled.

Sara wondered if she would feel the same for Lord Lyonsford. It seemed unlikely.

Cursing herself, she drew deep breaths in an attempt to soothe her frayed nerves. She shouldn't have been so forthright with a virtual stranger. While she had never been the type to strictly adhere to the expectations of a proper lady, she nevertheless knew exactly what those expectations were.

She didn't like feeling so unsettled, so out of control.

When had she sat down? Sara stood and began her morning duties as chatelaine, vowing to stay as far away as possible from the man who was responsible for her unease.

SIR GEOFFREY KNEW THE LAST thing he should do was waste time thinking of the pampered countess, but she confused him. Her gown was so much simpler and less adorned than the ones typically worn by women of her station. When he'd saved her from the impending fall, he'd felt the fabric press up against his skin. There'd probably been nothing but a chemise and a layer of cloth between his hand and her flesh. And when they'd looked into each other's eyes, Geoffrey had felt, not for the first time, a connection that unnerved him. Without a shred of doubt, she was beautiful, but more than that, he sensed a depth in her which most maids lacked.

Intriguing.

Off-limits.

Geoffrey strode purposefully out of the great hall and ran straight into the very man he was seeking.

"Good day, Peter."

Most of the household seemed to have been in the Caisers' service for generations, and Peter was no exception, according to Uncle Hugh.

"My lord," Peter said.

"Nay, sir. Not any longer."

Geoffrey could see the grimace behind the man's thick, greying beard.

"I've no doubt the title will be yours once again."

The man reminded him of his uncle, and Geoffrey couldn't help but admire his loyalty. "It's no secret along the border that we lost the feudal title along with Bristol, but we've not shared that fact with anyone here at Kenshire."

Before Peter responded, a servant approached, making his way around a wagon that had stopped not far from where they stood.

"My apologies, sir," the man said to Peter, "a shipment of spices awaits your inspection."

"I'll be along shortly, thank you."

When the steward turned back to face Geoffrey, he looked as if he wanted to say something. He must have changed his mind, however, because he simply said, "I apologize, my lord. I'm unable to finish our tour of Kenshire. Perhaps this afternoon?"

Geoffrey liked the man well enough, but that did not mean he was going to stand here exchanging pleasantries with him. He needed answers.

"What I'd really like to know is what we're doing here."

If he thought to get a better answer from the steward than his own uncle, Geoffrey was mistaken.

"You're here to protect Lady Sara's claim."

"If Randolf does attack, two are just two more men among a retinue stronger than most."

Peter glanced in the direction of the spice merchant making his way toward them. The man's velvet cloak and silk-lined hood reminded Geoffrey to add, "And I am no lord."

"In the eyes of the law, mayhap not," Peter said, wisely avoiding his question. "Now if you'll excuse me, I must do my duty."

After a quick bow, the second most important person at Kenshire walked away, leaving Geoffrey with more questions than answers. With his uncle overseeing the gatehouse fortifications and Lady Sara safe inside the keep as the household broke their fast, Geoffrey decided that some practice with his sword would suit him better than sustenance.

Once suited, he asked the staff for directions to the training yard. He wasn't surprised when the grunts, yells, and clanging of swords quieted as he approached. Knights, green young boys, and hardened men alike turned to stare at him. Most didn't know what to make of a border reiver turned protector. Hell, he didn't quite know what to make of himself.

He didn't belong here. Or anywhere.

Geoffrey strode through the yard, intent on finding the most highly skilled swordsman. Only by practicing with the best would he hone his own skills. With a few questions and even polite nods, he finally found his man.

He already knew of Sir Jerold, a knight who had served the Earl of Kenshire his entire life, as his father had done before him. The knight had made a name for himself well beyond the castle and its village. Each year during the Tournament of the North—the only time other than the Day of Truce when the English and Scottish, friends and enemies, set aside their differences—Jerold was a favorite, and he'd been the reigning overall champion more than once.

Even if the others hadn't told him which of the knights was best, Geoffrey would have picked Jerold from the crowd. His muscles bulged beneath his thin linen shirt, a sign of years of hard, dedicated practice, and the fact that he wore no armor, or even chainmail, spoke to his position among the other knights.

"Sir Jerold, care for a bit of practice?" Geoffrey asked.

The bearded knight, almost as large as he was, glanced around them. There were at least forty men in varying states of dress watching them. Several shouted encouragement to Sir Jerold.

"It seems I have no choice."

"You've always a choice. But if you'd rather not fight a reiver…"

"Knight, reiver, king. It matters naught to me."

A young squire handed each of them rebated swords. Most reivers favored the lance over the broadsword, but Geoffrey regularly practiced with both.

A smile spread across Geoffrey's face as the match began. Sir Jerold wielded his sword with deadly precision, and he had an easy grace for such a large man. They were well matched, but Geoffrey still had no doubt that he would win. Both of them had clearly benefited from years of devoted practice and natural skill; only one of them had a determination bred from a desire for vengeance. In feats of strength and skill, Geoffrey had never been beaten.

SARA, HAVING QUICKLY CHANGED AFTER her discussion with Sir Geoffrey, was finishing a light meal of freshly baked bread when she heard shouts coming from the courtyard.

As she made her way toward the commotion, she looked down at her admittedly odd attire. Would her new guests be there? What would they think of a woman in an altered version of men's breeches? The women in her family often wore them—a tradition dating back to Sara's extremely unconventional grandmother—despite the fact that it was still illegal for a woman to do so. Perhaps she should have let Faye talk her out of changing. Sara looked around for … nay, not Sir Geoffrey … her steward, and found she wasn't the only person both curious and apprehensive about the growing volume of noise from the courtyard. Dozens of people were headed in the same direction.

The shouts grew louder as Sara strode through the bailey and then headed past the stables. The crowd around the training yard was almost impenetrable. When she fought her way to the front, she realized why.

Sara had watched men train many times, though she found it uncomfortable when blood was shed. She herself was passing fair with the crossbow. Her father, who had insisted that she learn at least one skill to protect herself, had spent countless hours overseeing her training. Yet she had never seen anything like *this*.

No one ever defeated Sir Jerold. But apparently that news had not been shared with Geoffrey. He stood over the other warrior in naught but a light jack, his bare arms covered with sweat and dirt, his expression full of confidence and reserve.

Why does he look more like a seasoned warrior? A knight of the realm?

Geoffrey offered an arm to Jerold, who took it in stunned silence. Not used to being beaten, he was clearly both humiliated and in awe.

"Well played," Jerold finally said, lifting himself to his feet.

"Thank you, Sir Jerold. I'm glad to finally have a worthy training partner."

When the other knights and servants who'd gathered began to disperse, muttering reverently about Sir Jerold's defeat, Geoffrey looked up and saw her, his eyes widening in recognition. He stared for a moment, most ungentlemanly, and then nodded as if he'd made a decision. The hunger in his eyes at once excited and unnerved her

"Excuse me," he said to Sir Jerold. Then he made his way to where she stood.

Sara looked for an escape, but before she knew it he had reached for her hand, pulling her away from the crowd.

Protesting, Sara attempted to pull back from the vise-like grip. Rather than explain himself, Sir Geoffrey continued to drag her along, pausing only to hand his sword to one squire and to thank another for the cloth he'd been given to clean himself.

"Sir, I must protest."

She had wasted her breath. Since courtesy hadn't worked, she muttered a quite unladylike curse under her breath, but the cur didn't so much as turn around. He kept walking through the courtyard and inner ward, leading her toward a path few knew existed. Sara clenched her teeth, not sure if she wanted to slap away his hand or revel in the feel of it wrapped around her own.

For reasons she did not quite understand, she followed him.

GEOFFREY HAD MADE IT A priority to learn every inch of Kenshire, seeking out any vulnerabilities in the event Sir Randolf foolishly decided to use brute force to wrangle the title and land from Lady Sara. The battery gate and sea path had been built by the second Earl of Caiser as a secure passage to the coast of the North Sea, or so Sara's steward had told him. The sound of crashing waves and smell of the salt air became stronger as he led Lady Sara down the path. It had been rash of him to lead her away, but the feel of her hand in his, her skin so warm and soft and yielding, assured him he'd made the right decision.

He stopped so abruptly Sara nearly crashed into him. Her hand made contact with his bare arm as he spun around to face her, and Geoffrey knew from the look she gave him there'd be no protest. He reached behind her back to pull her closer, lowered his head and, without further warning, his lips were on hers.

Geoffrey knew this was madness, but he had felt an overwhelming desire to taste the fullness of Lady Sara's lips. He could feel her innocence, a fact that should have penetrated his need to pull her even closer, but he found himself coaxing her lips open with his tongue, raising one hand to the back of her neck to deepen the kiss. To his surprise, she tentatively leaned in.

Forcing himself not to focus on the feel of her breasts pressed against his chest, he moved his lips over hers as his tongue teased with the promise of more. He was determined to give her something to remember when she closed her eyes to sleep that night.

Geoffrey relented only when he felt himself harden.

Pulling back, he gazed into her liquid brown eyes, staring at him with a comely mixture of shock and desire.

"I'd apologize," he said roughly, "but I'm not in the least bit remorseful."

SARA TOOK A DEEP BREATH, but it did not calm her—instead, his masculine scent assaulted her senses. Stunned that he had actually dared to kiss her, she had a hard time reconciling her own feelings. Unlike the chaste kisses she'd experienced in the past, he'd used his tongue to open her mouth, sweeping it inside and touching it to her own. She was preparing to verbally eviscerate Geoffrey when she became aware of his hand on her neck, still in the same spot as when he'd kissed her. Hesitant to interrupt the slow, sensual pressure of his thumb, Sara merely glared back at him, showing rather than telling him she wasn't sorry either.

So much for acting like the countess she'd become.

Instead of explaining himself, Geoffrey lowered his head once again, claiming her mouth with more force this time. Sara's stomach fluttered as his tongue moved expertly with hers. A strange tingling shot from her core through every inch of her body.

With difficulty and indecision, she pulled away.

"Sir—and I use the address loosely—you insult me." Sara thought it was a good start and felt triumphant if somewhat unsteady.

"Insult?" Geoffrey's cock-sure smirk returned with a vengeance. "Make you hot, you mean?"

"I have never..."

"Aye, Lady Sara, I know. 'Twas evident from the way you kissed."

"I won't apologize for my lack of experience." Sara straightened her back, becoming emboldened as she spoke. "You know full well a lady in my station has no right to such a thing."

Geoffrey grabbed her hand once more, striding briskly toward an outcropping of rocks. Reluctant to return to the keep, she followed.

"Aye," he admitted, "I ken it well."

Sara thought briefly about pulling her hand away, but his slight accent startled her.

"You spent time in Scotland?"

"Aye, milady, us thievin' reivers know no borders," he said, slipping into a Scottish brogue.

Sara laughed and Geoffrey glanced sideways at her. "You should laugh more often."

When they reached a long, flat rock, he stopped walking. Turning toward her, he said, "My lady, I have no right to ask you to sit with me, especially after the liberties I took."

She knew she should agree. It would be the proper thing to do, the countess-like thing to do. Yet she found that she was not feeling very countess-like. Without responding with words, she found herself a comfortable position among the rocks, and he sat down beside her.

Sara noticed the sideways glance he gave her attire, and indeed, she was only surprised the conversation hadn't turned toward her wayward appearance earlier. It tended to cause quite a fuss among those unaccustomed to her habits.

Of course, there hadn't been much chance for conversation until now.

"I wore breeches precisely to traipse about the rocks this morn," Sara began, still not sure if she wanted to continue talking, admonish her protector for his actions, or be scooped up in his arms again.

Geoffrey looked squarely at her, his eyes defying her to lie.

"Are you disappointed I joined you?"

"No." Embarrassed by how forthright she'd been, Sara promptly changed the subject. "How did you know about the sea path?"

"I made it my business to know everything there is to know about Kenshire Castle when I arrived."

"Peter told you?"

"Aye, he did. And assured me it was safe despite being outside the castle walls. He claims your sentries can see for miles down the beach on a clear day. Although—" He turned toward the nearest watchtower. "I can't say I'm convinced."

"A point of contention between my father and me. It's good to know Peter has finally taken my side," Sara said, her voice nearly cracking as she thought about the countless arguments she and her father had had about her late night jaunts.

"I'm sorry about your father." The sincerity in his voice startled her.

"Thank you."

For the first time since they'd arrived on the beach, Sara listened to the sound of waves crashing against the shore. Odd she hadn't heard it earlier. That calming, rhythmic sound was what usually led her to this spot in the first place.

"Peter felt comfortable sharing information about our defenses." It was not a question. And she didn't mean to provoke Geoffrey. She meant it in earnest. Peter seemed very convinced of the reivers' value.

"Lady Sara..."

"Sara."

Geoffrey looked at her intently, the question clear in his eyes.

Not one to mince words, Sara got straight to the point. "I didn't want you here. After all..." She cleared her throat, wondering how to broach the topic delicately.

"I understand." It was obvious he meant it, though she sensed resentment in his tone. "I know my profession well," he added.

She considered the man sitting across from her for a moment. In some ways, he looked every bit the ruthless mercenary, and yet ... she'd met knights who'd sold their swords and was always struck by the coldness in their eyes. Geoffrey's lacked that same empty look.

"Be that as it may, I know my father. While it pains me to welcome a virtual stranger into our lives at such a difficult time, my father trusted your uncle without reserve. So that must be enough for me."

"Just so we understand, my lady, I have no desire to be here. With any luck, your betrothed will arrive shortly and Hugh and I can be on our way. But while I'm here, I plan to take this mission seriously."

"I'm your mission, then?"

"Your safety is, yes."

When Geoffrey narrowed his eyes and leaned forward, Sara resisted the urge to inch away. She was intimidated by no one. Or at least tried to convince herself as much.

"Tell me," he finally said, "what would make the daughter of a powerful earl offer a stranger, a reiver, use of her given name?"

Rather than answer immediately, Sara considered how much she should tell him.

Veritas facio semper, she reminded herself. It was their family motto. Her father's favorite saying.

The truth will always do.

CHAPTER 5

"I GIVE YOU LEAVE TO CALL me Sara because—" She hesitated and almost thought better of her characteristic bluntness before deciding to forge ahead. "Because despite my good sense ... I like you."

The admission startled her even as the words tumbled out of her mouth. Sara could sum up all she knew about this man in a few short words. Thief, intense, incredibly good-looking. And yet he made her feel startlingly safe.

Maybe it was the fact that her father had trusted Sir Hugh, and by extension his nephew, with her life. Or could it be Geoffrey's swift perusal and fortification of Kenshire? It certainly wasn't that kiss, however much it had moved her. Nay, kissing this man could only be dangerous for a woman in her position.

As she waited for Geoffrey's response, Sara studied his features. Everything about him was dark: his hair, his tanned complexion, his expression. Everything but his piercing blue eyes. Her gaze was drawn to his strong jaw—a slight tic had developed, making him appear even more menacing than he had moments before.

"And this from a lady who just yesterday said 'we'll make the best of a situation neither of us desires.' Interesting."

That bit of mockery made Sara stand in her own defense.

"Nay, milady." He shook his head, then amended, "Sara."

She slowly sat back down, not wanting to end their conversation.

"I apologize for throwing your words back at you. But you've said on more than one occasion you don't want us here. You spent the better part of the morning sparring with me. I'll admit that I've become a stranger to courtly manners these past years, given my current situation."

"Well, sir—" Her voice sounded curt even to her own ears. "I'd prefer to keep my own counsel, but as you're here and likely to stay until Lord Lyonsford arrives..." Geoffrey scowled at her words. "I thought it prudent to be honest and maybe even call for a truce."

SHE SOUNDED LIKE A QUEEN instructing her court. How Lady Sara managed to play the cool countess and fiery temptress all at once, he wasn't sure. Granted, his experience with women didn't extend to noblewomen, and Lady Sara was the daughter of an earl.

"In that case, *Sara,* please call me Geoffrey." He was pleased to see her eyes widen at that, though she couldn't have expected anything less. After all, he was the outlaw son of a baron. A man without lands. The use of his given name meant little; the use of hers meant much.

"Well, *Geoffrey.*" His name sounded like a caress on her lips. "It seems we've settled on forms of address. And yet I still know nothing about you." Her statement sounded like a question.

"You know the important parts. My occupation. What else would you like to know?"

She squirmed on her makeshift seat, making him intensely aware of her attire. Not accustomed to seeing women in breeches, he silently thanked whoever was responsible for her dress and tried not to stare at the shape of her legs. Interesting. He had never imagined breeches could be so provocative on a woman's form.

"That's precisely what I'm curious about," she said. "How did you ... well, what do you..."

His eyes had strayed to the beach, as they had done throughout their talk, searching it for any possible threats, but he returned his attention to her. "Reivers live simply, moving from place to place depending on the season. We take what we need, give what we can, and fight for survival," he said dispassionately.

"That's a fine speech." She all but rolled her eyes. "But it tells me little."

"Specifically, when word reached my uncle that he was wanted at Kenshire, we were camped just outside the village of Otterburn preparing for a cattle raid. Traveling by moonlight, I might add, takes considerable skill."

Sara gasped. "Are you mad?"

"Nay, milady, we do what we must to survive. It's a busy time of year for my people. The weather is still cooperating and court is out of session."

Appearing more indignant than sympathetic, Sara shifted in her seat. "You're stealing, plain and simple. How can you live with that?"

This time it was Geoffrey who stood. Who was she to judge him? They were both doing what they could to honor their fathers' legacies.

It had been a mistake to kiss her.

"Don't ask about what you don't understand."

Sara stood as well, the mood vastly different than just a few moments earlier.

"Are you coming, *Sara*?"

"Aye." The frosty countess was back, the fiery woman gone.

As they walked, Geoffrey cursed his impatience. His father had often regretted his decision to train Geoffrey as a knight himself rather than send him away to squire. *You're too rash*, he had told him often. And to soften the blow he would add, *As am I.*

Unlike his uncle, his father had always acted first and thought about consequences later. Geoffrey understood the merits of being patient even if he didn't always put it into practice. But the same decisiveness which served him well on the battlefield often made him retrace his steps.

While he regretted his harsh manner, he didn't look back. Nor did he offer an apology. Their mission here was to keep the lady safe, and that's exactly what he'd do. And nothing more.

THANKS TO THE WELL-TRAINED STAFF at Kenshire Castle, they had not been missed. Sara returned to the kitchen to find the noon meal already being prepared and the castle running smoothly.

It was close to the time of year when her father used to depart for a tour of his estates. Their family had amassed quite a few over the years across England. She'd been to all multiple times but preferred her home at Kenshire despite unease at the nearby border and the brutal winters.

It occurred to her, not for the first time, that her life would change quite a bit once she married. It was to be expected that Lyonsford would never approve of her current state of dress or propensity to wield a bow, but she was prepared to fight for visits to Kenshire as often as possible.

What would Geoffrey think about such matters?

A shout interrupted her thoughts.

"We have a visitor, milady." Faye at least was in good spirits.

Her heart plummeted. So he had arrived already. The man she was to marry, the one who held her future in his hands. Geoffrey's kiss flashed through her mind. Her future husband had finally arrived, and she was worried about a reiver? Maybe she should concentrate on the fact that Kenshire was saved. That the man trying to steal her inheritance would be thwarted. Indeed, the more she thought about it, the more she was ashamed to have allowed Geoffrey to take such liberties. A scoundrel, just as she'd suspected. An extremely attractive one, that was all.

"Let's meet Lord Lyonsford, then, and get it over with."

Faye's answer startled her. "'Tis not Lord Lyonsford, my lady, but Lord Thornhurst."

Sara fairly squealed with delight. It had been nearly a year since she'd seen William. "Truly? What brings him to Kenshire?"

"I know not, Lady Sara. He arrived but a moment ago and is

inquiring after you."

Sara glanced down at her breeches, briefly wondering if she should change before greeting him. While William was well-accustomed to her unusual garb, she was loath to take a meal in such a state. Shrugging her shoulders, Sara decided there were bigger issues at the moment than her apparel.

The scene that greeted her in the entrance to the hall was of Sir Hugh vigorously questioning one of her father's best trained and most trusted knights. Squired at Kenshire from a young age, Lord Thornhurst was now castellan of Camburg Castle, a Caiser property near the Welsh border. Travel was dangerous for her, which meant she rarely had an opportunity to visit the small yet pleasant estate, but she always welcomed visits from this knight who faithfully held Camburg in her family's name.

"No need for further questioning, Sir Hugh." Sara approached her old companion. He reminded her of Geoffrey in some ways. Though his hair was light where Geoffrey's was dark, William was as tall and well-muscled. "As my men have surely told you, Lord Thornhurst is a trusted friend."

The man in question spun around and swooped Sara into a brotherly hug, which was how Geoffrey found them moments later.

"My, my, isn't this a pretty scene?"

It was spoken in an ominous tone, and both Sara and William disengaged and turned to stare at the foreboding intruder. Was he always this rude?

"Forgive me, my lady," Geoffrey said, having found his manners. Still, he looked anything but pleased.

"And to whom do I have the pleasure?" William said, his cool tone at odds with his usual carefree manner.

"May I introduce Sir Geoffrey Waryn, nephew of Sir Hugh, whom you've already met. Sir Geoffrey, this is Lord Thornhurst, castellan of Camburg Castle, a friend and trusted servant of the Caiser family."

Geoffrey nodded and said, "Welcome, Lord Thornhurst. Kenshire could use a knight of your reputation."

It didn't surprise Sara that Geoffrey was aware of William's exploits on the Welsh border. He was making quite a name for himself.

"Thank you, Sir Geoffrey," William answered, his eyebrows furrowed. The charged atmosphere made her want to stand between the two men.

She needn't have worried. Leading William into the great hall, Geoffrey inclined his head in dismissal, leaving her to gape at his transformation. She couldn't quite reconcile the many sides of his character. There was the rude retainer, the gallant companion, and the man who had kissed her so passionately. And there it was again, the memory of that kiss. She felt her face flush.

"So, tell me more about Lord Thornhurst," Hugh said, interrupting her thoughts. "I remember the boy but don't know the man."

Sara took the older gentleman's arm and allowed herself to be escorted deeper into the hall.

"He squired with us," she explained, "and we were raised much like siblings. In fact, I was surprised my father did not appeal to Lord Thornhurst for further security. I know how much trust he put in him, and his reputation as a trained knight has only grown since leaving here."

Hugh stopped to face Sara. "And you were disappointed?" His tone was more straightforward than accusatory.

"I was," Sara admitted, "and confused."

Hugh nodded. "Asking two lawless reivers with no home to protect his daughter rather than trusting his own men both here and across England..." He drifted off as if lost in thought, then said, "You're still uneasy about our presence?"

Sara had the decency to blush. Sir Hugh had so neatly summarized her thoughts.

"I think it's nigh time for me to explain some things, my lady," he finished as they arrived at the dais in the great hall. "Things I'm told your father wanted you to know, eventually. Perhaps this eve after we dine?"

Eventually? What could that possibly mean? But she'd been

too rude already to ask. "That sounds like a wonderful plan, Sir Hugh," Sara answered, feeling both pleased and anxious for an explanation.

As Sara took a seat at her place at the dais beside Lord Thornhurst, her gaze settled on the trestle table where Sir Hugh was taking his seat. Shame clogged her throat; she'd asked for them to sit at the dais as part of the begrudging welcome she'd offered, but now it seemed wrong. She made a mental note to move them at the evening meal.

Knowing she would receive answers that evening, Sara shifted her focus to Hugh's companion, whose eyes bored into her own. Her breath caught. Geoffrey's expression could only be called feral. Sara quickly turned toward her old friend.

"Good sir, how do you happen upon our dwelling?" she asked, slipping into the lighthearted banter of their youth.

William laughed. "Hardly humble, my lady." Then, more soberly, he leaned closer and whispered, "I mourn for your father."

Sara inclined her head, tears quickly welling, threatening to spill over.

William tenderly wiped away a tear and held her hand, his touch a familiar one.

"I'm sorry you were unable to be at his side," she said.

"As am I. But the continued unrest with Wales has kept me busy, and there are mounting rumors of an impending invasion."

"How is it you came to visit Kenshire at such a time?"

"Well, little lass—" the endearment had roots in their childhood, "—'tis a good question. En route from the Scottish border, I received word of your father's death and came to see you. Against Lord Kenshire's wishes, I may add."

Sara drew her eyebrows together in confusion.

"On my last visit, your father's orders were strict. 'Should anything happen to me before Sara weds, secure our holdings in the west. Know she is well taken care of,' he commanded. Apparently he referred to Sir Hugh and his nephew," William continued, "although I was quite concerned at the time."

"But never one to argue," Sara finished for him, "you let the matter drop."

"Aye, I did. Although I doubt he counted on me being this close to Kenshire upon his death, hence my disregard of his wishes."

"I see." Sara picked at her food, refusing to look down, though she knew their conversation was being watched.

GEOFFREY REFUSED TO LOOK AWAY. His uncle had excused himself for a moment, so he felt no need to mask his emotions. Instead, he glowered at the couple sitting so prettily above him. Watching Lord Thornhurst touch Lady Sara, first by the hand and then more intimately on the cheek, he itched to force a separation between two obviously well-acquainted … what? Lovers?

Nay. She hadn't feigned innocence that morning. If they were lovers, Thornhurst certainly didn't know how to please a woman.

Geoffrey was appalled at his own lack of restraint. As his uncle had been quick to remind him once they were both seated, his attraction to Lady Sara was pointless. He knew that to be true. Nevertheless, he wished Lord Thornhurst would extricate his hand. Immediately.

"Stop staring, my boy," Hugh said as he sat down once again.

Rather than deny the obvious, Geoffrey changed the subject. "Do we trust this Lord Thornhurst, Uncle? Doesn't his timing seem overly convenient?"

Hugh watched the couple huddled in conversation. "Aye, I believe we do. Richard trusted him implicitly, which was one of the reasons he installed Sir William at Camburg."

"Only one of the reasons?"

"Yes, only one." Hugh used his knife to cut into the heavily seasoned pheasant in front of him. "As you know, he's a fine warrior, his skills in battle tested."

He knew his uncle well. The blasted man had left out something significant.

"And?"

Clearing his throat, he finally added, "As I recall, though the two were raised like brother and sister, William developed an affinity for Lady Sara, which Richard thought to mitigate by sending him off to the west." Having delivered the comment as if it was a mere comment on the weather, Hugh returned to his meal.

Geoffrey, on the other hand, did not.

I will kill him.

His body tensed as he stared up at the couple. As usual, his instincts had been accurate. He'd immediately sensed Thornhurst's special affection for Lady Sara, though her feelings were less easily discernible. Had they been intimate?

Knowing his thoughts led down a precarious path, he forcibly shifted his attention to the mug of ale before him and forced himself to think of reclaiming Bristol.

He was pulled out of his reverie when a young serving wench offered him some fine wine, which he turned down in favor of another mug of ale. Ale was a reiver's drink. Despite Peter's insistence they be treated like visiting nobles, he and Hugh were far from gallant rescuers. Sara had made that clear enough in what she'd said to him earlier in the day.

"I'll be fetchin' ale for ye then. Does milord need anything … other than ale?" the maid asked coyly.

"Just the ale."

She was comely, but a toss in the hay was the last thing on his mind. Well, at least not a toss in the hay with the serving wench. His gaze returned, unbidden, to Sara. At least she'd finally turned her attention away from Thornhurst.

His uncle was deep in conversation with a young knight, discussing border troubles, and Geoffrey nodded along, feigning interest, while his eyes stayed fixed on the dais. This morning's kiss had been a mistake; he knew that now. Fresh off the excitement of besting a skilled warrior, he had made an unusually rash decision. He had every reason in the world not to have led Lady

Sara down that path—yet he'd done so, and relished it.

Why?

Yes, she was beautiful. Desirable. But Geoffrey had bedded his share of desirable women. Besides, something told him it was not simple, unbidden lust. From the moment she descended down the stairs yesterday, he had felt a heightened sense of awareness every time Lady Sara was near.

The wise thing to do would be to distance himself, but it was a difficult task given Hugh's admonishment that he should not let the lady out of his sight. Perhaps he and his uncle should switch roles, and he should see to the castle defenses.

Uncle, I'm finding it difficult to restrain myself in the presence of the lady whom I adamantly refused to protect.

That would go well.

Nay, he could not do any such thing. He would simply have to remain as emotionally and physically distant as possible. And he would avoid repeating his mistake from earlier that day.

SARA WAS TRYING—AND FAILING—TO GIVE her full attention to William. He seemed as baffled by her father's decision to send for the reivers. Of course, she told him neither about her intense attraction to Geoffrey nor the kisses he had stolen—nay, she had freely given them—earlier that day.

Her cheeks flushed as she thought about the touch of his lips to her own. Remembered how he had opened her mouth with his tongue. Her eyes fell to the trestle table below the dais.

He was looking at her.

Nay, not just looking but *glaring*, as if he planned to pounce at any moment.

Geoffrey was jealous—a thought that sent an unexpected thrill through her.

"Is something amiss, Sara?" William was all concern, and he looked from her toward the table beneath them. He could not be allowed to learn of her attraction to the outlaw. There had to be some way to divert his attention…

"What if he didn't trust me?" she blurted out.

William looked confused.

"My father. Did he send Sir Hugh and his nephew because he didn't trust my ability to lead Kenshire in his absence?"

She'd never voiced the concern aloud, but it was too late to take the words back.

"Sara?"

The concern in William's face made her regret the hastily uttered words even more.

"Your father loved you. Believed in you. How could you think otherwise?"

How indeed. "He adamantly refused to consider my request to remain unwed. He sent these men we don't even know to *protect* me. What else am I to think?"

Curse Geoffrey for forcing this conversation, however indirectly. She wished William wouldn't look at her that way. With *pity.* It made her feel even worse.

"Sara. A woman in breeches who shoots a bow better than her retainers? You know 'tis not customary. I wish it were otherwise, but I have to agree with your father. Kenshire is vulnerable right now. It has nothing to do with your abilities."

Her only response was silence. Trying to convince him that he was wrong, that they both were, would be useless.

An inadvertent glance at Geoffrey didn't improve her mood. He looked positively menacing. Because of William.

"You know, Sara, you can ask them to leave."

She pushed the food on her trencher from side to side. She could. Now a countess in her own right without a direct male heir, the final decisions in Kenshire were hers. It made her slightly uncomfortable. "I can, but I won't. You and I seem to be the only ones who think a thief and his nephew are an odd choice for protection."

"Look at me."

As soon as she did, she rather wished she hadn't. His expression told her what she already knew in her heart. Though no one had ever told her so, she knew William had been offered the position in Camburg because his feelings for her had become more than brotherly. Even if his station had permitted them to be together—it didn't—Sara knew he wasn't the man for her. The love she bore for him was the kind a sister felt for a brother.

"Send him away," William said, his voice hoarse. "Break the betrothal. Sara, I..."

"William, please don't."

His handsome face, so dear, only not in the way he wished, refused to turn away.

"William, I would be just as disillusioned to think I can marry for love as to imagine I don't need a husband at all. My duty is to protect the earldom and its people from Randolf. I must marry the earl. And you know I love you ... like a brother."

William tilted his head back, took a deep breath, and squared his broad shoulders. For a moment, she thought he'd argue with her. But after a long, strained moment of silence, his mouth set in a hard, straight line. He nodded to the musician preparing to play in the corner of the hall near the dais. "I've seen him before."

It was the paunchy bard she and Geoffrey had spoken to earlier. She was glad for the respite the traveler brought to Kenshire, especially now.

"Yes, you have. He's been here many times before."

She caught William's look and felt a stab of sorrow. It hurt that she could not return his affections as he wished. Not that it would have mattered if she did.

The musician!

It wasn't his melodic, clear voice that caught her attention, but the words of the ballad he sang. Phillida and her suitor. She couldn't resist looking at Sir Geoffrey, and her pulse quickened when he gazed straight back at her. So the bard had taken the reiver's advice. What a traitor.

In the ballad, the lady's suitor turned his attention to another when Phillida refused to kiss him. What had Geoffrey said earlier? Desire wasn't the same as love? Apparently, the fickle knight in the song agreed. She'd do well to remember as much.

And yet the slow, sensual smile that replaced Geoffrey's intense, unhappy stare as they listened to the story unfold brought a small smile to her lips.

CHAPTER 6

AFTER THE MEAL, SARA MADE her way through the trestle tables, greeting vassals and guests alike. There was no sign of the blacksmith or his kin, so she inquired after his daughter, who was prepared to give birth any day. For as many years as she could remember, the Blake family had seemed like an extension of her own. The blacksmith's mother had once served as Kenshire's midwife. She'd assisted with the difficult birth of the old earl and was credited for having saved both mother and son.

The fresh rushes crunched under Sara's feet as she exited the great hall. Peter was deep in conversation with William, who planned to stay the evening, so she felt comfortable making her way to the stables. She breathed deeply, drawing in the misty sea air.

Her father had often said a brisk ride cleansed the soul. She missed him so much. If only she'd had more time to learn from him. Somehow he had always known the right answer to any problem, the way to make his people love him but ensure they never took advantage of his good will. She'd run the household in his absence plenty of times in the past and their staff was quite capable. But now all decisions fell to her, and it wasn't quite the same as leading in his stead.

She walked into the stable looking for the stable hand. The pungent, familiar smell made her feel more at ease.

"Oh, well met, Harold," she said, surprised to see the blacksmith emerging from a stall.

"Good eve, Lady Sara," he answered. "I was looking at a shoe that was recently fitted."

She walked toward her horse, Guinevere, and greeted her beloved palfrey, rubbing her neck. "I just inquired after your daughter. Mary's well but resigned to her bed?"

"Aye, milady, and none too soon if ye ask me. The midwife talked some sense into that stubborn girl. Her mother told her, 'There's a time for work and a time to rest,' but it seems we've done a fair job instillin' a proper work ethic," Harold said with more than a hint of pride in his voice.

"You've done a fine job and should be proud of your efforts as a husband and father," Sara praised him honestly.

The blacksmith, whose shoulders and arms were as thick as tree trunks, blushed. He cleared his throat as a stable boy prepared her horse for a ride.

"If I may ask, Lady Sara—" Harold barely disguised his desire to change topics. "Who will be escorting you this afternoon?"

During times of peace, a number of Sara's ladies accompanied her on rides. Of late, unfortunately, her father had insisted on a guard. As much as Sara relished the idea of riding unencumbered, she knew it wasn't possible.

"Mayhap—"

"I'll escort her." That voice. One of a great lord, someone accustomed to being in command. It was not the voice of a reiver.

She and Harold turned toward the stable door. Her eyes widened at the sight of Sir Geoffrey filling the entranceway, broad-shouldered and striking. She swallowed, taking in the slight shadow on his face. It was still clean-shaven, but not freshly so. She had the absurd notion to touch it, to feel the light stubble beneath her fingers.

It shocked her that Harold so easily relented. No comments were made about her virtue, no arguments were voiced about her companion's unworthiness to protect her. Harold merely stepped aside and inclined his head.

As if Sir Geoffrey were lord of the castle, he walked past Sara, took Guinevere's reins from the stable hand, and asked for his own horse to be saddled.

Sara was reminded why she found the man so insufferably arrogant.

"Sir Geoffrey..."

"Aye, milady, I know. You didn't request my presence and resent being told who will escort you."

Geoffrey mounted and indicated she should do so as well. Then he pointed to the sky. "But you may want to save your arguments for later. Our ride may be cut short due to the weather."

Sara looked up and silently agreed. The sky was layered with the shades of evening even though it was yet daytime. Rain, perhaps? Silently cursing her luck, Sara nimbly mounted Guinevere, aided by the breeches she still had not shed.

Trotting through the inner bailey, the pair fell into an amicable silence despite Geoffrey's high-handedness. Noises began to dissipate as they entered the open countryside, and they both quickened their pace. Kenshire's village dotted the landscape to the left. Open fields with white snowdrops, her favorite flower, dotted the still-green autumn grass.

Sara felt better the farther they went. She loved her home but also relished the freedom of riding. A secret grin spread across her face at the thought of how surprised Geoffrey would be if he were to learn just how adept she was on horseback.

FALLING IN LINE WITH SARA, Geoffrey caught her smirk and wondered what thoughts lay behind those big brown eyes. Her ever-shifting moods reflected an earnestness which was refreshing for someone of Sara's station. In two days he'd witnessed cool disdain, haughty anger, and simple pleasure from the pampered countess.

Well, maybe not pampered, but definitely sheltered.

He'd followed her from the hall, and it hadn't surprised him to find himself at the stables. It was fair to assume any maid comfortable leaving her chamber in breeches was also fond of outdoor pleasures.

Would Lord Lyonsford allow his wife to ride in breeches? Geoffrey had only met the widower, a powerful southern earl, once. He vaguely remembered the tall, commanding noble. While he knew little about the man's temperament, he could guess marriage to Lady Sara Caiser, Countess of Kenshire, would please any ambitious earl. Or any man with blood in his veins.

Geoffrey found thoughts of Sara's impending marriage distasteful. He pictured her lying beneath her future husband, her long, dark hair in disarray, her luscious body free of breeches. Shifting in his saddle, he picked up speed, leaving Sara to do the same.

Sara.

He really should think of her as Lady Sara despite the permission she'd given him to use her common name. Her safety was charged to him, and as much as he wanted to get the hell away from Kenshire, he was starting to believe she might need protection after all. Riding outside the gates with a madman on the loose … did she know the dangers that lay beyond her beloved castle?

Apparently not.

She rode well, outpacing him and grinning all the while. When they finally slowed to a trot, Sara pointed up ahead. "With the exception of the sea, you'll never see a more breathtaking view."

"Lady Sara, do you really think it wise to be this far away from the castle?"

Her sharp glance was all the answer he needed.

"And you wonder why your father thought you needed extra protection."

"I thought we had dispensed with formalities, *Sir* Geoffrey."

"Sara. Do you really think it wise…"

"Are you always this infuriating?" she asked, coaxing her horse to ride a little faster.

"By infuriating do you mean practical?" he said, matching her pace.

"No, I mean persistent."

"Like your knight, William?" Now where in God's name had

that come from?

"What does William have to do with anything?"

This time she slowed her mount, turning so she could look at him. He slowed his horse, too, and met her gaze. They were barely moving now. He tried not to notice the outline of her breasts, but it was impossible—he knew how they'd felt pressed up against his chest.

"He doesn't. I'm just looking after you as I have been ordered to do."

"If this mission is too hard for you, mayhap you should leave."

She thought *him* infuriating?

"Don't tempt me."

"It appears I already have."

With that, Sara rode off, leading him toward an area of dense trees. She dismounted when she reached the copse, tied her horse to a tree, and started walking down a small yet clearly worn path. Geoffrey became curious despite his mood. Dismounting, he saw nothing beyond the lady in front of him. Unbidden, he continued to picture her curvaceous bottom naked beneath Lord Lyonsford's hands. Sara turned at the sound he made and looked at him strangely.

A few more steps ahead, she turned once again, this time beaming at him as if she'd gifted him a grand treasure.

Indeed, she had. The view was spectacular. Weeping willow trees lined a small lake, which glistened despite the darkening sky. The salty sea smell of Kenshire had given way to a more woodsy but slightly floral scent. Tying his sturdy reiver's horse to a tree, Geoffrey followed Sara toward the lake, unable to decide if the scenery or the girl was more striking.

A jolt of lust reminded him of his earlier vow. He would not forget himself again; he could not.

SARA DREW A DEEP BREATH, feeling more like herself than she had in weeks. Putting aside thoughts of her impending marriage and the vile usurper, she walked to a nearby willow tree.

Holding her hand high, she allowed it to brush the lower branches, which glided across her arm as if caressing her. She understood why some thought the weeping trees symbolized death, but this haven, which she had discovered as a girl, reminded her instead of life. Everything about this place comforted her, making her feel as if all were right in the world once again.

And she was sharing it for the first time. The significance wasn't lost on her. She could have easily taken William or Gillian, the daughter of a northern baron and the only girl she considered a true friend, to this place. But she never had.

In truth, Sara could not say what had driven her to bring Geoffrey here. Upon leaving the castle, she had thought only about getting fresh air. But she'd turned toward her secret spot as they started to ride away.

"Well, what do you think?"

Geoffrey turned to her, detached. "I can see why you brought me here."

"You're the first."

It was impossible not to stare into Geoffrey's eyes as she said it. His face, a mask of indifference moments earlier, seemed to show a slight crack—the tic in his cheek gave him away. Saying nothing, he continued to stare at her. She stared back, shifting, waiting for a response. Any response.

When he finally spoke, he said, "This is not a good idea."

Sara turned her eyes to the mossy ground beneath her feet. On a whim, she had brought him to this place she loved above all others, the place she had visited in the days of deep despair following her father's death. Though his words were true, she knew it as well as he did, for some reason she had expected more.

GEOFFREY SAW THE HURT IN Sara's eyes before she turned from him, but he let her walk away. Lady Sara of Caiser was a fascinating woman, more so than any he'd ever met. And therein lay the danger—his lust for her, which had roared to life that first day and not abated since, was tempered by respect for her warmth and concern for the people of Kenshire. For her quiet strength. But it would not do to entertain those feelings. He had much to lose. She had even more so.

Nonetheless, he could soften the blow.

"Lady Sara," he began. She turned to look at him and Geoffrey amended, "Sara, this is one of the most breathtaking spots I've ever seen. Thank you for bringing me here."

Sara's smile barely touched her eyes, but it was more beautiful than a thousand weeping willows.

"You've given me nothing but honesty since we met, so I'll offer the same to you." The words came tumbling out despite his good intentions. "You're magnificent. This place," he gestured with his arms, "pales in comparison to the woman who brought me to it."

As he spoke, Sara's eyes widened. "Which is exactly why we must return. God is surely punishing me by putting me in charge of your safety." He forged ahead, his tongue ignoring his better senses. "The only threat to your person at this moment is myself."

He watched her toy with a low-hanging branch, wondering how that delicate hand of hers would feel on him instead.

"I can't say I know much about border reivers," she said, her voice throaty, "and I do know it's not wise to be here with you alone. We hardly know each other. By all rights, I should be afraid."

Yet she met his gaze without flinching, lifting her chin in defiance as if to tell him she wouldn't be the one to back down.

"I would never hurt you, Sara," he said, "but you already know that."

She continued to meet his gaze. He was hard as a rock, primed to take this woman of contradictions standing in front of him—to do what he knew he could not.

He looked down at the loose opening of her shift, a ridiculous garment for a gently bred woman to wear out of her bedchamber. He watched as her chest rose and lowered and knew he had but to reach out to claim her. Geoffrey imagined her breasts freed from the restraints of the shift, bountiful and soft beneath his palms, and knew she would burn for his touch.

That knowledge, and where it could lead, convinced him to turn and walk away. It was one of the hardest things he'd ever done.

THEY RODE BACK TO THE castle in silence.

When they reached the gatehouse, Sara watched Geoffrey dismount and speak to one of the guards. How had he so quickly ingrained himself with the men? While he had only been here for two days, he seemed to know everyone.

She rode past them toward the stables, anxious to distance herself from her protector, but he caught up to her in the hallway outside her chamber. Anger flooded her. Could she not be allowed her escape?

"You needn't accompany me to my chamber, sir."

"That may be so, Lady Sara, but I intend to join your guard at the top of the stairs if it pleases you."

"And if it doesn't please me?"

"Then I will join him anyway."

She let out a loud, impatient breath. "You presume much for a guest."

His blue eyes hardened—so different now from the heat she'd seen in them before—but thankfully he remained silent.

She turned into her chamber, leaving Geoffrey in the hallway looking quite furious.

Faye, who sat stoking the fire the chambermaid had started earlier, watched her with something like alarm. "My lady, if I may say so, I haven't seen you so angered since learning of Sir Hugh and his nephew's presence." She paused. "And I have a guess as to the cause."

While Sara normally loved the intimacy she shared with her maid, at this moment she had no desire to discuss her feelings.

"Faye," she began, a hint of warning in her voice.

"Aye, milady, this old maid knows you're wanting to be tight-lipped on the subject. And you may be the countess now with an earldom at your feet, but you're still a young woman—and an inexperienced one at that."

The knowledge that she was right did little to ease the blow. Finishing her task, Faye rose from the hearth and approached her.

"I know the woman who stood proud by her father's side holding court for some of the greatest men in the country." Reaching out to grasp Sara's hand, she continued, "I also know the girl who was coddled by her father as if she were a piece of precious glass. The girl who has very little experience with men."

Sara squeezed Faye's hands, plumper than her own but achingly familiar.

"Be careful, my Lady Sara. Lord Lyonsford will return to England anytime now. When he does, you'll marry and secure Kenshire. There's no place for Sir Geoffrey, as virile and handsome as he may be, in your life."

She knew Faye spoke without malice. And she was right—a fool could see that. Her duty was to the people of Kenshire, to her late father and to her future husband.

Who cared if Sir Geoffrey had snubbed her in her secret hiding place? He was not her priority, and soon he would be gone.

She would not give another thought to kissing that high-handed, devilish rogue.

CHAPTER 7

SARA LOOKED FORWARD TO HER discussion with Sir Hugh. Once dressed for supper, she sought out William, who had spent much of his afternoon in the village gathering goods for his return trip.

They walked the battlements facing the sea, the quiet punctuated by calls from the distinct orange-beaked puffins that congregated along the coast this time of year. Her sandy-haired companion, whose chiseled cheeks made the ladies swoon, brightened her dark mood despite the awkwardness between them earlier in the day.

"I'm so glad you came, William." She meant it. Her sometimes training partner and constant cohort in mischief was the closest thing to family she had left with the exception of Faye and Peter.

"Do you remember the time we stole the fresh crispels and brought them up here?"

"Aye, and we bribed the guard with pastries to keep him from revealing our hiding spot."

She could almost taste the honey, remembering the time before their relationship had become complicated. Or at least complicated for William. For her, the boy who had been sent to them to squire was the same one she walked with now.

"If I recall, it was the same guard who told my father about our crossbow lessons."

Unhurried, they continued to stroll side by side. William's grin told her he remembered as well as she did.

"He was more upset that I was your instructor. You've always been treated more like a son than a daughter."

"If that were true, I would have been left to fend for myself. My father would not have foisted some southern lord on me." The words sounded bitter even to her ears.

"Sara." William stopped, turning to face her. "I despise the thought of leaving you. Are you sure you'll be well?"

"Aye, we're safe. With any luck Randolf will wait to pay a visit until *after* Lyonsford comes to claim Kenshire."

"And you."

"We're well-suited," she said, forcing the words out. "And with Randolf at my heels, the partnership can't come soon enough."

"Marriage, you mean."

She had a hard time saying that word. "Yes. Marriage."

"I don't agree, you know."

She glanced up, not understanding. "Don't agree with what?"

"Your father, God rest his soul. Or Peter, who is convinced Lyonsford will come riding in on a white stag to save the day."

Sara rubbed her neck, trying to figure out how to defend a decision she didn't particularly agree with either. "You don't think Lyonsford will secure Kenshire?"

He almost responded but then stopped himself.

"What is it?"

After a long pause, William finally answered her question. "I think he will. But I don't think it's your only answer."

Finally someone who agreed with her.

"But the marriage is sanctioned," she said, knowing all too well what solution William would prefer. "The betrothal final. Even if there was another way, it's too late."

Worse, she had given her word. When the physician had told her father his illness was worsening, the earl's appeals had become almost panicked. What could she do but relent? After all, even without Randolf's claim to worry about, there would be others to challenge her. She shuddered to think what would happen to Kenshire, to her, without Lyonsford's support.

"Enough about me. Tell me how you've been. How is Camburg?" Sara asked.

He clearly didn't want to change topics, but hers was hopeless.

"Not without its own troubles, but all's well … for the most part."

They talked of his life along the Welsh border, and for a while Sara forgot about her blue-eyed protector. Until she spotted the area where they had shared a kiss. She still couldn't believe she'd allowed it! And yet the memory of his lips moving over hers sent a wave of heat through her.

"Do you agree?"

"Agree?"

William gave her a peculiar look, then placed his hand on her back, guiding her toward the narrow stairs that led inside.

"Come. You're distracted and rightly so. Let's see what masterpiece Cook has dreamed up for us tonight."

Distracted, indeed. But not for the reasons her friend probably assumed.

On the way down to the great hall for supper, William excused himself momentarily. She stopped at the entrance. An odd sensation assaulted her. It was as if she was being watched. Sara looked in every direction but saw nothing.

She continued into the great room. Hugh and Geoffrey were in their new seats on the dais, and she felt the need to apologize to both of them for their prior seating arrangements. At least Hugh's response was more akin to a refined gentleman than a lawless reiver.

"Please don't concern yourself about it, my lady."

Acknowledging his greeting, she glanced to her left. Had it been a bad idea to seat Sir Geoffrey and William together? She had to wonder, especially since the nephew was less than gracious about his altered seating arrangements.

"How quickly I seemed to have moved up in the world."

She glowered at him. The lighthearted banter they had exchanged yesterday was a thing of the past. "If only it were so easy to do so, *Sir* Geoffrey."

Sara had hit her mark.

"*Lady* Sara." The glint in his eye put her on edge. "It appears I have you to thank for the favor. With any luck, Lord Lyonsford will be as grateful for his elevation at your hands."

Did she dare? Spending time in the practice yard had its advantages. She often heard things that would have shocked her poor father.

Sara lowered her voice. "To which *elevation* do you refer?"

Somehow she managed not to blush while making the most forthright comment she had ever made to anyone. While still a maid, Sara was not ignorant to the ways of mating. To her father's chagrin, her unconventional ways had given her an education not deemed proper for a lady.

Having gained the upper hand, she turned away.

GEOFFREY WAS ANYTHING BUT PLEASED. He doubted Sara knew what her ribald comment implied. Nevertheless, it immediately evoked thoughts of her stroking him to an *elevation* of his own. He nearly groaned aloud. Lady Sara appeared more like a proper countess this eve. Her breeches had been exchanged for a light blue gown in stark contrast to the dark waves of hair cascading down her back. A gilded cord sat below her hips, which had swayed evocatively on her approach to the dais moments before. She made mention of her father's insistence she not adhere to the custom of mourning clothes. Geoffrey wished it were otherwise.

Sitting back, he found himself looking down at the table where he'd sat much more comfortably. Though Geoffrey was more than happy that his uncle had been given the honor of sitting at the dais, he didn't know if he could endure sitting next to Sara. She was close enough for him to smell a musky floral scent he couldn't identify.

He shifted in his seat.

Geoffrey had thought nothing of being seated among the other knights, and now, elevated above them, he felt like a fraud. The last time he'd sat in front of a room, he had deserved to be there. His mood didn't improve when Lord Thornhurst arrived offering his apologies.

"I'm sorry for my late arrival," the man said to Sara. "I had to speak with Peter about transporting some items."

"No apologies necessary, William. Come sit with us. Tell us what you've heard of the king's health."

As they spoke about King Henry III, speculating on how long it would be before his son, Prince Edward, rose to the throne, Geoffrey silently ate his meal.

While his actions at the lake and subsequent coolness to Sara were necessary, Geoffrey knew she was upset with him. Being at Kenshire Castle was dangerous—for him and for Sara—and he couldn't wait to leave, but he also couldn't imagine leaving Lady Sara unprotected. As hardened as he'd become since the day his parents had been killed and their land stolen, Geoffrey still sympathized with the lady's position.

And he wanted her.

He wanted Sara more than he'd ever wanted a woman before. At the lake he'd envisioned crushing her to him, wrapping her legs around him, cupping her bare buttocks as he lifted her onto him. Which was exactly why he had avoided being alone with her since then.

Well, as much as it was possible to avoid someone whilst guarding them.

Despite himself, he couldn't help but be impressed by the countess's careful handling of every situation she encountered. From her visit with the blacksmith's daughter, who was ready to give birth any day, to her meticulous inspection of the castle's food stores and her ready answers to Cook's questions about the menu, it was clear Lady Sara was entirely capable of managing a massive estate.

"You appear deep in thought, Sir Geoffrey," said Lord Thornhurst, who, blast him, was sitting right beside him.

"Aye."

"And not prone to conversation?"

He narrowed his eyes, not relishing the thought of conversing with a man who held such obvious affections for Sara. He might respect the man's skills, but he could do without William's presence.

"Not usually. I take it you are?"

William's smile appeared to be genuine. "I'm rarely in dour company at supper, Sir Geoffrey, so it's hard to say."

Pleasantries be dammed. It was his custom to get to the point. Ensuring Sara was deep in conversation with his uncle, Geoffrey lowered his voice. "You're in love with her?"

To his credit, William didn't flinch. Instead he leaned forward, glancing at Sara, and answered quietly, "Yes."

The two men stared at one another, neither saying a word, neither backing down until Lord Thornhurst ventured, "You are as well."

Geoffrey laughed at that, the deep sound attracting more than one stare.

"Nay, never that. I hardly know her."

Thornhurst pressed. "It's clear you desire her then, which is more dangerous in my mind."

Geoffrey had no wish to fight someone else's battles.

"Stand down, Lord Thornhurst. I'm here to protect Lady Sara, which I will do until her betrothed arrives. Nothing more," he assured.

Thornhurst refused to back down. "See that you do. I leave in the morn. If it weren't for Sir Hugh's presence, I would stay despite my charge."

"So kind of you to place your faith in our skills."

"The skills of Sir Hugh and the men of Kenshire. You, I'm afraid, are as much of a threat to Lady Sara as Sir Randolf is."

Geoffrey ignored the barb, which had an edge of truth he did not like. "As you were before Sara's father had you removed from Kenshire?"

Though he hadn't expected an answer, Lord Thornhurst gave him one. "Aye. I grew up here." He lowered his voice once more. "With Sara, there's everything to love and nothing to hate. When Lord Kenshire realized as much, he told me in no uncertain terms that had I been born with a more substantial inheritance, he would have happily given me permission to court her." William smiled. "Those were his exact words. Court. Do you know any earl who cared to give his daughter a choice?"

Geoffrey couldn't have answered if he'd wanted to. He wasn't acquainted with many earls' daughters.

William continued, "I'm a minor baron's son. I was lucky to even foster with Lord Kenshire. When my father died, I inherited a small manor with little land, so it was an honor to be named seneschal of Camburg Castle. But the appointment came with a price."

Geoffrey finished for him, "Leaving Kenshire and Lady Sara."

"Aye. I knew it was for the best. I never had a chance with her." Thornhurst straightened his slightly slumped shoulders. What a wasteful, debilitating emotion. Love made a man weak.

"You didn't consider fighting for her?" He wasn't serious and didn't expect to be taken so.

Lord Thornhurst gave him a sharp glance, his nearly black eyes piercing. "As you will do?"

Thornhurst was reading too deeply into his desire for Lady Sara. "I'm a border reiver who wants nothing more than revenge." He abruptly dropped the subject, unwilling to go into further detail. Before continuing, he took a swig of ale. "Despite what you think, I've just met Lady Sara. Even if I wished to marry, which I don't, I know my place well. If a minor baron's son had no chance with her, how do you think a reiver would fare?"

For the first time that evening, his dining companion didn't look like he wanted to run him through.

Lord Thornhurst nodded. "In that case, I wish you well in the days to come. Word has it the Earl of Covington has thrown in his support with Sir Randolf, making his threat to claim Kenshire very real."

"We've heard the same. Which is why, I believe, we're here."

Lord Thornhurst looked at him curiously. "You believe?"

"I understand the late earl's urgency to see his daughter protected, but it would seem there are more qualified candidates."

Thornhurst didn't disagree. "I've asked your uncle about the circumstances that led to your presence here." He thought aloud, "No one knows if Lyonsford has reached the shores of England yet. So I can understand the need for increased protection. But I agree. It surprises me that you and your uncle were Lord Kenshire's first choice." Amending quickly, he added, "I mean no disrespect."

"None taken. My uncle was apparently a childhood friend of the earl, and no one could argue his prowess in battle—"

"Or yours." Thornhurst frowned.

Geoffrey didn't need the knight's approval. "But two men against a potential army … the odds are against us unless Kenshire itself is well prepared, which, luckily, it seems to be."

Thornhurst agreed, his voice full of pride. "There's no finer place in the world than this remote corner of England. Its men are well-trained and the castle's fortifications are strong."

"Then why not trust in his own men, or even send for you?" Geoffrey asked.

"When I last visited, Lord Kenshire's instructions to me were clear. In the event that he passed away before Sara was wed, I was to remain at Camburg to protect it against potential unrest. But circumstances brought me too close not to call on her."

Geoffrey grimaced at his use of Lady Sara's given name.

"I respect the late earl's decisions and will return first thing in the morning."

His quiet voice told Geoffrey he didn't want to return. Geoffrey would have gladly changed positions with him, but stopped short of saying so. He didn't think the other man would take kindly to his reluctance to be Lady Sara's protector.

Both men, lost in thought, were startled when an older man rushed into the hall, causing a commotion near the entrance. He was visibly upset.

"Lady Sara, my apologies for interruptin' your meal," called the man, who Geoffrey recognized as Kenshire's blacksmith.

Without a second thought, the lady in question bounded up from her seat. Peter did the same.

"I'm coming, Harold."

"Not without me." Geoffrey stood, intending to follow whether or not she agreed.

"If you insist." And then to Harold she asked, "Is the midwife with your daughter?"

"Aye, milady," the blacksmith answered. "Adele's been there all evening, she says there's a problem with the babe. Thank you for coming so quickly."

Why was Lady Sara summoned with the midwife already in attendance? This he had to see.

THE BLACKSMITH'S SHOP, A MILL, and a chapel all lined the narrow road that ran from west to east toward the castle. Geoffrey, who'd been waiting for Sara for hours, watched as the village wound down, settling into sleep. All was quiet by the time Sara emerged from the small, thatch-roofed cuck house where she'd gone to assist the birthing. He held out his hand, which she immediately took.

They walked in silence to his horse, and he then lifted her onto his mount and swung up in front of her. Without commenting on the unusual transportation arrangements—they'd ridden here on separate horses—Sara remained quiet, taking slow, steadying deep breaths as they rode toward the castle.

Glancing behind them, Geoffrey saw a woman exit the home, a midwife perhaps, accompanied by the blacksmith himself. Though he was reluctant to upset Sara, Geoffrey's curiosity got the better of him. "She lost the babe?"

He stiffened when Sara's arms tightened around his back. This was as close as they'd been since he'd vowed to keep his distance between them. A good decision based on his involuntary response to her closeness.

"Nay, the babe is fine." She stopped short of explaining what had happened.

"You didn't have to wait."

"I toured the village but never took my eye off your location." Geoffrey's voice sounded unrecognizable to his own ears.

It sounded … protective.

As if suddenly aware of her position behind him, Sara shifted in the makeshift pillion he'd added for her comfort. "Where's Guinevere?"

He'd figured she would get around to asking about her horse. "I sent her back with Peter, who left hours ago. I assumed you'd be tired by the time you finished back there."

"For a lawless knight, that's quite chivalrous of you. I'm surprised Peter thought it respectable for me to ride back with you."

"I'd call it more practical than chivalrous. And he didn't think it was respectable, but he returned with your horse anyway."

He felt her shiver through the layers of their clothing. From cold? From something else?

"So why were you sent for when the midwife was already in attendance?"

"Adele is quite capable and rarely asks for assistance." Her voice lowered. The long night was taking its toll. "But when she does, I offer it gladly. I've been assisting Eddard in the stables since I was a girl. With birthings, that is."

She spoke as if it were normal for a countess to help a horse give birth to its foal or assist the midwife during a particularly difficult birthing. But given how she lost her mother, Geoffrey wasn't surprised she'd taken an interest in seeing babes brought safely into the world. The woman riding behind him was a beauty who loved her people enough to wish to help them however she could, and was competent enough to do so. Proud, yet most definitely passionate. Not a typical noble.

"My sister once happened upon a foal being born and nearly gagged." He smiled at the memory. "Her constitution for the sight of blood is not overly strong."

"Tell me of your siblings."

He sensed a wistfulness to her tone and wondered, for the first time, what it would have been like to be the sole child in his family.

"Emma is as kind a girl as any you'd ever meet. Some mistake her kindness for weakness. And that, she is not."

Although she'd be a handful to raise, Geoffrey rather liked Emma's strong spirit.

"I suppose stubbornness is a family trait, but none are more so than Bryce."

Sara sighed. Was she thinking of William? He was as close to a brother as anyone in her life.

"He is sometime so serious that even I wonder what the man is thinking. And he is completely unlike Neill."

Geoffrey shook his head. How to describe Neill?

"Impetuous, carefree, but unfortunately quick to temper, the youngest Waryn seems to have every one of our traits combined. With the exception of patience."

He stopped talking as Sara's breathing became slower … more even. They fell into an easy silence as they continued to ride past the small, tidy buildings of Kenshire, all blanketed by darkness. The only sound was a sole dog's bark.

Sara's arms wrapped tighter around his waist again, and he turned to see her head nodding in a light sleep.

She trusted him.

The thought struck him like a punch in the gut as he realized how easily she had taken his hand and allowed him to escort her back to the castle. He would have to speak to her. To trust so easily could be deadly, a lesson he had learned while living outside the constraints of polite society. Strangely, it also pleased him.

Sara awoke from her doze when they reached the stables, and Geoffrey helped her dismount. The stable boy looked at them strangely, but he took the reins from Geoffrey's outstretched hand. He escorted her toward the great hall with its slumbering guests strewn about. Having spent plenty of time sleeping on floors, or worse, he was thankful for the luxury of a bed. Even if it was temporary.

It occurred to him that Sara wasn't the only person at Kenshire given to trust. Her steward had allowed him, a reiver, to escort her home to the castle. He'd come to Kenshire expecting to be treated here the same way he had been while living on the run.

But the inhabitants of Kenshire were mostly accepting, if wary. Some were even welcoming.

As they reached the door to the lady's bedchamber, Geoffrey felt compelled to say something to her. He admired what she'd done this eve, the way she was with her people.

"You did well, my lady," he offered, prepared to turn her loose into her chamber.

More alert now, Sara looked down. If he hadn't known any better, he would have thought she was embarrassed. Shyness was one trait his lady lacked in abundance.

"'Tis a simple compliment."

"I…"

He held his breath, waiting.

Finally she looked up, her brown eyes peering straight into his own. Were her lashes always so pronounced?

"I know you're reluctant to be near me, but Faye is fast asleep."

He failed to see what her lady's maid had to do with anything.

"My gown," she explained.

He understood, and hardened, in an instant. The laces of the pale blue gown she wore, now wrinkled and stained from the evening's ordeal, were at her back. Taking a deep breath, he said a silent prayer for strength.

"Turn around."

She gasped, "Here?" They both knew there was a guard just out of sight, positioned at the top of the stairs around the corner.

God help me.

"Come then." He didn't intend the request to sound like a command, but he needed to end this quickly. He had made a damned vow and would honor it if it killed him.

Her chamber was warmed by a fire, which had evidently been tended by the maid before she retired. He couldn't help but glance around the large room decorated with a fair number of tapestries. Everything he'd heard of Lord Kenshire pointed to a well-educated, indulgent man of taste.

Breaking his reverie, Sara cleared her throat, presenting her back to him. He stared at the waves of flowing hair and ached to feel them beneath his hands.

Like his father before him, Geoffrey had fought countless raids and battles with steadfastness, but when he lifted his hand to untie Sara's laces, his courage faltered. Lady Sara was exhausted. Off-limits.

And then his hand touched the laces of her gown.

CHAPTER 8

SARA'S NERVES WERE AT THE breaking point. The moment she wrapped her arms around Geoffrey on the way back from the village, awareness had replaced weariness, even though it had been an overly long evening. The difficult birth, combined with her elation at the outcome, had been enough to leave her in tears as she left the blacksmith's family and its new babe behind. She had even forgotten about that much-anticipated meeting with Sir Hugh. But when she wrapped her arms around him, all other emotions faded away, and her attention was focused on the feel of his body beneath her hands.

And then she'd realized she needed his help with her blasted gown.

Though she'd briefly considered waking Faye, Sara knew her well-meaning maid would have a thing or two to say about how Geoffrey had escorted her home alone in the middle of the night. It was something she was too exhausted to face, though as soon as Geoffrey followed her into her chamber, she started to wonder if she'd made a mistake.

What could be taking him so long?

She'd shown him her back several moments ago—yet he had not started. Realizing her hair was in the way, she moved it to the side, giving Geoffrey access to the entire backside of her gown.

And then his hands were at her back, slowly undoing the laces. After what seemed like an eternity, they were finally undone. Sara started to turn around to thank Geoffrey and bid him a good night.

His hand on her shoulder stopped her. His touch was as light as a feather, his warm fingers tracing the exposed curve of her neck. Not for the first time that evening, she shivered. Not from the cold. She could hear the fire crackling intently, as if she were inside the hearth. She could hear his breathing, her own heart pounding.

Though she knew she should stop him, she didn't even consider it. After all, she would be married soon. She wasn't naive enough to think she'd feel this kind of desire for her husband.

What harm could come from another kiss?

Resigned and excited, Sara closed her eyes as Geoffrey's fingers dusted the tender flesh behind her ear. Surely he would kiss her again.

UNABLE TO RESIST A BRIEF touch, Geoffrey reached out to caress her before actually making the decision to do so. He saw her shoulders relax and couldn't decide if he was relieved or worried that she had not stopped him. Her shiver confirmed what he already knew.

This is wrong.

Despite that thought, he pulled her toward him and replaced his fingers with his mouth. Tilting her head to the side, he kissed the spots recently touched by his gentle perusal. Starting at her neck, he made his way toward the sensitive flesh behind her ear, showing her how much his actions at the lake were at odds with the desire he felt. He kept one hand on her waist, and the other moved silently to lower the soft fabric of her gown as his mouth moved its way back down to her shoulder.

"Geoffrey?"

"I'm the scoundrel you think I am, Sara."

She turned toward him, her look far from experienced but not quite naive either. "If you had no honor, you would have taken advantage of me at the lake."

They were mere inches apart.

"If I were any kind of man, I would have already walked out, leaving you in peace."

"Peace? Somehow I find it hard to be at peace with you near."

He knew how she felt. The attraction he felt for her—had felt since that first moment in the great hall—was so fierce he doubted it would ever be replicated.

He wasn't strong enough to resist it.

Honor be damned. When he lowered his head, their kiss was as rough as the first one had been gentle. Rather than coaxing her lips apart, his tongue immediately captured her own as he pulled her toward him, melding her to his body.

At first tentative, Sara touched her tongue to his. Her willingness made his loins ache. They drank from each other, the kiss deepening. He wanted this woman, needed her as desperately as any other. But he wanted to be sure.

Pulling away, he cupped her face and looked down at her. Her expressive brown eyes, wide with awakening desire, looked straight into his soul.

Geoffrey reached up to caress her bottom lip, glistening from the remnants of their kiss, with his finger. He groaned aloud when she opened her mouth for him. Realizing she needed to be shown the ways of love, he brought her slender finger to his mouth and kissed it gently. Then he brought it into his mouth, touching his tongue to the tip. Without breaking her gaze, he closed his mouth around her finger, sucking, then pulled it out slowly before continuing the sensual assault, mimicking an act she did not yet understand.

As her breathing quickened and eyelids hooded with desire, he placed both of her hands around his neck for support.

He tried his damnedest to move slowly, knowing full well what he had planned next was well beyond Sara's experience. But when she grabbed the hair at his neck, the hard-won restraint he'd spent his life honing deserted him in an instant. Kissing the sensitive lines of her collarbone, he glided his hand toward the neckline of her gown. She gave no protest when he inched it below her shoulder, so he eagerly tugged it even lower, revealing a thin shift below. He easily pushed aside the wide neck of the undergarment, revealing the perfectly shaped mound of her breast, which he'd spent more time imagining than he would care to admit.

Cupping her breast reverently, first with a light caress and then more firmly, he rolled its pink tip between his fingers. He closed his eyes at the sound of Sara's half-sigh, half-groan. Memorizing the shape of her, he teased and tortured her before opening his eyes to see the object of his pleasure staring at him in wonder.

Knowing he was well beyond any measure of restraint, Geoffrey lowered his head and trailed a row of kisses down her neck toward that perfect warm flesh, so responsive to his touch. When his mouth found its destination, Geoffrey used every sensual skill he'd acquired to make Sara's desire mimic his own.

Hot, ready, willing.

Reluctantly, he raised his head. How far should he let this go? He would have ripped her gown in two, thrown her on the bed, and ravished her luxurious body if she'd wanted it. If he hadn't known it would ruin them both. Instead he claimed her mouth in a searing kiss, thrusting his tongue inside, showing Sara—

There was a loud *crash* in the hall.

They risked being exposed. Acting immediately, he ran to the door, only looking back once as Sara lifted her gown to cover her breast.

SARA WAS STUNNED, IMMOBILE. ADJUSTING her gown as much as possible with loose laces, she finally found her legs and walked toward the door. Although she should care more about the source of the noise, Sara was more concerned with whether Geoffrey's presence in her chamber would be discovered.

The implications hit her as surely as a bucket of ice-cold water. She had been prepared to give herself to a man she'd known mere days. Her cheeks flushed with mortification as she made her way to the door, inched it open, and peered down the hall.

Nothing.

She didn't dare enter the hall in her current state of disarray. Moments after she peeked her head into the hall, Geoffrey turned the corner with one of her men-at-arms on his heels.

"Did the noise wake you, Lady Sara?" he inquired.

"Nay, Sir Geoffrey," she said, catching on quickly, "I was just preparing for bed. What has happened?"

Waving away the guard, Geoffrey leaned toward the door and whispered, his face so close she could feel his breath on her ear, "The guard was being relieved and lost his sword to the stairs below."

"He saw nothing?"

She could tell he wanted to touch her, and though it was wrong, she desperately wanted him to enter her bedchamber and continue where he'd left off.

But the spell had been broken, and Sara saw the intrusion for what it was … a blessing in disguise.

"Nay."

They stood for a moment longer, neither willing to be the first to relent, both understanding the enormity of the mistake they had very nearly made.

"Sara…"

"Geoffrey…"

Geoffrey looked over his shoulder, then turned to touch her, a brief stroke of her cheek before he walked away.

It was for the best.

Closing the heavy wooden door and leaning against it, Sara looked down at the state of her gown and tried unsuccessfully to slow her racing heartbeat. Could she learn to control herself around Geoffrey? She would need to if he was to continue guarding her.

She'd do well to take Geoffrey's own advice and remember the kind of man she was dealing with. He was used to taking what wasn't his, and she certainly fell into that category. She was a leader now, and it was about time to start acting like one.

CHAPTER 9

THE DAY AFTER GEOFFREY NEARLY took Sara's innocence—*surely it wouldn't have gone that far*—he gladly bid farewell to Lord Thornhurst. William saw fit to wholeheartedly return Sara's embrace after accepting a basket of food for his journey.

"'Tis unnecessary, little lass. I'm used to traveling with much less."

Rolling his eyes, Geoffrey would have walked away had he trusted the overly familiar lord with Sara's person.

Inclining his head for Geoffrey to follow, William finally mounted his destrier. Geoffrey stared at the magnificent creature. He could buy much needed support with the coin from such an animal, even without its armor. An unwanted image of his own war horse, a gift from his father after he was knighted, invaded his thoughts.

He would get it, and Bristol Manor, back.

"Ride with me, Sir Geoffrey."

Already irritated, he didn't bother being polite. "I don't take orders, Thornhurst."

Geoffrey only relented when nudged by his uncle, who had remained silent during the exchange. He'd regret his sharp tongue when Hugh got ahold of him later.

"I will look after Lady Sara, my son," Hugh said.

The endearment softened him slightly. Likely his uncle's intention. Geoffrey gave William a sharp nod and made for the stables. At least it would give him a brief reprieve from his beautiful tormentor.

"It seems a reminder of our discussion is in order?" William said, his tone firm, a few moments later as they rode side by side away from the castle. There was no sign of the smiling, amicable knight he was with Sara.

"I've never had a lady's maid, Thornhurst, and don't have a need for one now."

William grimaced. "You've been at Kenshire just a few days," he said. "I was raised here and have a vested interest in its people."

"Point taken. But I'll thank you to remember I'm not here by choice."

"Maybe so, but here you are. And you'll never meet a more honorable woman than Lady Sara. I ask you, one knight to another, to leave her as such."

He'd prefer not to hear his own thoughts uttered aloud to him by the gallant knight.

"Call me a reiver, a thief. I won't dispute it," he said. "But I've never taken a lady against her will in my life. Nor have I ever deflowered a virgin."

"How honorable."

"Did you ask me to ride with you so you could chastise me like you would a child? If so, I bid you a good day."

William switched topics, his point apparently made. "I spoke with your uncle at length last eve after you escorted the lady to the village."

He was becoming impatient with the censure he heard in Thornhurst's voice.

"And?"

"He told me a bit more about you."

"Is that so?" He didn't bother to hide his impatience. "Get to the point, and quickly."

"Are you always so prickly?"

Not usually. Although not quite as carefree as his youngest brother, he was usually less uptight than this, even in the middle of battle. It was his trademark, an ability to lighten the mood despite the intensity of a situation. He usually left the sullenness to Bryce.

Instead of admitting as much, he answered, "When being interrogated, yes."

"As I told your uncle last eve, if there's any way I can help reclaim your lands, you have only to ask."

It was the last thing Geoffrey had expected to hear.

"Why?" He no longer considered Lord Thornhurst a potential adversary, mostly because he was leaving—and because the lady did not seem to return his affections—but he was certainly no ally. Why would he offer to help a reiver reclaim his birthright along the tumultuous border?

"As repayment of your services to Kenshire."

There was a long pause as Geoffrey stared at Thornhurst, unable to understand what he was hearing.

"Sir Geoffrey, help Lady Sara secure her claim, and I'll do everything in my power to help you take back what the Kerrs stole from you."

With that, Thornhurst spurred his horse forward, leaving Geoffrey to stare after him. What he hadn't said was that Sara's claim would only be secured by her marriage to Lyonsford. As if Geoffrey needed another reason to stay away from the Lady of Kenshire.

For the next two days, he fell into a routine, trailing Sara while she visited tenants and settled disputes, keeping his distance as much as possible. Other ladies in her position might idle their time away with court gossip, but Sara was obviously accustomed to the duties required to manage an estate.

Despite his determination to stay away from Lady Sara, his interest in her only grew.

SARA COULD NOT CONCENTRATE.

Although her father had prepared her to run an estate, she'd had no mother to teach her about such things as desire. She thought back to the first kiss she had shared with Geoffrey and nearly laughed aloud at her naiveté. That was nothing compared with the way his mouth had felt along her neck, and—she was embarrassed to even remember it—her breast. For three days, she had thought of little else.

She wondered what might have happened if they weren't interrupted. Picturing every caress, she could almost feel his tongue claim hers. The memories assaulted her everywhere she went, and she found herself thinking about him again—his touch, his taste—when she met with Peter in the solar to sift through reports on taxes and rents.

Perhaps sensing her distraction, Peter leaned across the massive desk, taking a list of villagers' rents from the pile of parchments in front of them. "Lady Sara, 'tis my job to see to these. There's no need for you to be here."

Shaking her head, Sara repeated a phrase she'd often heard from her father. "If it's a part of Kenshire, it's a part of me."

She took the list from him, trying but failing to concentrate on its contents.

Sara was eager for a break from the tedious task by the time Sir Hugh appeared at the door.

"'Tis easy to find you, Lady Sara," he said, "I just have to look for the hulking form of my nephew. You're never far behind."

Sara stood and glanced to where Geoffrey waited for her outside. No one was more keenly aware of his presence than she.

"I'd like to speak with you, milady."

Peter indicated for Hugh to sit in the rich yet sparsely furnished room and then excused himself.

"I apologize for my absence these last few days," Hugh said. "We've been working hard to strengthen fortifications on the gatehouse."

Sir Hugh worked closely with Gerald de Winters, the castle constable, since he'd arrived.

"I know, Sir Hugh. I inspected the progress myself yesterday. Gerald told me you took a garrison to Dumridge for supplies."

"I hope you don't think my father remiss for failing to do so himself," she said, feeling the need to defend her father. "He knew it was necessary work, but his concentration was elsewhere."

She looked down at her simple but elegant surcoat, a blue so deep it appeared almost black. Too much like the mourning clothes she despised.

"That is what I'd like to speak with you about, milady. My relationship with your father." He paused. "I planned to speak with you the night of the birthing, and since then, I've been preoccupied by our preparations for Randolf."

"Please, no apologies. The men respect your knowledge, and I'm grateful for your help."

Sara wasn't too stubborn to acknowledge how much her opinion had changed in one short week. While she was anxious to hear what Sir Hugh had to say, she spoke the truth. The men with whom he worked spoke highly of his experience, which only deepened the mystery. How did a man without a home know so much about castle fortifications?

He nodded in acknowledgement, then said, "When I was a young lad, your father and I met at the first Day of Truce. I'd recently received my spurs from my elder brother, Geoffrey's father."

She felt a flutter deep inside her belly. It wasn't at all what she had expected to hear. Geoffrey's father had been a lord?

She couldn't hide her shock.

"Aye, my brother was a baron. He inherited Bristol Manor from our father." Frowning, he continued, "But that's a different story for another time."

Her head started spinning. A baron? But why were they reivers?

"Your grandfather negotiated the first Day of Truce in an attempt to find peace with the Scottish border clans. It was as tense then as it is now, and there was a murder attempt on your father."

"You saved his life."

A grin spread across his face.

"I did."

She had so many questions, but she held her tongue, deciding to let him speak first.

"Afterwards, we became very close friends." Hugh paused as Sara stared at him. Her father's savior. A noble family! It explained their grooming. And manners. Or Sir Hugh's manners, at least.

"Two and a half years after that day, Richard visited Bristol on an extended visit. While he was there, we were raided by Clan Kerr. Living so close to the border, raids weren't uncommon, but this particular time they were bolder than usual, driven by desperation to replenish their stores before the coming winter. It was during that raid your father saved my life. I'll spare you the gruesome details, but without his assistance, there's no doubt that raid would have been my last."

It made sense that such a thing would create a strong bond between two men, but she still had so many questions.

"Why did no one tell me earlier? Surely Peter must have known."

"Aye, I've visited Kenshire many times before duties kept me closer to the border. When we arrived, Peter instructed us to remain quiet."

"Why would he do such a thing?"

"It was at your father's request."

Of course. She should have guessed it immediately. A final lesson about acceptance, and one she would not soon forget.

"And the raid. Is that when you lost Bristol Manor?" She didn't want to pry, but she needed to understand.

Hugh sighed, looking distinctly uncomfortable.

"Nay. That happened years later, after Geoffrey and his siblings were born. I saw Richard less after he married. As the steward of Bristol, my duties kept me closer to home."

Sara's eyes shot to the doorway, and she couldn't help but wonder if Geoffrey could hear his uncle's tale.

"Life on the border was difficult, but Bristol Manor was our ancestral home. Though it was firmly English territory at that time, our land has been disputed by the Scots for as long as I can remember."

Perhaps the extreme measures her father had taken for her safety were warranted. She had assumed her father was just overprotective, that he didn't completely trust her to make the right decisions. Maybe he had simply recognized the very real danger of the border.

"Out of desperation, Clan Kerr's raids became more frequent and violent. One day, with the support of another lowland clan..."

His eyes were filled with pain, and while she wondered if she should stop him from continuing, he did not give her the chance.

"Bristol was devastated. I had taken Geoffrey and his siblings to a nearby village to visit a traveling market. My wife and I were never able to have children, so my niece and nephews are like my own. There's nothing I wouldn't do for them."

Hugh stopped again. As much as she wanted to hear the rest of his story, she was almost afraid for him to continue. She wanted to comfort the man who had been a friend to her father. A second father to Geoffrey. She had started to stand when another voice cut in, finishing Sir Hugh's story.

"My parents were killed. This time it was no raid but a battle for Bristol, and the Scottish bastards won."

Both she and Hugh looked up at Geoffrey, who walked into the room and settled a hand on his uncle's shoulder. Emotion welled inside of her as she looked into Geoffrey's eyes. She knew what it was like to live without a parent, the overwhelming despair of having a loved one taken too early, but to have one's parents and one's home taken in the same afternoon? Words seemed inadequate.

Feeling like she had intruded on a private family matter, she forced her gaze down to her hands. "I'm sorry," she said. It was all she could say. Why hadn't Geoffrey told her all this sooner? Why had he let her think the worst of him?

Hugh stood, clapping Geoffrey on the back and turning to Sara.

"Thank you," he said. As if he heard her silent question, he continued. "As you can imagine, it's a tale I'm reluctant to relive. But you deserve to know who you invited into your home."

With that, he winked and walked away, leaving her alone with Geoffrey.

Everything had changed.

Geoffrey had taken his uncle's chair, as if realizing Sara would not let him go without asking any questions. She blurted out the first thing that came to mind. "You're the son of a lord?"

"Aye. Or *was* the son of a lord. My father's barony wasn't quite Kenshire. We lost two manors along with the lordship and a very small village."

"Why didn't you tell me this before?"

Of course he was of noble descent. Everything about him told her as much, from his proud bearing to his ability with a sword. And yet he stole from others for a living. He sat across from her with no hint of embarrassment, only pride and his usual hint of arrogance.

"I didn't know you were curious."

"Of course I'm curious. That day on the beach, you refused to even discuss it. But I did ask."

Geoffrey shot back, "The murder of my parents is a topic I'd rather avoid."

Immediately contrite, she tried to explain. "I didn't mean it in that way. It's just … well … I can't help but wonder how you came to your profession. A baron? Didn't you have family to turn to?"

"My brothers and sister live with family now." At her questioning glance, he clarified, "Two brothers and one sister, all younger. But my aunt and uncle were barely surviving themselves before we arrived with extra mouths to feed."

"Aunt and uncle?"

"My mother's sister. The daughter of a physician, Lettie was too proud to accept charity from my parents. She and her husband lived humbly but comfortably. But they took us in without question. Hugh's intention was to eventually take us south on a campaign to find additional men to support our claim."

Sara could guess at the outcome, having already worked out the timing in her head. The tic in his cheek hinted of impatience. But she pressed anyway. She needed to understand.

"But civil war was brewing."

"Aye, the undercurrent of the baron's war changed his plans, and instead we landed further east. We were still close to the border with extended family, but far enough away from the clan who took everything from us."

Geoffrey looked remarkably like his uncle. Elbows propped on his knees, he leaned forward as he told his story. His carriage reminded her of the time he'd appeared at the stable entrance and insisted on accompanying her for a ride—relaxed but very much in command. Her heartbeat quickened.

"With four children at his heels, my aunt and uncle's family couldn't possibly support us. A displaced knight has few options, as you can imagine, so Hugh joined a local reiving family across the border."

"Did they accept an outsider so readily?" She knew little of reivers but remembered hearing of their fierce loyalty to family and clan.

"One built like my uncle?" he said with a grin. "What do you think?"

Understanding, she guessed what happened next. "And you eventually joined him?"

"Aye. It's too dangerous to stay in one place for long, so Hugh and I typically roam the border, living off the land and returning to give our family much needed supplies."

"So you don't often see your siblings?" She had always wanted brothers and sisters.

"Not as often as I'd like. But their safety is of the utmost important to me."

"Have you been back to Bristol since you were a child?"

"So many questions for one day. Mayhap it's your turn to answer a few?" Geoffrey sat back and crossed his arms. The sleeves of his white linen shirt were rolled slightly, revealing dark hair underneath. She stared at his arms, remembering what they had felt like around her waist.

This was the longest they'd spoken since the incident in her bedchamber.

"What do you want to know?" She hoped her voice sounded dispassionate. Somehow she knew his question would have nothing to do with her past.

She was right.

"Have you thought about that night?"

Of course she had. She had thought of little else. But it was the one question she did not wish to answer. Still, she was opening her mouth to do just that when Peter came running through the open door, face flushed and panting.

"My lady. He's here!"

CHAPTER 10

GEOFFREY SPRANG OUT OF HIS seat. Sara's face blanched. This was the moment he'd been waiting for since Hugh had brought him on this fool's errand. But could he relinquish Sara to her betrothed so soon?

As if he had a choice.

What the hell are you thinking?

"Sir Randolf is at the outer gatehouse asking for permission to enter."

Sir Randolf?

He shouldn't be relieved. When Lord Lyonsford arrived, he'd be free to continue gathering the support he needed to take back Bristol. It was the only thing he cared about. Or was it? There was no time to sort through that now.

At the moment, he needed to concentrate on the fact that the man who wished to wrest Kenshire from Sara had arrived at the castle gates. Good. He was itching for a fight.

All three made their way down the stairs forthwith. They met with Kenshire's marshal in the great hall, and Sara began questioning Peter and Gerald.

"Does he bring many men?"

"According to the tower guards, it doesn't appear so, milady," the marshal said, "but we've sent scouts ahead to be sure."

"Good. I assume you've put everyone on alert?"

"Aye. And Sir Hugh is in the guardroom as we speak."

"I won't ask you to intervene, Sir Geoffrey," she said, turning to him, "but I'm sure you know what this means." The woman who addressed him was self-assured and clearly in charge. It was remarkable reversal from the empathetic Sara he also knew existed.

"If it's a battle Sir Randolf wants, it's a battle he'll get."

They received word that Randolf was indeed escorted by less than twenty men-at-arms, and after consulting with her officers, Sara decided to allow him entry. She waited for the arrival of her archenemy with more composure than Geoffrey himself would likely have mustered if a member of Clan Kerr stood outside the castle gates. Chin lifted slightly, Sara appeared calm, collected, and regal. Yet he noticed she was biting her cheek. While she was in control, the countess was very much annoyed.

Geoffrey knew he had no business thinking of her cheek or any other body part, for that matter, but damned if he didn't itch to throw caution to the wind and claim those pursed lips as his.

Although common courtesy demanded Sir Randolf be announced, this was no ordinary circumstance. This was the man who had forced Sara into the match with Lord Lyonsford. The man who wished to steal her home and title. Geoffrey gritted his teeth. If the man looked at Sara the wrong way, he'd enjoy sending the greedy bastard to his maker, lofty connection be damned.

Moments later Sir Randolf was escorted, alone, into the keep. Geoffrey immediately despised him. Tall and thin, with brown hair hanging around his shoulders in the current fashion and more jewels than Geoffrey had seen on Sara during his entire stay, Sir Randolf Fitzwarren belonged at court.

Or in hell.

He declined to bow and instead stared straight at his hostess.

"You're in the presence of a countess, *Sir* Randolf," Geoffrey said. "You obviously haven't been taught any manners." It wasn't his place to speak, but he took immense pleasure in the man's discomfort.

Though not extraordinarily broad-shouldered, Randolf was nevertheless imposing, his bearing that of a man who fully embraced his station. He hadn't noticed Geoffrey's presence earlier, but he did now.

Good.

"I'd bow if the countess were keeping her title, but alas, she is not."

Sara snaked out her hand and slapped Randolf hard enough across the cheek to snap his head back.

"That, you coxcomb, is for causing my father worry in his last days."

When Randolf took a step toward her, Geoffrey shifted to block her from him. "That's close enough."

"I don't believe I've had the pleasure of your acquaintance." Randolf's terse reply and combative tone were at odds with his words.

Geoffrey felt a feather-light touch on his shoulder. They stood apart from Randolf as if a line had been drawn. But now Sara's captains closed ranks and began to encroach on that invisible line.

"A fine show, Lady Sara," Randolf said, glancing around the hall. "Where is that lovely Faye? A flask of wine would be much appreciated."

Aside from a slight lift of her chin, Sara hardly moved a muscle. "It has obviously escaped your notice that you are not welcome here."

"I see. Then mayhap we should take a seat while we discuss the terms of your surrender?"

Geoffrey's hand twitched.

Sara laughed. A perfect, hearty sound that filled the otherwise eerily quiet hall devoid of its usual flurry of activity. "Go to hell."

Geoffrey nearly smiled at Randolf's reaction. A lady simply didn't demand one's departure to the devil's lair. Well, most of them didn't anyway. But Sara, as he'd learned, was special.

His beady eyes narrowing, Randolf finally got around to the purpose of his visit.

"Well, since you're obviously not inclined to offer a weary traveler succor, here are my terms. Vacate Kenshire within two days, or everyone you hold dear will be destroyed."

It was Geoffrey's turn to laugh. From all he had learned about Randolf, the man had never enjoyed a warm welcome at Kenshire. The loose ties to Caiser went back generations, though it was only in the last years of his life when Sara's father had explicitly forbidden Randolf from his holdings. If the man had not been so politically connected, his claim would have been laughable. As it was, he would have to fight his way to her inheritance, but his well-placed allies emboldened him.

Looking Geoffrey straight in the eye, Randolf made a bold prediction. "I'll start by destroying this arrogant oaf."

Robbing Randolf of the pleasure of the response he so clearly wanted, Geoffrey stood immobile, his face a mask of indifference.

Randolf's ears turned bright red as his eyes narrowed.

It was almost too easy.

"If that's all you've come to say, I bid you adieu." Sara spoke slowly, as if she were dismissing a young child.

Spinning on his heels, Randolf started to leave the hall, followed closely by Eddard and Sir Jerold, but then he turned back, leveling his gaze on those who had dared to mock him.

"I would be amiss not to mention that the Earl of Covington not only supports my claim, but backs it with a full force of men. I'll return with them in two days' time. Send your scouts a bit farther west to confirm, if you'd like. Or not. It matters naught to me."

Turning to leave with his escorts, he called back, "Oh, yes, and your betrothed has finally landed on England's fine soil, but alas, he's more than two weeks' ride from Kenshire."

With that, the impertinent pretender finally left the hall, having thoroughly cast a black cloud over its inhabitants.

"Do you want me to kill him?"

He was glad Sara appeared to seriously contemplate his offer before answering him. Because he *was* serious.

"Nay, the consequences are too uncertain," she finally said with a sigh. "My father would've done the deed ten times over if

Sir Randolf's friend Lord Covington didn't have the king's ear. The earl's reach is broad."

Sara tapped her chin with her finger, deep in contemplation.

"A word, Sir Geoffrey?" she asked.

Hell, you can have anything you'd like.

While the others began to issue orders, he followed Sara to a private corner of the hall. They were still visible to all, but their conversation would not be overheard.

"If you're going to tell me that I overstepped by addressing Sir Randolf that way, send us away now. I'll not stay silent while that scum insults you."

She startled. So that wasn't it.

"I wasn't planning to say any such thing. In fact, I wanted to thank you for your assistance."

He had jumped to the wrong conclusion, but his pride wouldn't allow him to apologize for it.

"I wanted to ask your opinion."

"Me? A common thief? Are you sure?"

"Aye, I'm sure. Though you're apparently no common thief at all, but a displaced lord."

"Displaced. What a pretty word."

It was impossible not to stare at her lips.

"What is wrong with you?"

You.

"Nothing," he snapped, his tone belying his answer. "I shouldn't be surprised that my past matters so much to you. Yesterday I was one step away from being a rapist and murderer. Today I'm treated like a noble. 'Tis enough to turn a man's head."

"Sir Geoffrey Waryn..." Sara spoke for only his ears, but her sharp tone convinced him to cease talking. For the moment. "I have not treated you differently. If anything, I've given more of myself to you than to any other man. *Before* I knew anything of your background. Take your self-loathing elsewhere."

He grabbed her arm before she walked away.

"Even Lord William?"

Her narrowed eyes widened.

Where the devil did that come from?

"You don't deserve an answer, but I'll give you one anyway. Aye, much more than Lord William. I don't feel sisterly toward you."

"How do you feel?"

Suddenly aware that his hand remained on her arm, he released her. From his grip, not from answering his question.

"Confused."

She pulled her arm back and walked away.

Confused.

At least he wasn't the only one.

Sara walked toward Faye, who was huddled in conversation with his uncle. He didn't even notice them enter. Luckily, their discussion seemed to have gone unnoticed.

He walked toward Hugh, wanting to hear his uncle's take on the situation. The uncivilized part of him wanted to follow Sir Randolf and slay the man's black heart before he could do Sara any damage, but he was keenly aware of the delicacy of the situation.

"The bloody bastard," he said to Hugh. "Did you hear his demand?"

"I did. How fares Sara?"

"Fine. She handled it remarkably well."

Hugh did not look pleased. It was obvious he'd noticed their semi-private conversation.

Geoffrey amended his hasty reply. "She's off with Faye at the moment. If you ask me, it's the servant who needs smelling salts, the poor woman."

"I'm not sure that's true. She seems a sturdy sort to me."

It was the first time he could remember his uncle remarking on a woman. While it was true the maid was handsome for her age, he couldn't imagine thinking about her as anything other than Sara's servant. But there was something in Hugh's tone that gave him pause. Could his uncle be interested in her? His wife had passed away when Geoffrey was just a babe, and his uncle had been alone since.

"Do you think he's bluffing?"

"Well," Hugh began pacing back and forth. "It's certainly possible. Richard never trusted the man. And his father was just as wily. Eddard isn't taking any chances. He's planning to send his fastest riders in every direction to investigate." He paused. "What do you think?"

Geoffrey considered the question, weighing all the possibilities. "With an ally installed at Kenshire, the earl would be as powerful as any in England. Which is precisely why I don't believe King Henry would allow it."

"With Prince Edward abroad again, mayhap Covington sees an opportunity? Everyone knows the king's health is failing."

"It's just as likely Randolf is bluffing, though to what end I'm not sure."

But he had an idea.

A SHORT TIME LATER, GEOFFREY WAS summoned to a meeting with Kenshire's other top officials. When he and his uncle entered the solar, its inhabitants quieted and turned to look at them. They were outsiders. Everyone knew that. But Geoffrey didn't sense the distrust he had expected. He felt welcome, and a surge of electricity filled the air the moment his eyes met Sara's. She was the only one in the room who didn't appear to be overly happy about his presence. He wasn't sure why he had given her such a hard time in the hall, especially since he was so proud of the way she conducted herself.

Sara's nemesis was a greedy bastard who was abusing his connection to an equally greedy noble known for his role in the baron's war against the king. The Earl of Covington was lucky not to have lost his head in the war. Although direct ties could never be found, most knew he colluded with the English barons responsible for the revolt. Given the extent of his power, most were afraid to cross him. Somehow Randolf had convinced the earl to take up his cause against Sara. Geoffrey was determined to do everything in his power to take him down.

As the meeting went on, Geoffrey could feel himself getting sucked into a battle that wasn't his. He silently nodded to Sara, who was engaged in a lively discussion with her marshal, and she acknowledged him with a nod in return. She was sufficiently protected at the moment, so Geoffrey headed outside, intending to inquire after Gerald to discuss his plan. He had exited the keep and was walking toward the east when the hair on the back of his neck stood up. Barely in his line of sight, a servant Geoffrey recognized as John, the cupbearer, was having a heated conversation with a woman dressed as a noble. Though she was vaguely familiar, Geoffrey couldn't place her.

Something told him to investigate, so he waited until John moved on and followed him discreetly through the inner ward toward the back of the main keep. After looking in both directions, John entered a door. Geoffrey followed close behind. He'd entered the kitchen, and all eyes turned toward him. A swift assessment confirmed John had moved on.

He'd use this opportunity to learn more about the man. With a bow, he found the person in charge, a rotund woman ordering the staff about.

"Well met. I apologize for interrupting … preparations for supper?"

The woman wasn't that easily won over.

"What else? Now out of my kitchen!" She turned away from him without another glance, but had a more difficult time reining in the younger kitchen maids. "What are ye starin' at, ye witless girls? Haven't ye seen a man before?"

He looked at Cook as if she were the fairest maid in the world. "Of course they have, just not one as enamored of your fine talents."

Turning to him and shooing the young ladies back to work, the cook stood as tall as her short stature would allow. "Take your charms elsewhere, Sir Geoffrey. I've got a meal to prepare."

Undeterred, he offered her a lopsided grin, holding his hand to his heart. "I'm wounded that my reputation precedes me. You don't believe me to be sincere?"

Cook's talents were indisputable. Much better than his typical fare, especially during the harsh winter months.

Not completely immune to his charms, she finally relented slightly. "If ye like fish pie, wash yourself and get thee gone."

She reminded him of the healer at Bristol who could fix a broken bone in the dead of the night with one hand. He alone could make that cranky woman smile, which was a good thing. They had become well acquainted; she'd patched him up more times than he could remember.

"Aye, Cook, I'd never argue with the most important person at Kenshire." He bowed again. "Good day to you."

With a wink he took his leave, stopping to whisper to a young kitchen servant, "A man by the name of John came through before me?"

"Aye, milord."

His bearing, if not a title, had elicited the greeting. Geoffrey usually corrected it; this time he did not.

"Does he visit the kitchen often?"

"At times, milord."

While considering how to phrase another question without raising suspicion—he did not want the servant to find out he'd been asking after him—he wasn't completely surprised she continued to offer information.

"He keeps to himself mostly. He's been at Kenshire mayhap three years?"

Not one to push his luck, he changed the topic.

"What's your name, fair maiden?"

He spoke the truth. She was indeed comely.

"Margaret, milord," she said, blushing.

"Pleased to meet you, Margaret." He noticed Cook's stern gaze out of the corner of his eye. "I'll leave you to your work."

Stealing a handful of raisins, Geoffrey grinned and took his leave. Giggles trailed him out of the door.

A quick search failed to turn up the servant, so he decided to return to his chamber to clean up for supper. When Hugh had committed them to protecting the countess and her title, he had done so with the knowledge that it might thrust them into the middle of a war. And Geoffrey was sure he'd stumbled onto something important. He'd learned to rely on his gut and would continue to ask after the servant. Like it or not, he was thoroughly, if temporarily, ingrained in the affairs of Kenshire Castle.

CHAPTER 11

THAT EVENING, GEOFFREY WATCHED JOHN closely at supper. He also searched for the lady the cupbearer had spoken to earlier, but there was no sign of her.

Randolf's visit had cast a pall over the gathering, and it was a more subdued meal than usual. Hugh had left earlier that evening with a scouting party.

Sara entered the hall accompanied by her maid. Typically, her attire reflected the active role she took at Kenshire—most of her gowns were less ornate than custom dictated, their hems falling short of the ground—but this eve she'd dressed the part of royalty. She walked toward him in a bright lavender dress pooling around her feet.

Sara made her way toward the dais with her head held high, her clasped hands hidden by folds of hanging fabric. As she approached, he spied rich gold thread delicately framing a neckline that offered a tantalizing glimpse of the creamy skin below.

Another image flashed through his mind … her breast being freed from the fabric of the dress she had asked him to unlace. The perfectly shaped mound had come alive under his fingers. And he would never forget her look of wonder when he bent his head to circle her hard nipple with his tongue, finally taking it in his mouth. Standing to greet her, Geoffrey forced his mind elsewhere.

"Good evening, my lady."

"Good evening, Sir Geoffrey."

John approached to fill her chalice, but she didn't pay him any heed. "My apologies for being late."

"The meal waits for you." Geoffrey gestured to the hall filled with vassals, servants, and visitors. Every detail so richly appointed. "I noticed a noblewoman at the castle earlier," he said after waiting for the cupbearer to walk away. "Shouldn't she be seated with us?"

"Lady Maude. Before you arrived, Peter apprised our visitors of the position we've found ourselves in. Most left for their own holdings, with the exception of Lady Maude and her husband, Lord Edmund.""Yet she's not in attendance?"

Sara gave him a strange look. Too many questions. "I was told they left earlier this evening. It's curious they'd not wait till morn, but even more curious they stayed so long. Still, Kenshire never turns away a guest. With the exception of Sir Randolf, of course."

They exchanged a smile, but Geoffrey decided to keep pressing her. Something just wasn't right about that woman.

"Tell me about her."

Sara grabbed her cup so quickly a drop of red wine splashed onto her sleeve. He stared at the spot she attempted to remove with the dining cloth, his gaze moving toward her fingers before stopping on the long, slender one he had taken into his mouth not so many nights before.

"She's quite beautiful, although you seem to have drawn that conclusion already."

He could enjoy this. "Jealousy becomes you, Lady Sara. I find it quite endearing."

"How absurd," she sputtered. "If you're tempted by the likes of Lady Maude..."

"I'm tempted by only one woman here, and you know it." He leaned closer. "One who makes the room come alive when she walks into it. A lady as comfortable in breeches as she is in a dress fit for a queen."

Sara cast her eyes downward. Was she embarrassed to be the object of his endearments? She was trying hard not to look pleased, but he was learning to sense her moods. At least she was no longer angry.

He lowered his voice. "One whose flesh is as creamy and delicate as the finest silk. A lady unlike any I've ever known, one I'd lay down and make love to this very moment if she were mine."

Her lips parted. He'd give no quarter. "Are you remembering how I tasted your finger—" His voice lowered even more. "Or my hand on your lovely breast?"

She swallowed hard. "Why?"

He knew what she was asking, so he didn't waste their time with questions.

"I'm not sure, since I'm torturing us both."

THAT MUCH WAS TRUE, AND two could play this game.

Warming to the exercise, Sara took a deliberately slow sip of wine before turning back to her target. Could she say it out loud? If Geoffrey could do it, so could she and they were, after all, seated alone.

"If you must know, it's your mouth on my breast I was remembering."

As if they were discussing something so mundane as the latest fashion at court, Sara turned back to the first course being served. If the sound he uttered was any indication, her barb had found its mark. Pleased with herself for maintaining her composure, she continued to press.

"Actually, upon further reflection, I wonder what would have happened had we not been interrupted."

This time his guttural groan was unmistakable. Taking a dainty bite of cheese, she presented him with her nicest manners.

"Thank you for allowing me the finest portion. It seems you do know a thing or two of courtly manners."

"I know a thing or two about many topics more interesting than proper manners," he said in a near growl. "Shall I enlighten you?"

There was a strange, clenching sensation in her core. Was this desire? It left her breathless and wanting … something.

"Please," she said. "You're obviously much more worldly than I."

His look told her he wasn't fooled by her mock deference.

She had once thought this man a dishonorable thief. There was no doubt Sir Geoffrey Waryn was not everything he seemed. If he had been completely lacking in honor, it would have been easy for him to take her virtue.

"Well, I could tell you why you've been so sheltered here at Kenshire. I've tales of the border that would shock your innocent ears."

"With a battle coming to my own gates more likely than not, I'd prefer not to speak of such things at the moment." That was precisely why she was enjoying the conversation so much. She had no stomach to dwell on the troubles that awaited her outside the safety of this hall.

"Fair enough. Maybe you'd like to talk about politics. I have a lot to say about the taxes levied to finance our prince's crusade." Geoffrey took a bite of the fish pie.

It was an exceptional meal. She would have to be sure to thank Cook. But at the moment, Sara couldn't stop staring. Wiping her mouth, she pretended to consider it. "Hmmm. It sounds stimulating, but I'll have to decline. Any other ideas?"

Geoffrey tilted his head up and clenched his jaw in mock concentration. She nearly laughed aloud at his attempt to be serious.

"Aye. Since you mentioned stimulation, what if we venture back to our original conversation?"

"You are incorrigible."

"I've been called much worse, milady."

"What think you to add to our discussion?"

He leaned even closer to her. Scandalously close. A musky, distinctly male scent filled her nostrils. "While you were thinking of my hand's exploration of your breast, I was imagining my body pressed against yours. Free of clothing, of course."

She willed her hands not to tremble. The intensity of his gaze made her nervous. Excited.

Though she willed it otherwise, her father was right about one thing. The world did not look kindly on a woman alone, and as much as she cherished the independence her father had allowed her, she knew it was his strength and authority that had made it possible. Would Geoffrey be as indulgent with the women in his life? Did it matter?

It didn't, but she wanted to know anyway.

"I've heard it said a woman is good for wedding and bedding but not much else. It seems you agree, Sir Geoffrey?"

Again, mock contemplation. "Come to think of it, yes, Lady Sara, I believe you have the right of it. Wedding and bedding. I couldn't have said it better myself."

"Ugh!"

His laugh stopped her from physically assaulting him. She liked when he forgot to be serious.

"I seem to have misspoken," he said, putting his chin in his hand as if deep in thought. "They may be useful for other things."

"Such as?"

"Well, that depends."

"On?"

"On the station of the lady in question."

Sara dreaded his line of thinking but forged ahead. "For a noblewoman?"

"If she's a typical noblewoman, she's likely good for wedding, bedding, and bearing children. And maybe overseeing servants if the lord is lucky."

"'Tis as I thought."

Why should she feel disappointed?

"On the other hand, if she was raised by an overly indulgent but intelligent parent, surrounded by the love of her people, it's just as likely she'd be 'good' for much more."

"Such as?"

He paused for so long she thought he might not continue.

"Such as aiding in the birth of babes, nearly outriding an expert horseman, effortlessly commanding castle officials." He shrugged negligently. "Stirring the passions of at least one man but likely more."

Unable to look away, she stared into his eyes.

"A woman any monk would envy with her extensive education. A lady with such an unconventional upbringing may also have learned to use the bow on horseback, reputably better than many knights."

She was speechless.

Luckily, Geoffrey had more to say. "Of course, such a woman would be extremely rare."

Sara knew why his answers were so important. She was falling for the reiver.

"And if you found such a woman?"

GEOFFREY FINALLY BROKE SARA'S GAZE, looking instead at the great hall around them. How could he answer that question? Every day for the past five years, he had wanted nothing more than to take back what had been stolen from him. He had no time for a relationship. Even if such a thing were possible.

His first instinct was to brush off her question with sexual innuendo, but he changed his mind. She deserved the truth.

"If she were mine for the taking, I'd thank the heavens for my good fortune. But I'd tell her the time wasn't right. There's something I still need to do."

"Bristol."

"Aye. I was raised there—my brothers and sister deserve more than to live off the charity of relatives.

"And *you* deserve your inheritance. You're a lord."

"Was a lord. Bristol was a land grant. I lost the right to that feudal title when our land was taken."

"I understand. But you're a lord in the ways that matter."

No, he was not. According to the law, he was nothing. But he didn't want to argue with Sara. He wanted her to think he was worthy of nobility.

"If this extraordinary woman was not mine, I'd memorize

every detail of her beautiful face and every curve of her luscious body for the inevitable day ahead when I find myself lying on the cold, hard ground before a raid, wondering why a baron's son keeps company with men who steal cattle for a living."

They sat in silence. He had nothing more to say. Or to offer. Just words.

"Thank you." Sara's soft voice was barely louder than a whisper.

"No thanks are necessary. 'Tis the truth."

CHAPTER 12

AFTER SUPPER, THE SUBDUED MOOD sent most of the castle's inhabitants to their respective stations. Sara was loath to leave Geoffrey's company, but Faye whisked her away to retire early. She was hard-pressed to disagree; it had been a long day and she knew tomorrow would be just as taxing.

After bidding Geoffrey good night, she made her way through the hall as the servants moved the benches to prepare the area for sleeping.

"Faye, I'll be along in a moment." Sara had nearly forgotten. "I've a quick errand to run.""My lady, your guard is watching your every move. He'll be at your heels unless we retire as planned."

Would that be so bad?

"I'm just visiting the kitchen. I'll be but a moment."

Without waiting for a response, she found her way to the building behind the main keep. She stepped inside, nearly running into the very person she sought.

"Cook! There you are."

"Aye, Lady Sara, right where I should be."

Sara put her arms around the portly woman. "Imagine finding you in the kitchen."

"My lady, how many times do I have to tell you not to come in here when you're in your finery? Your gown will get soiled. Wearin' the purple to show who's in charge, are you?"

Purple indeed. She would not be driven from her birthright.

"You'll have to tell me as many times as I have to tell you that

I don't give a fig about my gowns." She planted a kiss on the side of Cook's cheek."And what was that for?"

"That should be obvious. Do not deny it. You went to great pains tonight to lift our spirits with that meal."

Cook beamed. "Well, Sir Randolf's visit was a trying ordeal for you, milady. Don't *you* deny it."

Sara twisted one of her soft waves of brown hair around her fingers. "I'd never argue with you, Cook."

"There you are!" A booming male voice shouted from the door. "Is this how you retire to your chamber?"

Sir Geoffrey needed to be reminded of exactly who was in charge here. The purple dress clearly hadn't conveyed its message to *him*. But Cook replied before Sara could answer his high-handed greeting.

"And who are you to speak so harshly to milady?" The fact that Cook, a servant, would admonish Geoffrey spoke of her high regard at Kenshire Castle.

Visibly more relaxed, he smiled at Cook. "You missed me then, my buxom miss?"

"Hmph."

If Sara didn't know her better, she'd say Cook was blushing. Staring from one of them to the other, she was about to ask how they could possibly have become acquainted when Cook stumbled through an explanation.

"This lumbering knight thinks to charm me as he does all the ladies." Cook gave the knight in question a blistering stare. "But this old *gal* is on to him."

Winking at Sara, Geoffrey challenged the truth of Cook's words. "Thank you for the meal. As you promised, it was a culinary treat." Taking the woman's hand, Geoffrey raised it to his lips for a quick kiss, his eyes never leaving her face.

Then, lowering his voice, although not enough to conceal his words from everyone present, he unabashedly flirted. "And I know 'twas a special treat for me."

A sterner woman than Cook couldn't be found in these parts, and Sara's father had often joked that she could frighten even the most fearsome warrior. And yet here she was, taken with an outsider.

Geoffrey turned to Sara. "When your business is finished, will you allow me to escort you back to your chamber, my lady?"

"Thank you, Sir Geoffrey, I'm finished here." Nodding to Cook, she said, "Thank you again. It was a fine meal indeed." She took Geoffrey's extended arm, making a grand show of accepting his offer to escort her—just for fun. It was impossible to stay angry with him when he was this charming.

She could hear Cook remark to Faye, who'd followed Sara to the kitchen, "I never thought I'd see the day."

Her quick acceptance of an escort was a bit unusual for her, but Sara couldn't deny she wanted his company. Still, he'd taken a tone with her when he'd first followed her into the kitchen. "I've been coming and going without you for some time. There was no need to panic over a quick visit to the kitchen."

"That may be so, but with a madman at your gates, I'm not taking any chances." He looked behind them. "I expected to find Faye at your heels. The woman does travel close."

"Aye. Faye is dear to me," she said in an undertone. "She and her husband were never able to have children, so she treats me very much like her own daughter, especially after her husband passed away."

They walked the short distance back to the hall, but for the second time that week Geoffrey tugged on Sara's hand, changing course.

"Where are we going?"

"Your favorite place."

"The lake is in the other direction. And out of the question with Randolf so near.""Your second favorite place, then."

She sucked in her breath. Would he really take her there now? What would he do with her when they got there?

"Is it safe?"

"Aye, never safer. Randolf is being closely watched. Lord Henry's men arrived this morning. Eddard stationed them as extra guards at the north and south towers."

"He told me as much. I'll have to thank our vassal when I see him."

As they made their way down the path, a few passersby shot curious glances their way.

"My men will wonder where we're going." She wasn't very concerned, but there would be questions.

"Aye, they will. I'll spread the word that you offered to show me Kenshire's dungeons. They're located that way, no?" Geoffrey pointed to a narrow hallway before continuing on toward the secret entrance to the beach.

"They are, but they've gone unused for years. That's a curious excuse."

"Not for someone fascinated with dungeon lore."

"You're fascinated with dungeons?"

They exited the hidden archway, following the path that spilled onto the beach. The clear, salty air filled Sara's lungs and the sound of ocean waves breaking in the distance became louder with every step. Geoffrey wasted no time with words. He spun her around, pulling her into his arms. "Nay. But I am fascinated with you."

With that he claimed her lips, kissing her as fervently as if this was to be their last encounter. His tongue dove into her mouth, and she met it with her own. One of them groaned, she couldn't be sure which, as he deftly untied the laces at her back and pulled her gown down from her shoulders.

She let him. Didn't even consider telling him to stop.

When both of her breasts bounced free, he explored them with his hands.

Geoffrey's mouth ravished hers. His warm hands cupped her breasts and his thumbs teased the hard tips. The double assault to her senses was almost more than she could handle. Then, without warning, her lips were bereft of heat as his mouth replaced his hand. Grasping his hair, she moaned, unable to reconcile the feeling building deep within her.

Geoffrey lifted his head and his eyes bored into hers. "Sara." The intimacy of hearing her given name on his lips sent a thrill through her. "I want to please you."

"Geoffrey, you already do."

"Nay, I want to give you the kind of pleasure you've never experienced before."

Not understanding, she said, "You wish to make love to me?"

A sound of half pleasure and half torture escaped from his lips. "There's nothing I'd like more, but we cannot. As I said at supper, you're not mine to take."

"That's where you're mistaken. My virginity is mine alone to give."

That apparently startled him. "And you'd give it to me?"

Her answer was instantaneous. "Aye."

She wouldn't take it back. The rest could be worked out later. She had been raised to be decisive.

Well … she was making a decision now.

Geoffrey took a deep breath and squeezed his eyes shut.

What was he thinking?

The moment he opened his eyes, she could tell he was going to refuse her. He cupped her face in his hands and kissed her softly on the lips. "Tis the finest gift I've ever been offered, but one I must decline. I won't jeopardize your marriage to Lord Lyonsford, as much as I wish it were otherwise, for my own pleasure. He is your future and Kenshire's security."

"I know my duty well." And didn't need to hear it from him.

"It's not so easily done," he said, caressing her cheek, "fooling a man into believing he's taken a virgin."

She'd thought of that, of course. But there were ways around it.

"When I said I want to please you, I meant it. It's anyone's guess what tomorrow will bring." He inclined his head toward the castle. "Your men prepare for battle even now. Let me help us both forget for a short time."

She swallowed hard before nodding. What could he mean? Had he changed his mind?

GEOFFREY RECOGNIZED HER CONFUSION AS innocence. He placed another soft kiss on her lips, but she held out a hand to stop him.

"You have me at a disadvantage." She nodded toward her naked chest and then at his own torso. "I want to see you."

Never predisposed to patience, he quickly dispensed with his padded leather jack. After he shrugged it free, Sara stepped forward and shakily untied the laces of his undershirt herself.

Geoffrey couldn't recall ever being so aroused by the simple act of having his shirt removed. Once the garment was discarded, Sara ran her hands along his chest muscles, touching her finger tentatively to one nipple, staring in apparent fascination as it hardened, reacting to touch much like her own did.

He hadn't counted on her curiosity, her sense of open wonder, when he'd vowed to leave Sara a virgin. The tantalizing touch of the woman in his arms had him rock hard. Ending the sweet torture, he pulled her closer so their bare chests came in contact. Her soft "Oh!" shot straight to his manhood.

He kissed Sara while moving her toward the same rock outcropping where they sat days before. The one he knew was not in view of the lookouts. "Step out of your gown." Sara complied without question, and he silently helped her.

Kneeling at her feet, Geoffrey reached under her shift and removed her fine hose one leg at a time. He allowed his hands to brush her firm legs, smiling as a sigh escaped from her lips. Reverently, he eased her into a seated position beside her fine, discarded gown. Her shift was already pulled low, giving him access to her beautiful breasts.

Kneeling below her, Geoffrey murmured, "Trust me."

Moving closer, he once again traced his hand up her well-formed calf, teasing the soft flesh of her upper leg and splaying his hand across her inner thigh. Her eyes were closed, head tilted back. Asking for her trust was unnecessary. When his hand found an undergarment, he expertly brushed past it, willing his lady's eyes to open. He was most anxious for her response. It didn't take long. Sara's eyes shot open at the first stroke of his finger.

Their gazes locked. "Nay, don't close your legs, love."

When she started to argue, he cut her short. "Look how your body responds."

With that, he thrust a finger inside, smiling at her throaty gasp, and continued to distract her from embarrassment.

"Your wetness tells me what I already know." Allowing her enough time to adjust to the new sensation, he began to move his finger. Keeping time with the sound of the waves as they crashed ashore, he picked up and then slowed his pace, using his thumb to tease the nub that lay at the core of her building passion.

"Close your eyes. Forget about everything save my finger inside you." Her arched back told him the gentle assault was working. "Let me pleasure you, Sara. Feel it build and let go when you're ready."

He knew his words meant naught to her, but he was desperate to bring Sara to her first release. Moaning, she pushed her hips toward his hand. When he knew she was close, Geoffrey used his free hand to toss the hem of her shift even higher. He trailed kisses up her leg until his lips found the soft flesh of her inner thigh.

He felt her body tightening as her breathing turned heavier and heavier. Kneeling at her feet, he used his hands and mouth to bring her to the brink of a passionate release. Finally, Geoffrey felt her clenching around his fingers. He watched her fingers claw at the rocks from the corner of his eye. Not allowing her climax to subside, Geoffrey continued to tease with his fingers until her thighs slowly stopped trembling. Eventually, her body began to relax.

He considered showing her how quickly she could climax again but decided to forego the idea. Much more of this exquisite torture and he'd forget his honorable intentions. As it was, he needed to relieve himself—and quickly.

Geoffrey looked up as he lifted Sara's delicate foot to replace her stockings.

Clearly disheveled, beads of sweat at her brow, Sara looked as though she'd been thoroughly ravished.

It was the loveliest sight he ever beheld.

"I don't trust myself to speak."

"Then don't." He moved to sit beside her.

"But I have … I mean, I want…"

He rescued her. "It seems I've rendered milady speechless."

This woman had faced her archenemy with cool disdain, but he'd pleasured her so well she was unable to formulate a coherent thought.

He was inordinately pleased.

"What do you find so humorous, pray tell?"

"You. If I'd known that's all it would take, I'd have pleasured you at our first meeting on the beach."

"I'm sure I wouldn't have allowed it!"

He wasn't so sure he agreed—this connection between them had been out of control even then—but didn't think she'd appreciate hearing his opinion.

"What about you?"

He deliberately feigned ignorance.

"What of me?"

"Well, I … don't you, you know?"

Geoffrey had not been dissembling when he'd told William he had never taken a virgin. He'd never had a conversation like this with a woman, but he was enjoying himself immensely. "You're wondering about my own pleasure?"

"Aye." She was clearly relieved to be unburdened from putting her thoughts into words.

"That will have to come later."

Eyes wide, she obviously jumped to the wrong conclusion.

"Nay, my lady. Not by another." He continued unabashedly, "I'll have to see to it myself. Or take a cold swim instead."

"Oh." Her lips formed a perfect circle and he couldn't resist putting his lips to them. His hand closed around her neck, and he marveled at how aroused a simple kiss could make him.

He pulled away before the entire household came to look for them. "I'm loath to let you go, but Faye must be near mad with worry."

"Faye!" Sara exclaimed. "What will I tell her?"

Standing, she allowed him to help her dress, the deep violet fabric wrinkled beyond repair after being discarded on the dune.

"I'll tell her I begged you to allow me solace on the beach."

Laughing, Sara took the hand he offered, weaving her fingers around his. They walked hand in hand, the castle looming above them.

"Geoffrey? Was that, um, the usual way?"

For him, definitely not. He couldn't remember a time when he had felt quite that way without even taking his own pleasure. "I don't believe so."

Shy wasn't a word he associated with Sara, but he was sure she opened and closed her mouth at least three times before speaking. He didn't want to press her, but he ached to hear what she would say next.

"I mean to say, is that what it feels like every time?"

He stopped, turned her toward him, and brushed his thumb across her lower lip. This was madness, but he couldn't keep his hands off her.

"Nay, not always."

Not ever.

CHAPTER 13

FAYE MOVED AROUND THE ROOM, instructing a young chambermaid to stoke the fire and take away the wash bowl.

"One minute you're visiting the kitchen and the next you're jaunting down to the beach—all while your cousin is practically at Kenshire's gates."

If Faye had been a typical servant, Sara would never have allowed her to be so bold. But theirs wasn't a normal relationship, and most of the time Sara was glad for it.

Just not at the moment.

Using her most authoritative tone, Sara said, "Firstly, I was not jaunting but walking. I desperately needed to clear my head. And secondly, as well you know, Randolf is *not* my cousin." She looked pointedly at the young maid, whom Faye promptly dismissed.

Faye put her free hands firmly on her wide hips. "Call it what you will, but your father would have never allowed you to roam free under such circumstances."

Sara sat on the edge of her bed, feeling slightly guilty for omitting much of the true story. "He would never have known unless someone was keen to tell him, Mistress Faye—just like someone did the last time I was caught there after sunset." She gave her an arch look.

Faye made a most unladylike sound.

"I was well-protected, in any case."

"Aye, I imagine you were."

Sara didn't know if it was her imagination, or if Faye truly did suspect what she and Geoffrey had done on the beach. Willing herself not to blush, she said, "Besides, my men are following Randolf and his small retinue. I was never in any danger."

"I don't doubt Sir Geoffrey is well-suited to protect you, my lady. But who will protect you from him?"

Before she could answer, the chambermaid rushed back inside, apologizing profusely. "I'm sorry to interrupt, my lady, but Sir Hugh and the scouting party have arrived. They're asking for you."

Faye looked down at Sara's thin chemise and sprang into action. "The breeches will be quicker." Then Sara said to the maid, "Tell Hugh I will receive him and the captain in my solar."

When Sara walked into the solar, it was already occupied by Sir Hugh, Peter, Eddard, and Gerald. Sir Geoffrey was notably absent.

Peter spoke first. "We apologize for the late hour, my lady."

Sara waved him off. "What news?"

"We're still waiting for the search party. They traveled southwest—the most likely path for Covington's army," Eddard began, "but the rest of us saw no sign of any of his men, Lady Sara."

"What's your current assessment then?"

"We've no evidence that Covington is backing Randolf's claim other than his own words and a rumor which he himself may have started."

All eyes turned to the door that had just opened. *Geoffrey*. Sara's heart thumped at the sight of him. "As you know, gentlemen," he continued, "besieging a castle such as Kenshire would involve assembling and paying an army, gathering supplies, and hauling them here at considerable expense," said Geoffrey. "In my opinion, it's unlikely Covington would go to that trouble on behalf of anyone other than himself, especially at the risk of angering the king. Again."

It seemed as if everyone began talking at once after that.

Sara found it hard to concentrate with Geoffrey looking at her, his hair wet—had he taken his cold swim after all?—his eyes boring into her own.

Willing herself back to the conversation, she spoke over the volume of opinions. "If Sir Geoffrey is correct, we must assume Randolf is planning something more nefarious than a siege. Else it would be foolish indeed for him to arrive at Kenshire with less than twenty men and a tenuous 'claim.'"

"And if he's wrong?" Eddard asked. The gruff middle-aged man had a plentitude of scars that attested to his battle record.

"Kenshire is prepared for Sir Randolf and Covington both," she said. "Hugh has overseen much-needed fortifications at the gatehouse, and my father's improvements to the castle in recent months have made it stronger than ever. We've plenty of food and water stockpiled in preparation, and only those essential to Kenshire's safety remain as mouths to feed. All of our remaining visitors have left. We've been preparing for this day since my father took ill."

Warming to her topic, she continued. "We're not ruling out a counter-attack if an army does arrive on our doorstep, and Lord Thornhurst is only one of my family's many vassals who have pledged men if necessary. Messengers are already in position awaiting our signal. If Geoffrey is wrong, which I don't think he is, we're as prepared as we'll ever be."

Though Geoffrey grimaced at the mention of Lord Thornhurst, he looked … impressed.

Everyone was quiet for a moment before Eddard, who had been in Kenshire's service since he was sent to squire at Kenshire, said, "Lady Sara is right." Then, for her ears only, he murmured, "Your father would be proud."

She couldn't help a small smile at that.

"Come, we've work to do," Eddard said. "Hugh, may I speak with you a moment?"

Eddard and the other men filed out of the solar one by one. Peter beamed at her on his way out. Eventually only she and Geoffrey remained. He approached her slowly and deliberately, but stopped a good distance away. Both of them were aware that his uncle stood outside the door with Eddard.

"It seems every time I bid you a good night, circumstances

intervene to bring us back together."

She couldn't think past Geoffrey's potent, distinctive scent, now layered with the smell of the sea. She attempted to steady her voice. It was easier addressing a room full of warriors than it was this one man. "Why is that, do you believe?"

"That's the very question I pondered in my chamber before being summoned to you once again."

It was pointless to speak her truth—their situation had not changed—but she could not stop herself. "Do you want to know what I think?" she said softly.

"Aye."

"We share a connection unlike any I've ever known. I think I'm drawn to you, and I think you feel the same."

"Sara..."

"Nay, don't say it. I already know. I beg forgiveness for rushing to judgment when you arrived and for not allowing you and your uncle to prove yourselves." She hesitated before adding, "But most of all, I mourn that this cannot be."

She knew her duty to her people and would not abandon it. But she also cared for this man who was so much more than a reiver.

There was nothing more to say.

With a quick squeeze of his hand, Sara turned and walked away.

JUST A FEW HOURS AFTER their encounter, Kenshire was buzzing with activity. Outside the castle walls, the rising sun heralded a new autumn day as villagers went about their routines. Inside the castle, it was a different story. Pots of water were placed on walls and in towers to detect mining tunnels in case Randolf attempted an underground entry. The granaries were inventoried, additional guards were put on alert, and catapults were placed into position.

Geoffrey had taken part in similar preparations on a smaller scale many times in Bristol. Life along the border meant maintaining constant vigilance. Not that it had done them any good. In the end, they had failed. He had failed. He should have been there to help his sire defend their home. Instead, his home and his parents had been taken from him.

He'd be damned if he let the same thing happen to Sara.

He wasn't sure when or how it happened, but her battle had become his. His uncle was right—Bristol could wait a few weeks longer. He would see Sara safely wed.

The thought formed a knot in his stomach.

While he longed to be preparing for battle with the others, Geoffrey was grateful duty required him to keep Lady Sara in his sights. He trusted no one else, even her own men, to keep her safe. In the meantime, he continued to quietly inquire after a certain servant, but he learned nothing of import. Peter informed him that no suspicions had ever been raised concerning the cupbearer.

During preparations for the midday meal, usually the largest and best attended, he pulled a serving maid aside in the hopes of gleaning information.

"A word?" He recognized the girl from the kitchen the day before. She'd been following him with her eyes, and he hoped her interest would incline her to help.

"With pleasure, my lord," said the blonde-haired maid.

"Margaret, correct?"

"Aye, milord."

He allowed the courtesy again, using his perceived station to his advantage.

"I hesitate to ask you something, but I feel you're able to keep a secret."

Margaret moved closer, deliberately misunderstanding.

"You can *ask* me anything ye please," she answered.

Geoffrey was surprised at his body's lack of response. She was beautiful, obviously willing, and yet he didn't feel the slightest stirring.

"I might have a different sort of … question for you later," he said, hinting at future pleasures that would never be. "Do you recall how I asked about the cupbearer yesterday?" He could only hope her interest in him would be enough to sway her loyalty to another member of the staff.

She nodded. "You wanted to know if he visits the kitchen often."

"Aye, but I never asked about his disposition."

He left the inquiry open.

"Coy, fer sure. Never met a man who kept to himself more than John. He's been here a few years, but I'd hardly say I know him. Why do ye ask, milord?"

"He's been attentive these past days, and I wondered how to show my gratitude." It was a lame excuse, to be certain, but it was the best he could offer.

Margaret gave him a knowing smile. "He fancies himself the cupbearer, though truth be told, he's no more esteemed than I am."

Geoffrey knew it was an honored position in some households, though at Kenshire the servant seemed to have many duties beyond bearing the lady her drink. Margaret's next words sparked his interest.

"There be rumors of a relationship with Lady Maude, if you'll excuse me saying so." Lowering her voice, Margaret added, "Her husband is an elderly baron past the age to give her a child."

And then, as if she feared she said too much, Margaret swiftly changed topics. "Is there anything else I might do for ye, my lord?" Her light hazel eyes finished the thought.

From the corner of his eye, Geoffrey caught Sara's quick glance from across the hall. "Not at the moment, lass. Thank you for keeping our conversation private." He emphasized that last word, giving her a playful wink.

Giggling, Margaret moved on. The Countess of Kenshire's frown turned into a scowl as the pretty blonde walked by. If only she knew how little he wanted to bed the girl.

Sara was cool and quiet to him when they took their meal. Geoffrey considered explaining his conversation with the maid but thought better of it. Perhaps he should allow her to think the worst of him. Although he was unable to understand the connection between them, he could not longer deny that it existed. He did, however, question his own ability to remain detached.

As the day wore on, Geoffrey continued to turn to the question of the suspicious cupbearer and Randolf's threat. Finally, he could keep his suspicions to himself no longer. He asked Peter to keep a close eye on Sara, left the hall, and made for the stables at the other end of the courtyard. While he waited for his horse to be saddled, he considered informing his uncle of the impromptu plan, but Hugh would either attempt to stop him or accompany him on this fool's errand.

Neither possibility was acceptable.

Riding past the gatehouse, Geoffrey admired the work his uncle had commissioned. The castle was, to his mind, impregnable, which only made him more suspicious of Randolf's aims. Acknowledging the guards, he sped away without giving another thought to potential danger.

Locating the camp was easy—finding Randolf proved more difficult.

As he charged into the encampment, Geoffrey dismounted and held his hands into the air. He was immediately surrounded by a half dozen men-at-arms, their swords raised.

"Sir Geoffrey Waryn," he announced, his voice loud and strong, "from Kenshire Castle. I mean no harm."

"State your business—immediately." The man who addressed him was armed and suited for battle, his chainmail and weapon proclaiming him a knight of means. He was fully bearded, though, and looked more like a reiver than Geoffrey did.

"I seek Sir Randolf with a message," Geoffrey said.

"From Lady Sara?"

"Nay, from me."

Eyeing him warily, the bearded man, evidently the spokesman of the group, gestured for the others to put down their weapons. "Randolf is not here, nor does he care to receive messages from anyone other than the Lady of Kenshire."

So much for cordiality.

"Then kindly deliver a warning to your lord." Lowering his hands, Geoffrey stared directly into the eyes of the leader as the others began to back away, still eyeing him intently.

"If Sir Randolf dares to take Kenshire by any means other than those considered honorable, I will hunt him down and slit his cowardly throat."

It took a moment for the words to sink in, but when they did, the mood shifted immediately. One overzealous knight charged him, sword held high as if to decapitate him. He drew his own sword just in time to deflect the worst of his attacker's thrust.

His opponent gave him a sizeable gash in the lower arm, but Geoffrey quickly relieved the man of his sword. The man toppled backward, and before the others could do aught to stop him, Geoffrey stepped on the man's chest and lowered the point of his weapon until it hovered just above his throat.

"Stop!" the bearded man shouted.

Having made his point, Geoffrey took his booted foot off the man's chest, backing away. He sheathed his weapon and looked at the men surrounding him. It was just as he'd thought. Less than twenty men rushed forward in total, though Randolf had claimed to be accompanied by at least twice that number.

"I have no quarrel with you, sir," Geoffrey spat, walking away, somewhat surprised the path cleared for him. "I expect the message to be relayed."

Without waiting for a response, he mounted and rode back toward the castle. His arm hurt like the devil, but the scratch hardly mattered. He'd achieved his purpose.

THE EVENING MEAL WAS ONCE again more subdued than usual. The second scouting party had not yet returned, and Randolf's two-day deadline was fast approaching. Sara, who still seemed aggrieved by the attention Geoffrey had given Margaret, gave much of her attention to Sir Hugh. The conversation turned to Sara's mother, whom Hugh had met several times.

The talk made Geoffrey think of his own parents, and how

his youngest siblings had come of age without them. His hands clenched into fists as he thought about Bristol Manor and the bastards who'd stolen it. Even now the border clan lived in his home, among his people. How he wished to send them back to Scotland, or preferably to hell.

A hand on his arm brought Geoffrey back to the present. He looked up into Sara's concerned gaze. It was enough to remind him that they were where they needed to be for the time being. The bastard Kerrs could wait. But not for long.

"Is something amiss, Sir Geoffrey?"

"Nay, my lady."

She clearly didn't believe him. What could he say? *I was remembering my murdered parents, relishing the moment I can exact revenge on the blackguards who killed them.*

Instead, he changed topics. "It seems your mood is improved." At least that made one of them.

SARA STRUGGLED TO KEEP A smile on her face. As if Randolf wasn't enough to worry about, she hadn't been able to banish the image of Geoffrey and Margaret laughing and flirting.

"It will be improved when we have confirmation that Randolf has naught but a small retinue of men and his own empty threats."

"And with any luck, the Lord Lyonsford will be riding in to your rescue at any moment."

There was something about his tone that sounded almost … jealous. "Aye, with any luck he will be," she said. She hadn't yet forgiven him, and his mood was apparently as sour as her own.

She was about to turn away when she noticed a thin line of red on his arm. His gaze followed hers, and he rolled back his sleeve to reveal a bloody bandage.

Without thinking, she grabbed his arm to inspect the wound. "How did you get this?"

They exchanged a look, and Sara became acutely aware that she was holding his arm in full view of a roomful of people.

Her pulse raced as he parted his mouth to answer. What an inopportune time to think about the feeling of his lips on her own. So soft and hard at the same time. She swallowed, watching his eyes darken, knowing his thoughts mirrored her own.

Realizing she was still gripping his injured arm, she forced herself to release it.

The momentary spell was broken.

"Excuse me." Geoffrey stood abruptly, taking his leave.

So much for protocol, which dictated she be the first to retire. She watched him walk away, only then realizing he had not answered her question about the injury.

"I apologize for Geoffrey," Hugh said from his seat on her other side. "He's not usually quite so rude."

Sara decided not to disagree. "We're under tremendous pressure at the moment. And I know it wears on him to remain by my side when he'd prefer to be with you and the men."

"Aye, it's a different role for him. But an important one."

Sir Hugh seemed to read her thoughts.

"Unlike my nephew, I'm not ashamed at what we've had to do to survive these last few years. Just as your father wasn't ashamed to house a minor baron's brother in the same quarters as an earl and his family. The character of a man, or woman, is more important than their station. I believe that, and your father did as well."

Sara considered his words. She knew her father would agree. Although he'd urged her to cultivate the respect that was due of an earl's daughter, he had also warned her not to take it for granted.

But why was Sir Hugh telling her this?

"But it doesn't explain why my father didn't just tell me of your close friendship."

Sir Hugh ate a bite of bread and followed it with a swig of ale. He looked at her expectantly.

Of course her father hadn't told her. It was a lesson he'd expected her to learn on her own. There was a difference between decisiveness and making judgments without all of the facts.

"Thank you."

And she meant it. Talking to Sir Hugh made her feel as if her father sat beside her again.

Sara raised her cup. "To Lord Kenshire."

Hugh lifted his mug. "To your father. The finest man I've ever known."

One of the finest, she amended to herself.

CHAPTER 14

WITH SARA SAFELY SEATED BESIDE his uncle, Geoffrey left the hall. He wasn't sure what had tempted him to goad her by mentioning Lord Lyonsford. That the earl would be the one to secure her title and save the day irked him immensely. But taunting her with that fact had done nothing more than irritate them both.

"My lord?"

The voice beckoned to him from a small antechamber adjacent to the hall.

Seeing no one about, he made his way toward the room. Margaret, the blonde-haired servant, stood just inside the doorway. Geoffrey felt immediately uneasy.

"Were you inquiring after me?" he asked, keeping his distance.

Certain of the answer, he looked up and down the hallway. Nothing appeared out of order.

"Aye, milord. You asked about John earlier. I have information ye'll be interested in."

He stepped closer, relaxing a little when he realized the small reception room was empty.

But she was up to something. "There's no need for further inquiry. 'Tis nothing to concern yourself with."

Lowing her voice and reaching for his hand, Margaret said, "But you do concern me." Pulling him into the room, she leaned closer as if conspiring with him. "And this should concern you as well. It's about Lady Sara."

Slowly retrieving his hand, his curiosity allowed him to continue the conversation, though he couldn't temper the sharp edge to his voice. "What about Sara?"

Listening for footsteps or other unusual sounds, Geoffrey awaited her answer. Her demeanor indicated there was something more at play, but for the life of him, he couldn't work out what it could be. Had she told John about his inquiries?

The room was one Geoffrey had only seen briefly before. It was more richly appointed than the neighboring hall, though dwarfed in size by the great room. Coats of arms hung from the ceiling, and each wall was bedecked with an oversized tapestry.

"Please. I don't wish to be overheard." She moved closer in a way that reminded him of a practiced courtesan. Could this be nothing more than an attempt at seduction? If so, he wanted none of it.

Then she leaned in close enough for him to feel her breath on his ear. "You were right to question John," she whispered.

Stiffening his shoulders, Geoffrey followed her farther into the room.

"Please, milord." Without warning, she lunged toward him, wrapping her arms around his neck and pressing her lips firmly to his own. He sensed a presence before seeing one and attempted to disengage himself from Margaret's grasp. Unfortunately she was tenacious, and rather than allowing herself to be dislodged, she moaned as if in the throes of pleasure.

A gasp at the entranceway told Geoffrey what he had already suspected.

He'd been deceived.

He was able to pull away from the amorous servant just in time to see Sara's back as she practically ran from the room, but before he could hurry after her, a familiar voice stopped him.

"You don't want to do that."

The very man he'd inquired about walked toward them. Short and stocky with balding hair, John's dress was plain and drab. His manner was tinged with an air of superiority not typical of a man in his rank.

"And why is that?" With one fist clenched, he moved his other hand to the hilt of the sword at his side.

"I'd like a word with you, sir." The servant remained calm, as if he hadn't witnessed Geoffrey's embrace with the servant girl or Sara's subsequent departure.

As though he didn't understand the threat.

"That's too damn bad." He turned to leave. Whether by bad luck or something more sinister, Sara had been positioned to see him with Margaret at the worst possible moment, and Geoffrey wanted to know why. But finding Sara was his main priority. He would handle this fool later.

"You've been asking about me." It was John's tone rather than his words that stopped Geoffrey in his tracks.

A chill ran down Geoffrey's back. John turned to Margaret, who'd been quietly retreating from the room. "Don't go too far, Margaret. I'd like a word with you when we're finished here."

She bobbed a quick curtsy. "Aye." Turning, she ran away from them.

"How may I be of assistance, Sir Geoffrey?" John said, turning to him.

It was obvious the man wasn't at all interested in being helpful. But what *was* he up to?

"Now that you mention it—" He walked toward the small man, the hand at his side never moving from his sword. Standing more than a head above most men, he dwarfed the servant. "I wonder if you know the whereabouts of Lady Maude?"

John's face went decidedly pale.

"I'd say she left Kenshire a few days ago," he hedged, "but can't tell ye more than that. I'm but a humble servant, after all."

To his credit, the man finally seemed to realize his perilous situation. He took a step away from him. Good idea. Geoffrey didn't bother to hide his displeasure. "I know you're acquainted, having witnessed a discussion between you."

John's shoulders relaxed. "Ahh, that. 'Twas nothing but a small disagreement. She's overly indulgent, at times, though it ain't my place to say so. Her husband asked that I water her wine.

When she discovered it, the lady confronted me."

He was a liar. But Geoffrey was eager to ensure Sara's safety and explain the situation she'd witnessed. He'd act like he accepted the meager excuse. For now.

"In that case, it seems we've nothing more to discuss."

Before waiting for a response, Geoffrey left the room. The man called after him, but he did not slow his steps. He took the stairs leading to Sara's chamber two at a time. Pleased to find the door unlocked, he virtually slammed it open. A quick perusal confirmed his fears.

No Sara.

CHAPTER 15

BACK IN THE HALL, THE servants were cleaning and stacking the trestle tables against the wall to prepare for the night. It was quite different from the mood on Geoffrey's first night at Kenshire when the great hall had buzzed with music and guests. With Kenshire Castle preparing in earnest for battle, only knights and servants remained.

Geoffrey found Peter and Eddard talking in the corner of the hall.

"Have either of you seen Lady Sara?"

Her two trusted advisors exchanged a glance as they both shook their heads.

"We'd ask the same of you," said Peter. "You've not been more than ten feet away from her for days."

Rather than waste time responding, Geoffrey bellowed commands over his shoulder as he raced toward the door. He didn't care that he wasn't in a position to do so; he only cared about finding her. And John must be detained.

He searched the kitchen next, though Cook's bemused expression told him before he had a chance to ask that Sara wasn't there. Everywhere he went, Geoffrey issued the same order: "Find Lady Sara." Within minutes the castle was abuzz with activity, the search for its lady well underway.

Standing in front of the main keep, Geoffrey tried to decide if he should head toward the gatehouse, where his uncle was likely stationed, or in the opposite direction toward the stables.

Geoffrey assessed the situation and considered Sara's most

likely location. She was clearly upset over having seen him with Margaret, but she was also smart and level-headed, so he discounted the possibility of her traveling outside the outer curtain wall toward the village. She wouldn't consider such a thing with Randolf just beyond Kenshire's gates. But his gut told him something was wrong. The staged seduction, John's behavior—somehow it was all tied to Randolf. Geoffrey knew it. He just didn't understand how.

A young knight came running toward him. "Sir Geoffrey!"

Darkness had begun to descend, and it took Geoffrey a moment to make out the source of the voice. The lad looked fairly young. His dark hair and youthful face reminded him of his youngest brother Neill.

"Has she been found?"

The boy looked confused. "She? Your uncle sent me to find you. There's movement at Randolf's camp. We're not sure..."

Fear like none Geoffrey had known since the raid on his village gripped him. He started running before the lad could finish. It had suddenly occurred to him where he could find Sara. As he ran toward the sea gate, one thought overrode all others. *Please let her be safe.*

Geoffrey cursed himself as he traversed the narrow passageway. He should have immediately thought of the beach. An image flashed through his mind of her head tossed back, her features alive with pleasure

Making his way through the bluffs, Geoffrey could hear nothing but the sounds of the waves, see nothing but tall grass on the horizon. While just a few days earlier the chorus of the ocean had evoked a sense of peace, now it sounded foreboding to his ears.

His heart slammed in his chest, in his ears. Geoffrey recognized the primal fear that gripped him and knew if anything had happened to her, he'd never forgive himself.

Please let her be safe.

With the moonlight as his only guide, he made his way toward the water to get a clearer view of the coastline.

And then he saw it. A shape? Or was it two? They were heading toward the bluff where he had stood just moments ago. No sound could be heard over the waves, and he'd almost missed them.

Charging toward the movement, he unsheathed his sword—the same one his father had given him when he was knighted. A sword made for revenge. As he came closer, his view became clearer and he began to hear muffled sounds. Sara was being held from behind by a man he couldn't identify. He could see the train of her gown though not her face.

Somehow, his presence had gone unnoticed so far. But there was nowhere to hide, and he knew the element of surprise was his best hope.

He moved stealthily, his soft leather boots not making a sound on the dry sand. It was the one and only time Geoffrey had ever rued his large size. All it would take was one look in his direction for the attacker to see him clearly. Luckily, the man's back was to him, and Sara's attempts to struggle free were commanding his attention.

Though he couldn't, *wouldn't*, take chances with Sara's safety, Geoffrey was straining against the urge to charge forward, pull her from the man's grasp, and unceremoniously slit his throat. Instead he crept closer and closer, waiting to be discovered.

That moment finally came when Geoffrey's sword scraped a rock. The man turned sharply and spotted him. The moonlight cooperated, and he was granted a clear look at the man's face.

How the hell did Randolf get inside the castle walls?

CHAPTER 16

GEOFFREY BEGAN TO RUN FASTER than he'd ever run in his life. Just before he descended on the man whose life he would end that night—there was no way in hell Geoffrey would let him live—Randolf stopped him dead in his tracks.

"One step closer and she dies."

He immediately halted. Randolf had tugged Sara around so that both of them were facing Geoffrey. There was fear in her eyes, but they were also full of fight. His fierce countess. Randolf's hand covered her mouth as she struggled.

"Be still, wench!" He was clearly having a more difficult time with his captive than he'd expected.

Geoffrey smiled. A cool, mocking smile meant to inflame the man standing across from him.

"I wouldn't be smiling if I were you, Sir Geoffrey. You're going to die tonight."

He laughed in response, as if it were the most amusing joke he ever heard. Sara stopped struggling and looked at him as if he were mad.

"Throw down your sword, bastard!" Randolf commanded.

"Landless, yes. But a bastard? Nay, not that."

"Are you witless? I came here to force the lady's hand in marriage, but I can just as easily slit her throat. I said throw down your sword!"

The man was desperate enough to do something rash. Geoffrey took a deep breath, remembering the many times he had landed flat on his back in training because he was "too rash." He silently thanked his father, who had always encouraged him to bring a cool mind to conflict.

Geoffrey thought of everything he learned about his adversary, deciding which pieces of information should guide his next actions. A third son who had outlived both parents and brothers. An accident and whispered rumors. Ties to Caiser that went back generations. Alliances in the baron's war. Traitor. Dangerous. Envious.

Tossing his sword aside, Geoffrey crossed his arms, still smiling. "I'm most anxious to see how you think to leave here alive," he said, acting as if Randolf were an old friend.

The pretender looked toward the castle.

Geoffrey continued to mock him. "Ahhh, you're waiting for company." He still wondered how the hell Randolf had managed to get past the guards, but he didn't voice that particular question.

Sara began to struggle again in earnest. Geoffrey forced himself to hold his concentration on the man who held her. If he looked into her eyes at this moment, he'd very likely lose the composure he was struggling to maintain.

Randolf sneered, "You forget, reiver, I know the secret passageways as well as anyone."

Geoffrey wanted him to keep talking. "And John?"

Randolf laughed. It was a high-pitched, overly confident sound.

His suspicions about Margaret and John were confirmed, but was anyone else involved? He began to applaud. "Well done. I just wonder, if you will indulge me, what Lady Maude had to do with your design?"

Randolf looked confused. "Lady Maude? I know nothing of a Lady Maude. John was told to get Sara alone and unguarded, and he did."

Geoffrey pretended to ponder that. "Hmmm, but I wonder how you knew precisely when that would happen." Every time Randolf answered, Geoffrey inched his way forward, using the other man's distraction against him.

Glancing back at the secret path from the castle, Randolf appeased Geoffrey's curiosity.

"A signal from the Constable Tower solved that problem easily enough."

Geoffrey could sense the man's rising panic. There was no sign of any helpers, and Randolf had no hope of escaping alive without any aid.

"If your purpose is to dispose of Lady Sara—" Geoffrey said. His composure nearly cracked at the thought, "—why not just have your man John do it rather than risk coming here yourself?"

Randolf clearly had difficulty deciding whether to sneer at him or formulate a new plan.

Sara stopped fighting, most likely surprised to learn that the man who had served her household faithfully for these last three years was a traitor.

Randolf's laugh made Geoffrey's blood run cold. He was getting impatient, but he needed to know who else was embroiled in this scheme to wrest Kenshire Castle from Sara.

Accommodating for a miscreant, Randolf indulged him. "The original plan was for him to dispatch her with a few drops of poison in one of the drinks he poured. But the coward thought it could be traced back to him." Randolf shifted his weight back and forth. He was tiring. "He proved useful, however. A forced marriage will do just as well." Another quick glance toward the castle.

"Waiting for your men?"

"My men?" Too quickly, Randolf added, "Aye, and when they arrive, your meddlesome presence will no longer be an issue."

He didn't dare move any closer, but Randolf had just confirmed that he was waiting for just one person. One who would never arrive. Geoffrey had seen to that.

Sara caught Geoffrey's gaze, and he was nearly undone. Despite her obvious terror, she was composed, aware. He nodded his head, and she somehow seemed to understand. Struggling like a wildcat, she kicked Randolf squarely on the shin. Later Sara would say she hardly saw a movement before being thrown to the ground.

In one fluid motion, Geoffrey grabbed his sword, charged the pair, and twisted Randolf's arm until his weapon fell to the ground. After recovering from his surprise, Randolf unsheathed his sword and simultaneously jumped back. A wave of relief washed over Geoffrey—Sara moved away from them. She was safe

While Randolf was surprisingly adept with the knight's broadsword, he stood no chance against Geoffrey's strength and vengeful fury. He had dared to threaten Sara's life—his only option was to die. With a bellow of rage, he ran his sword through the traitor's gut. The fool wasn't even wearing chainmail.

Falling to the ground, Randolf clutched at the sand below him, his eyes wide with shock. Geoffrey felt nothing but satisfaction as he watched the life drain from Sara's relative. Gurgling now, attempting to talk but unable to do so, the last man with any blood ties to the Caiser family finally succumbed to his destiny.

RANDOLF WAS DEAD. BEFORE THE thought could fully register, Sara ran to Geoffrey and clung to him as if her life depended on it. The rage and despair she'd felt upon seeing him with the beautiful servant didn't matter.

He had saved her.

Geoffrey wrapped his arms around her, dropping the sword that dripped with Randolf's blood.

"Shhhh, you are safe now," he murmured, his voice barely a whisper. Sara could feel his heart pounding against her chest.

Tears streamed down her face. She sobbed uncontrollably for everything that was lost. The life of the man who had threatened Kenshire. Her father, whom she thought of every single day. The love of the man whose arms held her now.

She should never have come down here alone. But she hadn't stopped to think after seeing him in an embrace with the comely servant. Pain and rage had swallowed her whole. He belonged to her. Of course, he didn't, not really, but she hadn't been thinking rationally. She had alternated between wanting to tear out the girl's hair and weeping like a child.

She'd hardly noticed her surroundings. Only when she heard the sound of the water did she realize she'd run toward the sea. She hadn't noticed Randolf until he was upon her—and by then it was too late to escape. She'd never been as scared in her life.

Randolf had come to take her castle, her inheritance. Her people. She'd struggled with all her might, ignoring his frantic pleas to calm down.

Never. She would do right by the people of Kenshire if it killed her.

Luckily, thanks to Geoffrey, it hadn't come to that.

PULLING HER FACE FROM HIM, Geoffrey stared into the eyes of the woman who had just brought him to the brink of terror-induced madness. Her eyelashes still glistened, so he carefully wiped away the tears with his thumb and leaned down to kiss every inch of her face. Her eyes, her cheeks, her lips. His mouth moved over hers in a kiss that conveyed everything he'd been feeling that night. The kiss was tender at first, his only thought to erase the pain of what she'd endured, but Geoffrey felt powerless to stop. Desperate to taste her, he thrust his tongue inside her mouth, twining it with hers as he pulled her toward him.

He eventually pulled back, cupping her beloved face in his hands. "You scared the hell out of me."

Sara's unsteady smile and drying tears made his countess look more vulnerable than usual. He wished he could wipe away her worries as easily as he had her tears.

"I'd say I'm sorry, but I'd be lying," she said. "I've never been happier to see anyone in my life."

Knowing she meant it, he reached for her hand. "Come." He nodded to Randolf's dead body. "He must be taken care of."

"Randolf said he was waiting for his men?"

"There is no one. I'll explain everything. But Kenshire is safe."

Her shoulders relaxed.

He looked up at the castle, seeing nothing out of the ordinary above the high outer curtain wall. Reluctantly, he tugged Sara in that direction, hurrying his steps. There was a full-fledged search underway, and none of Sara's people would rest until they knew she'd been found safe.

Lifting the hem of her torn dress with her free hand, Sara followed, looking as if she wanted to ask him something.

"What of the embrace I witnessed?"

He stopped in his tracks. "Of all the questions you have, that is the most pressing?"

Sara stopped alongside him, close enough for him to reach out for her, which he was sorely tempted to do.

"Aye."

"It was a trick, a way to separate us. Effective, it would seem."

She looked into his eyes for a long moment, studying him, and by the time she looked away, Geoffrey knew that she believed him.

"The perfect timing," he admitted, "eludes me still." Grabbing her hand again as he led them through the bluff toward the gate, he thought aloud. "Something about John piqued my curiosity enough for me to inquire after him."

Sara interrupted, a common but endearing trait of hers. "What could possibly have interested you about the man? He's as quiet and nondescript as any servant at Kenshire."

"I witnessed a discussion between him and Lady Maude." He struggled to find the right words. "It's difficult to describe. Something just wasn't right."

He could hardly tell her about his uncanny sense of intuition, which had gotten him out of more situations than he could count.

"And then I spoke to his men." At her quizzical look, he explained, "The night my arm…"

"You went to his camp,"

It was a statement, not a question.

"What happened tonight?"

Straight to the point, as always.

"I'll explain everything, but first I need to know." He took a deep breath. "Did Randolf hurt you?"

Mercifully, Sara was quick to answer. "Nay. He wasn't gentle by any means, but other than a few snide remarks and his filthy hand gagging my mouth, he didn't hurt me." She amended, "He never had a chance. You came upon us not long after he found me on the beach."

He didn't have to ask what had brought her there, alone, in the first place. They both knew.

"How could he have possibly known you'd be down there?"

"When we were young, before my father and Randolf had a falling out, he spent enough time at Kenshire to know about my affinity for this secret path. As I said, it was a sore subject between my father and I, enough so that he built that tower—" Sara pointed to a tall building he knew as the Vale Tower, "—for extra eyes on the coast." She smiled at the memory. "He said, ''Tis an expensive habit, your late night jaunts on the beach,' though I knew it wasn't for my benefit alone. Ever since the castle was built, there's been discussion about how best to secure it along the coast."

Geoffrey conceded it was a reasonable guess that a distraught Sara would seek solace in a spot she revered. But he found it hard to believe a plan would hinge its success on that likelihood. Unless, of course, Randolf really was that stupid.

Nearing the entrance, they stopped, knowing what their arrival on the castle grounds would bring. "'Twas a risky plan on Randolf's part."

"Aye, but my father always said Kenshire would be nearly impossible to breach by force. It's not uncommon for treachery to be the sole means into an impregnable fortress."

On that point Geoffrey agreed. "I've seen it often enough, which is most likely why your father entrusted your safety with someone he'd known since childhood."

Neither spoke, the implications of Randolf's demise clear to them both.

"You'll be leaving?"

"I don't know." A pinch in his chest reminded him of his need for this woman he couldn't have. "Hugh will decide our next move."

He grasped her other hand, their slight trembling nearly enough for him to toss out his good intentions. But Sara's people were searching frantically for her; it wouldn't be right. "I'm glad you're safe." His words and tone seemed foreign to his own ears. "If anything had happened to you…"

Tears welled her eyes. "Thank you."

"You're welcome." With a quick kiss, he let go of her hands and led her through the gate.

Walking behind her … she was so graceful … an uncomfortable thought tightened its hold on his mind. The possibility had first occurred to him when he'd discovered she was missing. It had shifted to near certainty the moment he saw her with that man.

But wasn't he immune to love? He'd always thought his heart was too full of vengeance to make room for any other emotion. Others succumbed to love, and it usually led to sorrow, but not him.

Yet his heart knew a truth that his mind would rather not acknowledge.

CHAPTER 17

WHEN SARA AND GEOFFREY ENTERED the courtyard, they were greeted by a sky lit with torches and shouts of joy. "She's found!" one man yelled. "It's Lady Sara."

The blacksmith rushed toward them, engulfing Sara in a hug. If Harold had not been so much older than Sara, Geoffrey would have bristled at his familiarity. "God be blessed," the man muttered as more people, servants and knights both, gathered around their lady.

Geoffrey allowed himself to be pushed back by the crowd. The people's relief was palpable. It was nice to see their love for Lady Sara, though it did not surprise him. He'd witnessed her gentle ministrations to Kenshire's people for days now.

A panicked woman's voice could be heard above the crowd. "Oh thank ye good Lord, thank ye." Running toward them, a disheveled Faye wept and prayed simultaneously. The circle around Sara parted to allow her into its midst.

"What happened?" Hugh asked. Geoffrey turned to look at him, and his uncle clapped him on the back. "Come," Hugh said. Nodding to the crowd, he continued, "She's well taken care of."

They walked to the side of the crowd, and Peter peeled off from the gathering to follow them.

"Sir Geoffrey, I'm glad to see you unharmed."

His smile for the man was genuine. It was obvious Lady Sara's steward cared for her—just as his father had done before him.

"And in good humor," Peter continued. "Tell me what happened."

"Gladly, sir. But first, John's secure, I assume?"

"Aye, securely guarded at the moment."

"Good, I'll be back momentarily to explain. In the meantime, there's a body to recover on the beach below the sea gate," he said as if talking about a dead stag. It was as much respect as Randolf's remains deserved.

"Very good." Peter needed no more prompting to move in that direction.

"The man respects you," Hugh said.

"Aye." He couldn't understand it, but he'd counted on that fact earlier in the evening when he'd given him the order to apprehend the servant.

They walked toward the keep, watching more people converge on the celebration that had broken out near the stables. No one was quite sure what had happened save that their lady had gone missing and now was safe.

"It's easy to see why," his uncle said. "You've grown into a fine man, my son." Hugh crossed his arms. "Now tell me what happened."

My son. It felt good to hear those words—to feel a sense of belonging.

"I told you about the conversation between John and Lady Maude. It unsettled me enough to inquire after him."

"But how does that..."

"John was Randolf's man. It was he who filtered information out of Kenshire. And, I suspect, the one who planned to allow Randolf access ever since he arrived. I'd bet my life the other team of scouts will return with confirmation that the Earl of Covington doesn't support Randolf's claim." He then amended, "Didn't support his claim. The man is now dead."

"I suspected as much."

"I'm not sure whether he came to speak to his traitor or merely signal it was time for action, but Randolf's visit was nothing more than a ruse to put his treacherous plan into action. It seems my presence was a burden which needed to be overcome."

"If Randolf had no support for his claim and his intention was to murder Lady Sara, why not have John do the deed himself?"

"I asked that very question before sending him to hell." His hand rose unbidden to the hilt of his sword. He'd send the man to hell again if he could.

"And?"

"John was a coward. He was apparently afraid of the deed being traced back to him. The lackwit's job was to ensure Sara was alone and possibly help Randolf escape notice."

"Which is why," Hugh mused, "his men left their camp earlier this eve."

Geoffrey stopped short. "Why the hell are we standing here chatting like old maids if his men are unaccounted for?"

"I didn't say they were unaccounted for, only that they'd abandoned their camp." Hugh's tone implied he didn't care for Geoffrey's tone. "They were tracked down easily enough and are being questioned as we speak."

It was Geoffrey's turn to be surprised. "Who gave the order to secure them?"

"Eddard. When Sara went missing, it put everyone on high alert."

"But you couldn't have made the connection. Sara was only 'missing' because she was upset."

"Your order to Peter to secure John did that. There are no coincidences, and her men know it well. Logic told us Randolf was involved, especially when he wasn't found among his men."

"Somehow Randolf found his way to the bluffs not far from St. Oswald's Gate. I suspect a secret entrance, which is most likely why he was alone. Bringing a retinue of men would have been impossible without notice. It would take just one man to do the job, and Randolf clearly thought he was that man."

"But he was not?"

"Nay. I discovered Sara's location too quickly for him. When I found them, he had her at knifepoint. At first I thought he awaited relief from his men, but then I realized John was the only one who knew Randolf's whereabouts. Or," he amended, "who had access to our position."

"And you already knew he had been obtained?"

"Or hoped so, at least." Geoffrey had trusted Peter to carry out his orders.

As they reached the keep, Geoffrey finally asked his uncle the question that had been torturing him from the moment Randolf fell down dead.

"What happens now?"

Hugh misunderstood. "I imagine there'll be an inquiry, though I've no fear you'll be acquitted of wrongdoing."

Geoffrey could care less about an inquiry.

"Kenshire is more secure than ever," Hugh posited, "but until Lady Sara weds..." He paused, then seemed to come to a decision. "She's still vulnerable. Perhaps she'll agree to send a party to Elmhurst Manor to check on the children."

Geoffrey wondered what his siblings would think of being referred to as the children. Even the youngest of them was ten and six and could hardly be considered a child any longer. And thanks to the bastards who'd stolen their home and livelihood, they weren't in a position to have Neill fostered or knighted.

Goddamn the Kerrs!

His uncle seemed to warm to his decision. "The earl would have wanted me to stay, and so we will. Lord Lyonsford must be on his way. Hell, once he claims Lady Sara and the Caisers' land, he'll be among the most powerful men in England."

So they wouldn't be leaving on the morrow as Geoffrey had feared. Or hoped. He couldn't decide how he felt about the news. But Hugh's next words stopped him cold.

"And when he does, he'll find a virgin bride waiting for him. Sara's future, the future of her people, depends on it."

Of course he knew. Hugh was one of the most perceptive men alive. Even Randolf had suspected their feelings for each other enough to use their bond against them.

And Hugh was right.

"He will, Uncle," Geoffrey agreed.

"Damn right, he will, or I'll cut your bollocks off myself, my boy. Now come inside, you've had a hell of a night."

AFTER THE INITIAL EXCITEMENT WORE off, Sara called for a meeting in her solar. She knew it was important to take charge of her officers as she'd done the night before. As soon as all of the officers were seated, she ordered them each to give their account of the evening's events.

One by one, they told her about the diversion Randolf's men had created by abandoning their camp. Peter relayed the order Geoffrey had shouted to him before pursuing Sara—and told them all how John had been captured while attempting to slip through the Battery Gate. Randolf's men were less than loyal and the profile that emerged from the reports was that of a man desperate to claim a land and a title. One hired soldier admitted Randolf had failed to obtain the Earl of Covington's support. Another particularly loose-tongued traitor had given up the same piece of information.

"You're confident the threat is contained, then?" she asked no one in particular.

A chorus of "ayes" confirmed that fact.

"As Countess of Kenshire and primary witness to Sir Randolf Fitzwarren's death, I will personally speak to the sheriff about what happened. But consider yourself exonerated, Sir Geoffrey. There's no need for you to remain at Kenshire for a trial."

Sara tried hard to appear composed, but she wanted nothing more than to retreat to her bedchamber and be left alone with her thoughts. Hugh and Geoffrey would be leaving, and there was naught she could do to prevent it. She thought she wanted them to leave, but it was difficult to imagine Kenshire without Geoffrey.

Geoffrey started to say something, but he was interrupted when Peter agreed. "Aye, Lady Sara, you have the right of it. We've also to decide how to deal with Randolf's men."

Not having committed a royal offense, their only crime had been their allegiance to a man without scruples or morals.

"I will hear them on the morrow," she said. "In the meantime, we have to confirm that Randolf truly acted alone."

"The scouting party should be back any time, my lady," Eddard said.

"And John?" Geoffrey asked. All conversation ceased.

"Let the bastard rot in Kenshire's dungeons," Eddard suggested.

Hugh agreed. "Allowing him to disappear would be the least he deserved for his treachery."

Sara seriously considered their advice. The man had conspired to put her in danger. She knew what her father would have done in the same situation, and she would do the same. Had he struggled to make difficult decisions, or had leadership come as naturally to him as it had always seemed to?

"I will hear his case on the morrow."

Geoffrey spoke up for the first time. "It's been a long night. Perhaps we should reconvene in the morn."

Sara suspected his words were for her benefit. His arm must have been injured anew. A nasty red gash bled through the bright white of his shirt. Apparently reivers didn't believe in much protection beyond a simple leather jack. It struck her that this might be the last night Geoffrey Waryn resided at Kenshire. She couldn't bear to end the meeting, but the decision to retire was taken from her by her steward.

"Aye, Faye is waiting to assist you, my lady," Peter said. "Come." And before she could think of a reason to stay, Peter led her from the solar as the men bid her a good night. She longed for a moment alone with Geoffrey, but Peter walked upstairs with her.

It was a comfort to return to Faye—and her maid awaited her with a wooden tub of steaming water. Sara knew the effort that went into preparing a hot bath and was grateful for it. When she said as much to Faye, the woman waved her off and spun her around to help her undress.

"Fie. This dress was ruined by that swine."

"A torn dress is the least of my concerns."

Faye was immediately apologetic. "I'm sorry, my lady. You've been through a hellish ordeal and this old ninny is worrying about a dress."

"No need for an apology, Faye. I was teasing."

Sara had told Faye earlier about her encounter with Randolf—her mad dash to the beach and the final confrontation that had led to Randolf's death. Oh, how maddening it had been to be in that man's power…

He'd never been particularly intelligent. His greed, apparent from a young age and finally resulting in his exile from Kenshire, was the only thing that had ever truly frightened her about her distant relative. Without the support of the Earl of Covington, Sir Randolf Fitzwarren had been nothing more than the son of a baronet with tenuous familial ties to her father.

And now he was dead. She was the only remaining member of the small but powerful Caiser family. That realization made her feel lonely, but also free.

Unclothed, Sara stepped into the tub and sighed. It felt heavenly. As she sank into the warm water, she thought of Geoffrey's arm. Had someone tended to his wound? Where was he now? And, most pressingly, was he leaving on the morrow?

He and Hugh would have no reason to remain now that the threat to her person had been eliminated.

Should she go to him? The idea was both dangerous and foolish, but this might be her only chance to see him alone again. She couldn't squander it.

She told Faye she'd prefer to finish her bath alone, and asked that the tub be left in her chamber for the night. An abundance of reassurances were required of her, but her maid did as she asked.

When Sara finished her bath, she dressed in the finest chemise she owned, a white silken shift embroidered with silver thread that shimmered in the candlelit chamber. After drying and brushing her wet hair as thoroughly as possible, she grabbed the closest candle, said a quick prayer, and opened her door.

Nothing.

Would he be in his chamber? Ruing the fact that the lord's chamber was so close to the top of the stairs, she forged ahead.

She dared not knock for fear of alerting the guard, so she opened the door as quietly as possible, stepped inside, and closed it behind her.

The chamber was much darker than hers—only two candles flickered and there were no windows to usher in the moonlight. Even so, she immediately sensed she wasn't alone. As her eyes adjusted, she saw Geoffrey sitting in a large chair adjacent to the canopied bed. His eyes widened but otherwise his expression was inscrutable.

Would he welcome her presence or would his honor prevent it? He cared for her. She

had felt the desperation in his embrace on the beach. Naive to the ways of men and women, she instinctively understood his kiss was not just one of passion. There was an undercurrent of something more. And this eve she was determined to find out what it meant.

He rose and came toward her.

SURELY HE WAS BEING PUNISHED for his all-consuming thoughts of revenge. Or maybe for the lives he had taken. He wasn't sure what he'd done, but Geoffrey knew it must have been very wrong, for it had brought the one person who could make him forget his duty into his bedchamber.

After the meeting in Sara's solar, he had returned to the sea path, just as he'd taken to doing every evening after Sara retired. He'd stripped naked and dived into the frigid sea, letting the salty water cleanse the innocuous wound on his arm.

Though Sara no longer needed to be watched every moment of the day and night, Geoffrey had nevertheless returned immediately to his bedchamber after speaking to Faye, who'd assured him Sara was safe inside her own chamber.

Geoffrey had reached for his sword upon hearing the door open, but quickly retracted his hand. His midnight guest was the very person he'd been thinking about.

Sara stood as erect and proud as the day she glided down the stairs when he first arrived at Kenshire. There were two differences. This time she was even more assured.

This time she wore nothing more than a thin chemise.

Geoffrey himself was naked but for his braies and woolen hose, and he throbbed beneath them as the vision before him moved closer.

God have mercy.

Her hair was just wet enough to make him inhale deeply. Rosewood.

Would she be wet for him?

The unbidden thought was the one that broke him. Closing the remaining distance between them, he grabbed her head and pulled her toward him, claiming her mouth. Unrelenting, he slanted his head to give himself greater access than ever before. Sara met his tongue thrust for thrust. He reached for the candle she held and placed it on a nearby table.

A low groan escaped his lips as he allowed his hands to roam free. Cupping Sara's backside, he pulled her closer, allowing her to feel his need for her. A mewling sound told him she was pleased, though he had never doubted it. Gripping the soft fabric of her chemise with both hands, he pulled it swiftly above her head, disposing of the offending garment.

Sara instinctively crossed her arms over her chest in the dim candlelight.

"Nay." She had nothing to be ashamed of. "Don't hide yourself from me. You're too perfectly formed for that." Taking in the sight of her luscious breasts, narrow waist, and perfectly rounded hips, Geoffrey had to remind himself to breathe. He wanted to touch every bit of her all at once. Reaching out, he cupped one breast, flicking his thumb against the pink nipple. He couldn't resist.

Frantic with need, he allowed his hands to explore. Her waist, hips, buttocks … he couldn't get enough.

She stopped his exploration. "I want to see you."

Groaning, wanting nothing more than to feel her soft hands on his throbbing cock, he began to loosen the drawstring at his waist. Sara pushed away his hands. He stood deathly still, staring into the depths of her deep brown eyes, not trusting himself to move as she loosened the fastening at his waist.

He pulled down the last barrier between them but was distracted by the sight of her pink, hardened nipple. Pausing, he couldn't help but cease his own undressing to pull the taunting morsel into his mouth. Sara's hand gripped the back of his head as he suckled and nipped her, and he was so flooded by desire he nearly forgot her earlier request.

"Please," she begged. He quickly dispensed of his clothing, and his manhood sprang to life. A gasp told Geoffrey she'd likely never seen a man naked before, or at least not one standing so close to her. He stood erect, towering over her petite form.

"Is that … normal?"

He couldn't help but laugh. "Nay."

Evidently her curiosity overcame shyness. "May I?"

He was, as always, brutally honest.

"Sara, if you touch me, I will explode."

He realized belatedly she was ignorant as to what that meant.

How innocent she was. What was he doing? It didn't matter that she had come to him, this could not be.

Perhaps sensing the shift in his mood, she explained the reason for her late night visit.

"I can't let you leave on the morrow without knowing you." She quickly amended, "All of you."

So that was it. As they stood blissfully naked, Sara now attempting to cover herself, he felt compelled to admit the truth.

He did it while caressing her bare shoulders, his hands trailing a path down her arms. "We stay at Kenshire." For this moment at least, he was quite glad for it. "If you'll have us, Hugh believes it best we stay until your betrothed arrives."

"That changes nothing," she said in a tone that brooked no argument. "You'll leave before long, and I'll never forgive myself to not have known you."

Why was he surprised at her forthrightness? Sara had been raised by an earl who'd encouraged independence. Decisiveness.

But she deserved better than a landless reiver.

"Do you have any idea how much I'd give to throw you on my bed and show you how this—" he gestured down toward his erection, "—will very easily fill you?"

"Then show me how to please you."

She was making it very difficult to remain honorable.

"Nay, I can't let you do that," he choked out. "You're innocent of such things."

"You'll not decide for me. You've given me pleasure, and I will do the same for you this eve."

She meant it.

He couldn't fight it. Didn't want to. He grasped her soft fingers and guided them toward his hardness. He jerked when her hand first touched the sensitive flesh. He'd dreamed of this but never imagined it would ever come to pass. He clenched his jaw, trying with every muscle in his body to remain in control.

SARA KNEW SHE PLEASED HIM and felt strangely warmed by the knowledge. He guided her to move her hand up and down. She remembered the way he'd teased her with his finger, fast and then deep and slow. She mimicked the pace, pausing to wrap her palm as fully as she could around his manhood. It felt strangely soft for something so hard.

And she was in control.

Relishing that fact, Sara moved her hand more quickly, sure he was on the verge of the same experience she'd felt when he'd pleasured her with his hands and mouth.

"Oh God!" Geoffrey closed his eyes, tilting back his head. He reached for her, holding the nape of her neck as she guided him to a powerful climax.

"Ahhh yes," he cried as Sara felt an unexpected wetness. Looking down, she stared at her hand in surprise and awe. So, this was what happened when a man experienced pleasure? She barely had time to register it before Geoffrey grabbed her under both arms and carried her to his bed.

Not knowing what to expect, she was startled when he climbed over her and forced her mouth open. His lips moved expertly over her own, gently nibbling and tasting. Her eyes were closed, so she felt rather than saw his hand moving toward her core. When his fingers thrust inside her, Sara pushed against them, remembering. The dual sensation of his tongue and fingers, which slipped so easily inside, was her undoing. Pushing against his hand, she felt the same incredible sensation as before. This time his naked chest rose and fell just above her own, his muscled back hard and hot under her fingertips. It was too much. With a cry Geoffrey muffled by closing his mouth around her own, Sara came beneath his fingers.

He collapsed against her then, one arm draped around her chest, the other still between her legs as she continued to pulse beneath his touch.

GEOFFREY LAY BACK ON THE linen covers, looking up at the posts of his fine four-poster bed, wondering what the hell had just happened. His eyes landed on Sara's naked body, barely illuminated by the flickering candlelight. He'd thought about seeing her like this, of course—enough to almost drive him mad—but all his imaginings paled in comparison to the real thing.

She was perfect.

"You're embarrassing me."

He ran his fingers upward from her thigh, grazing her breast, cupping the perfectly shaped mound. "You're pleasing me."

Sara laughed, a melodic sound that made him smile. "I can see that."

"I was afraid I'd never hear that sound again."

She ignored the observation. "I find it hard to think when you do that."

"Do what, my lady?" His hand traced her breasts, then dipped between them, traveling across her abdomen and then over her hip.

"You know very well, blackguard."

"Blackguard, is it? If I be a pirate, this must be me bounty." He moved his hand over her black curls, cupping her as he leaned forward and took a firm nipple into his mouth.

She pushed him away. "You can't do that again already!"

She had challenged the wrong man.

His palm pressed against her, his finger teasing but not entering her. She pushed against his hand.

"Come for me again, sweet Sara."

Lying on his side next to her, he continued to tease her with one hand while propping himself up with the other. He brought his mouth down to her ear and whispered, "What did you say?"

Sara tilted her head back, licked her full lips, and wisely stayed silent.

Not so easy.

"Tell me," he lowered his voice, "what can't I do?"

He slowly eased his finger inside her … and then stopped. When she tried to push her hips up to meet him, he withdrew.

"Sara?"

"Geoffrey, please."

"Please what?" he said, though now he was teasing both of them.

"You *can* do it again. Please."

Not yet.

"Aye, and I will."

He thrust his finger inside her again as he kissed the sensitive flesh behind her ear. This time he met her thrust with one of his own. Her breathing was heavy, and it wasn't long before he once again felt her throbbing around his fingers. He was ready to explode.

He concentrated instead on watching Sara's face. She opened her eyes and looked into his own.

"My amorous little minx."

"My knight in shining armor." She traced the scar along the

side of his face.

A shiver ran down his body that had nothing to do with sexual pleasure.

"What are we to do?"

He knew neither of them wanted to consider the honest answer to that question—but he wouldn't lie to her.

"There's naught to do but savor tonight as a memory. A delicious," he kissed her neck, "sensual," he moved his mouth toward her breast, "tantalizing memory." His mouth moved lower, kissing her stomach as his hands explored the luscious legs splayed on the bed where he had lain awake more nights than one imagining this very scenario.

He considered bringing her to climax with his mouth, but her eyes were closed when he glanced up to gauge her reaction. Sara was exhausted. The incident with Randolf seemed days ago, but in truth her life had been in danger just a few hours earlier.

His countess needed sleep. After giving her a final soft kiss on the lips, he scooped her up as if she were a feather pillow and carried her toward the door.

Sara came awake then, horrified.

"You don't mean to carry me into the hall like this!"

"Aye, and why not? 'Tis a most glorious state of undress if you ask me."

Placing her on her feet next to the discarded chemise, he reached down and grabbed the slip of silk. It was as fine a fabric as he'd ever touched.

He kept letting himself forget, but Sara was a lady of the realm. A noble with lands scattered throughout England. He was the son of a baron whose birthright had been stripped from him. A thief and a blackguard.

Unworthy. You never should have touched her.

Though he'd intended to slip the chemise over her head, Geoffrey handed it to her instead.

Sara slipped into the fine piece of silk. When she reached the door, she peeked into the hall, glanced back, and gave Geoffrey her brightest smile and then disappeared into the night.

Evidently she hadn't noticed his changed mood. It was just as well. Tomorrow would be soon enough to face reality.

CHAPTER 18

WHEN FAYE ROUSED SARA FROM sleep, the sun was higher in the sky than normal. The thought of the day ahead was enough to make her groan. She would need to deal with Randolf's men and the servant John this day, not to mention the uncertainty of her relationship with Geoffrey. She wished she could remain in the soft bed and told her maid as much.

"You're not often so slovenly, my lady. Missing morning mass? Talk of staying abed?"

"If you'll recall, I was held at knifepoint last eve by the man who attempted to wrest Kenshire from me. Mayhap this weary body can stay abed a few moments longer than usual?"

Faye sat down next to her mistress, smoothing out her unkempt hair. "Aye, it can. I'm only teasing. You've done well, Sara. I overheard the men talking about how you handled Randolf. You've made them proud."

Smiling, Sara accepted the praise with her silence, something her father used to do. Sometimes, he'd say, silence was the best response.

"Hugh and his nephew are stayin' on a bit longer."

She'd heard that very news from Geoffrey last eve. It was hard not to show any reaction.

How could she have ever thought him without morals? A thief, yes. But not by choice.

Geoffrey was easily the most honorable man she knew, save her father. As Faye prepared her gown, Sara closed her eyes, thinking of last eve.

A sudden feeling of melancholy pressed down on her.

She'd fallen in love with a border reiver, but there was no way they could be together.

Even if she were willing to risk a match that would put her people—and her father's legacy—in jeopardy, the betrothal with Lyonsford was quite final. A broken betrothal with a man like him was no small thing. He could choose to attack out of vengeance. Or appeal to the king and have her title stripped from her. The outcome was uncertain, but she could be sure Lyonsford would not simply accept a reversal of their marriage agreement without a severe repercussion.

With a strangled sound, she leapt up from the bed, frustrated and angry.

"A tigress," Faye said.

Sara reluctantly smiled. "Aye, and 'tis time to show Randolf's men my claws."

If Faye was startled by her choice of words, she didn't show it.

"Good choice, Faye," she said, looking down at the gown her maid had selected. The deep purple gown with its gold-embroidered surcoat was a perfect fit for her duties this morn. Randolf's defeat was a cause for celebration. She had already ordered a thorough cleaning of the great hall, which reminded her… "Did you tell Cook to prepare a special dish at the evening meal?"

"Aye," Faye said as she helped Sara into the heavy gown. "I did, though she was confused when I asked her to make supper the highlight of the day."

The men and women at Kenshire deserved to rejoice, but there was much to do and Sara wanted no distractions. Their celebratory meal would have to wait until the evening. First, she had to deal with the unpleasant task of administering justice to the traitor. She would also have to arrange for Randolf's body to be taken back to Meeringha and deal with the sheriff.

Impatient now, she sat and waited for her hair to be dressed.

As she finished brushing Sara's long, thick tresses, the older woman said, "You look every inch the countess this morn."

"The breeches will have to wait." She gave her maid a peck on the cheek on her way out the door.

WHEN LADY SARA CAISER WALKED into the great hall that morn, she looked every bit the conquering noble. The vixen who'd so eagerly responded to his touch last eve had been replaced with the self-assured countess he'd first met upon arriving at Kenshire. Geoffrey knew that she would administer justice for all of the crimes that had been committed in Kenshire. The decisions were hers alone to make, and she looked prepared to do just that.

He watched the proceedings from his position across the hall. The trestle tables had been cleared and the prisoners stood, in shackles with guards, below the dais where Sara sat with her officers. Sara had asked him and Hugh to sit with her, but they agreed the people of Kenshire would benefit from seeing fewer people in charge. Better they focus on their lady.

Geoffrey saw only the tops of the prisoners' heads, with so many people crowded into the hall prepared to witness their lady's administration of justice.

"You look pleased with yourself," Hugh said from beside him.

He had to be more careful. There was no doubt his uncle suspected the connection between him and Lady Sara, and without Randolf's threat to occupy Hugh, his perceptive eyes would be watching them more closely.

"The scum believe they'll receive mercy with a woman to hear their case."

Murmuring his agreement, Hugh watched as the men who once belonged to Sir Randolf were made to swear fealty to Lady Sara.

Her strong, even voice carried to the back of the great hall.

"Report to Lord Thornhurst at Camburg Castle. I've no desire for you to remain here among my people. Fail to do so and I will put every vassal to Caiser on alert. And know this—if you fail to arrive, you'll be found and hung as traitors. That is my promise as Countess of Kenshire, daughter of the late Richard Caiser, third Earl of Kenshire." Geoffrey reminded himself never to get on her bad side.

As the men were escorted from the hall, Hugh grinned at his nephew.

"If you knew the man, you'd appreciate the daughter."

Geoffrey held his tongue. His answer—"I do"—had almost slipped from his lips.

She dealt next with John, who was dragged into the great hall in chains. The people of Kenshire loved their lady, just as they had loved her father before her. As the former cupbearer was led to the front of the hall, every foul name imaginable was hurled at him.

"Enough!" Sara snapped, instantly putting a halt to the crowd's antics.

The proceedings continued, Sara explaining to the servant that he wasn't entitled to the shire court as a freeman would have been. Though she was outwardly calm, he knew her well enough not to be fooled. Her eyes burned with fire.

Would Lord Lyonsford appreciate how lucky he was? He didn't know the man but was sure he didn't deserve this jewel that stood in front of the hall.

And you do?

Landless and penniless, he could barely support his siblings, let alone bring anything of value to a marriage with a countess. He had nothing to offer except his desire for revenge. Even if he'd retained his station as eldest son to a minor border baron, she'd still be well out of his reach.

The crowd erupted into cheers after Sara heard witnesses, precious few for John, and consulted with her steward. It was decreed that the servant would die a traitor's death, no surprise to anyone, for the crime of conspiring to murder among a litany of other charges. Sara had decided to spare him a public execution, so the jeering spectators would have to make do with seeing the man taken away in chains. The impudent look on the man's face made Geoffrey long to run him through.

He was stopped by that tenacious voice in his head: *She's not yours.*

"Where are you going?" Hugh asked as Geoffrey began to push his way through the crowd.

"The training yard."

He walked from the hall, long strides taking him to the one place he felt entirely at home. The shouts and clanging of swords were a much needed reminder of his real duty. To find men. To fight for what was his.

This was where he belonged.

SARA WATCHED GEOFFREY LEAVE, STARING at the spot where he had stood moments before. He might not be leaving yet, but he would no longer be at her heels now that Randolf's threat was removed.

The second scouting party arrived that morning to confirm what they already knew. The Earl of Covington was not bringing an army, nor had he ever supported Randolf's claim. On their journey back to Kenshire, her men had learned that word was beginning to spread about her father's death. Rumors about her tenuous position gave way to talk of Kenshire's future.

After the Baron's War, questions of Henry III's ability to tame the border still prevailed. She was glad for more reasons than one that Geoffrey would be staying at Kenshire.

As she continued to stare at the spot Geoffrey had vacated, attempting to sort out her feelings, the dissipating crowd made way to allow Peter through. For the second time in a few short weeks, Sara found herself staring at a handsome stranger in her hall. With his dark hair and light eyes, he closely resembled the man she'd grown to love. It could only mean one thing.

So this is the brother.

Every female servant turned to stare at the newcomer, some obvious in their perusal, but the thing that interested Sara most about him was his connection to Geoffrey.

He knelt on his right knee in greeting.

"You are Sir Geoffrey's brother," she said, waving him upward.

Though it wasn't a question, he answered anyway. "Aye, my lady," he said as he stood. "Sir Bryce Waryn at your service."

Peter formally introduced them.

Hurry, Peter! She had so many questions.

"Sir?" She was finally able to interject. "You are a knight?"

"I am."

"I squired with Lord Huntington, a close friend of my father's, and remained with his household until..."

He stopped abruptly.

"I imagine you want to see your brother." Sara spared him the need to continue his story—she knew it did not end well—and stepped down from the dais to take the knight's arm. Sir Bryce's courtly manners weren't lacking. She looked up, assessing the similarities and differences between the two brothers. The strong resemblance didn't end with their hair and eyes. With the same high cheekbones and square jaw, Bryce could practically be his brother's twin. But his demeanor was much sterner than that of his brother. Sara was sure this man had never smiled or laughed once in his life.

She quickly revised that opinion moments later after learning Geoffrey's whereabouts and leading his brother to the training yard. Though the gathering wasn't quite as large a group as last time, there were more spectators than on a typical day. As soon as he saw the combatants—Geoffrey and Ralph, one of Sara's retainers—the big man grinned.

Her throat constricted as they watched the match. She had never enjoyed watching men train. While she knew sword training was both a serious endeavor and an ideal way for the men to build their strength, she typically avoided watching it. It seemed to her someone would be injured at any moment.

Swords clashing, the warriors thrust and sliced at each other as if they were enemies in truth. Both men moved constantly, attempting never to be on the defensive. But Geoffrey's skill and strength were remarkable, and it was only a matter of time before he disarmed his opponent.

GEOFFREY HAD HASTENED TO END the match after glimpsing Sara from the corner of his eye. He was normally annoyed by any interruptions to his practice, but his pulse raced at the thought of her watching him train. Ending the match, he wiped the sweat from his face and began walking toward her.

He stopped so suddenly, the servant who'd handed him a cloth to clean up with ran into him from behind.

"Bryce?"

Geoffrey closed the gap between them and engulfed his younger brother in an embrace, clapping him on the back.

"What the hell are you doing here?"

Bryce gave him a rare smile. "That's a fine greeting to give your little brother."

"Who's protecting Emma and Neill?" he asked as the shock of seeing his brother at Kenshire began to wear off.

"An interesting question," Bryce said. "Lord Wellingstone paid a visit and was injured on a stag hunt. He and his men are currently recovering at Elmhurst."

"Ahhh, so the overlord comes to visit. You trust his knights to be well-behaved?"

Bryce bristled at the slight criticism. "I'd not have left otherwise. And Uncle Simon is more than capable of watching our brother and sister, Geoffrey."

He disagreed. "Simon isn't as young as he looks, Bryce. But I do think Wellingstone can be trusted to take care of his own. It's just a shock to see you here." He may have been too quick to judge his brother, but Geoffrey hated apologizing and rarely saw the need. His uncle was fond of saying his stubbornness would get him into trouble. And it often did.

Suddenly aware of Sara's presence, he felt as if a knife had been thrust into his gut. He wasn't too stubborn to recognize the emotion. Jealousy practically smacked him in the face. Would Sara be taken with the man known as The Slayer? Bryce despised the name, but it had followed him from Huntington where he'd squired. Apparently it referred to the trail of broken hearts he left everywhere he went. Geoffrey would love to meet the woman who could actually break the icy shell of his brother's infamous cool composure. Even as children, Bryce had been the most serious of them all. But for some inexplicable reason, his little brother attracted the ladies en masse.

"You've met my brother?" he forced himself to ask.

"Aye." Sara glanced at Bryce.

His younger brother gazed back at her, clearly appreciative. Another trait they had in common was the ability to recognize—and appreciate—a beautiful woman. That uncomfortable feeling of jealously welled in him again, and he rather ungraciously grabbed his brother's arm and excused them both.

"Walk with me."

"Well, I'll be damned." Bryce turned his head to look back at Sara. "A countess. Sure set your sights high, don't you?"

Geoffrey refused to respond. Ignoring his brother was always the best way to shut him up.

"You don't look happy."

Sometimes it was easier to accomplish than others.

Geoffrey took him toward the gatehouse. Hugh had been staying in the living quarters on the upper floor. With two portcullises, heavy timber doors, and multiple murder holes to prevent enemy attacks, it was as well-defended a gatehouse as any in England. Not surprisingly, they found his uncle trading barbs with one of the guards when they approached.

"Well done guarding the entrance, Uncle. Look who they've let though."

Both Hugh and the guard turned around.

"Bryce! What are you doing here?"

Scowling, Bryce said, "I've had a warmer welcome from the seneschal than my own family."

Hugh embraced him, and Bryce heartily returned the welcome despite his harsh words. "We're surprised is all, my boy."

"How did he get past you, Uncle? I was shocked to see him in the training yard without you nearby." Bryce was crafty, but hopefully not wily enough to evade the defenses they'd sought so hard to maintain.

His normally easy-tongued uncle actually looked embarrassed. "I've only just returned." From where? He'd been in the great hall with Hugh not too long ago. But rather than explain his answer, his uncle left it at that.

He was deliberately being evasive.

Bryce apparently didn't notice anything suspicious, though, and he could tell from the look on his brother's face that he had come with news.

"Lord Wellingstone was injured on a hunt and recovers at the manor house as we speak—"

"Aye, you said," Geoffrey interrupted him, "so you thought to journey to Kenshire during what could have been the middle of a siege because you missed your brother's good humor?"

If he sounded cross, it was only because he tried to protect his brother. Bryce had no sense of self-preservation. He chafed at being left behind while Geoffrey and Hugh struggled to gather the resources to wrest back their land.

"Aye. Your good humor," Bryce said. "And I sorely missed being chastised as if I were a lad of one and ten. "

"Bryce, we've been through this. Our aunt and uncle are aging..."

"I know, and our brother and sister need protection.'"

Hugh intervened, halting the familiar argument. "What does bring you here, Bryce?"

"Wellingstone is willing to help," he said, his eyes lighting up with something Geoffrey had rarely seen in his little brother—excitement.

He froze. Hugh looked at Bryce as if he were speaking in a foreign language.

What the hell had Bryce been thinking?

"It wasn't your place to approach him," Geoffrey snapped. "We agreed when the time was right we'd make our case. Who gave you leave to talk with him about Bristol?"

"No one." Bryce was anything but defensive. "But if I waited for the two of you to get around to it, we'd spend the next five years listening and waiting."

Geoffrey looked at Hugh, but his uncle's face was inscrutable.
"I'm tired of waiting," Bryce said. "Aren't you?"
"Aye," Geoffrey said. "But that doesn't mean we can rush into a battle alone."
Hugh shot Geoffrey a look that clearly indicated he shouldn't intervene. Only one person in the world could quiet him with a glance.
Make that two. Sara had a similar effect, but for very different reasons.
"Bryce," Hugh said, "what exactly did Wellingstone say?" Hugh began to pace. He may have sounded calm, but Geoffrey knew better.
"He supports our claim…"
"He's always supported our claim," Geoffrey interrupted.
"Aye, but now he's willing to commit troops to help us take Bristol back from the bastard Scots," Bryce finished.
"Why would he do that?" asked Hugh.
"'Tis well known Father's wool was the finest in the region, and now our enemies use it to fill their chief's coffers," Bryce said. "Wellingstone will aid our cause in exchange for a share of future profits."
Silence hung in the small room, devoid of embellishments and constructed for defense. They all understood the implications of such a deal, the politics of aligning with the northern lord and paying homage to him. While their present position was less than ideal, presently they answered to no one. The Waryn men relied on charity and the spoils of Geoffrey and Hugh's unrespectable work, but at least they had no overlord to shackle them.
Hugh was the one who finally broke the silence. "What's his timeframe?"
"He leaves for London within the fortnight. No plans to return to his northern holdings anytime soon."
He already knew what his brother would say next, which explained his sudden, unannounced presence at Kenshire.
"It must be now."

The tension in the small room was palpable. Clearly Bryce had made his choice, and he could guess at his uncle's response. His uncle would not leave. He'd given his word to Sara's father, and no man was more loyal than Hugh.

Eager to stall for time—he needed to collect his own thoughts—Geoffrey voiced a question he'd been harboring for weeks.

"Uncle, why didn't you ever ask Lord Kenshire to support us?"

Despite the many different scenarios they discussed, Hugh had never raised the possibility of becoming a vassal to Caiser.

"A good question."

Both men waited for an answer.

"Richard was able to stay neutral for a time in the Baron's War. Aiding your father could have jeopardized that."

"But our own overlord abandoned us." Geoffrey began to pace.

"Aye, he determined the ongoing conflict with the Scots was not worth holding his northern lands, including Bristol, at such considerable losses."

Geoffrey began to understand. "Then the battle at Lewes and Evesham."

"By then Richard was forced to take sides, sending men to Prince Edward in the name of the king. He was firmly not in the baron's camp."

"And afterward?" Bryce watched his pacing with quiet reserve. He'd give him one thing: his little brother was more patient than he.

"Richard was fighting his own battles fending off Fitzwarren."

Geoffrey finished the thought. "And now his daughter attempts to hold Kenshire. And if she succeeds—" He knew before being told. "You planned to seek aid from her and Lyonsford?"

Hugh nodded. "I've considered the possibility."

The men fell silent once again.

"I won't leave."

It was exactly as Geoffrey had expected, though he understood Bryce's anger.

"Uncle." Bryce's voice rose as he spoke. "This is the best chance we've ever had. We may not have another anytime soon."

To an outside observer, Bryce would probably appear mildly agitated. But Geoffrey knew better. His brother was furious.

"You're probably right, Bryce. But as I told your brother, I made a promise to Sara's father that I intend to keep. Until she's safely wed, she and Kenshire are under my protection."

Wed. Geoffrey was beginning to hate the word.

They were both looking at him, waiting for his answer.

Stay to protect Sara, who was already well protected? Or take the chance he'd been waiting for, dreaming of, every day for more than five years? He didn't like the idea of involving Lord Wellingstone as an absentee overlord who cared only for the profit he could reap from their land.

Could he really leave now?

He needed time to think.

"Hell."

He turned from their scrutinizing stares. "I need a moment," he said over his shoulder as he hurried down the steps. He could hear his uncle trying to fill the gaping silence he'd left behind.

"Bryce, it's good to see you…"

But Bryce wasn't to be denied. He made the uncomfortable situation even worse by following Geoffrey down the stairs. "Shall I guess where you're off to, brother?"

In no mood to jest, he said, "It's none of your damned business."

"I'm not sure what madness has taken you, but be careful, brother." He lowered his voice. "Falling in love with a countess is a dangerous undertaking for someone in our position."

With those parting words, Bryce turned back up the stairs. Geoffrey stopped and stared after him. He wasn't sure how his brother had discerned his feelings in so short a time. His brother wouldn't know love if it hit him on the head with a war hammer, but he couldn't deny that he'd guessed correctly.

Geoffrey had never met a woman like Sara … and was doubtful he ever would again.

He *loved* her.

He'd known this stay at Kenshire would be trying, but the war they'd averted was nothing compared to the onslaught that was Lady Sara Caiser, Countess of Kenshire, soon to be Lady Lyonsford.

It mattered naught.

He could not have her, as well he knew.

Mayhap it was time to leave. Randolf was no longer a threat, and Sara would be safe with his uncle. Geoffrey would return with Bryce, and the two of them would take the chance they'd been waiting for. It killed him to think of bending the knee to Lord Wellingstone, but nothing mattered more than taking back Bristol.

Nothing.

He groaned aloud when a vision of Sara in his mind was replaced by the real thing as he walked through the inner bailey toward the keep. The subject of his thoughts strode purposefully toward him.

It was as good a time as any to tell her he'd be leaving after all.

CHAPTER 19

"IS SOMETHING AMISS?"

Sara lifted her impractical gown for what seemed like the hundredth time that day. "Aye, a man has information on the maid, Margaret. Will you come with me to question the stable hand? I was on my way there when I spotted you."

"Of course." Geoffrey walked alongside her toward the stables. "You have people to handle such matters, you know."

"Peter's already there, but I'm worried for her safety."

She glanced sideways at Geoffrey, unable and unwilling to forget the intimacies they had shared the night before. Visions of their encounter had intruded on her thoughts all morning.

"You failed to mention your brother is nearly your twin," she said.

"But much less handsome, of course," he replied, the ever-so-slight crinkles at the corner of his eyes making her want to lay her hand on his cheek and touch the lines there.

She took in his purposeful strides, perfect profile, and air of confidence, and vehemently disagreed. "I do believe you tease me, sir. I've no doubt who is the more handsome brother."

"Please enlighten me, fair maiden."

"Why—" She couldn't resist, "Bryce, of course."

"Wench," he whispered as they entered the stables.

Sara had to bite her lip to keep from smiling.

The stable hand began talking as soon as they entered. "I know yer lookin' for her and don't mean to get her in any trouble, but she was here."

Geoffrey and Sara glanced at each other.

"We had, er, a relationship and she came ta see me. She's hiding out in the cottar's house." He shrugged. "It seems I weren't the only one she had … relations with."

Sara thanked the boy. "My thanks for sharing this information. We do have some questions to ask her."

They left the stables in search of Peter.

Geoffrey thought aloud. "There's no doubt she ambushed me. The only question is how involved was she in Randolf and John's plan?"

"Do you believe John when he says she knew about the plot and was as guilty as he?"

"Nay, I don't. Whether he harmed her or not, I can't be sure, but I'm certain she knew less than he claimed."

Switching topics, Sara asked him about Bryce.

"My aunt and uncle's overlord was injured and is recovering at their manor home. Apparently Bryce thought Emma and Neill were protected enough to ride here to speak to Hugh and me."

"May I inquire why he found a visit so urgent?" Sara was used to speaking openly to her father about matters some would consider inappropriate for a woman.

Without hesitation, Geoffrey told her about Bristol, expanding on the story he'd already told her. They walked companionably toward the keep, Sara feeling a nervous jitter each time she looked at Geoffrey's profile. She knew last evening wasn't far from his thoughts either. She could see it in his eyes when he looked at her.

Sara tried hard to attend to their conversation.

"What are you not telling me?" she finally asked.

"My lady?"

"I think we're beyond formalities, Geoffrey."

Instead of answering her question, the scoundrel grabbed her hand and tugged her behind the kitchen. Moments later, Sara found herself in a little-used stairwell. Without preamble, he pushed her gently against the wall and brought his lips to hers in a welcome onslaught. His hands bracketed the wall on either side of her face as he leaned closer and slipped his tongue into her mouth for an increasingly familiar mating. Even through the blasted heavy gown, she could feel the hardness of his chest. She grabbed one of his outstretched arms for support, easily able to feel the line of muscles underneath his linen shirt. For all the strength there, his demanding lips moved gently across her own.

Geoffrey abruptly pulled back, his hands still braced behind her, and looked deep into her eyes. She loved the tic in his cheek—a sign that he was losing control.

If they were caught, it would be her ruin. Sara opened her mouth as if to speak, but then closed it abruptly.

She didn't want to talk. She definitely didn't want to stop him.

It was her last coherent thought before he claimed her lips once again.

WHEN SARA ALLUDED TO THEIR breach in conduct the previous evening, Geoffrey could think of nothing but being inside her. He wanted to devour her, make her his in every way.

Pulling away once more, he carelessly shared his thoughts. "I want to make love to you with everything that I am. If I stopped thinking through the consequences, I would take off every piece of your clothing and show you the meaning of desire."

His voice, raspy and belabored, sounded to his own ears like a lover's entreaty.

Her whispered response nearly brought him to his knees.

"I would that you could, sir."

Their lips met again, this time less frantic, in a kiss meant to arouse passion. Geoffrey teased and tortured them both. He knew this was a dangerously exposed spot for such an encounter, but couldn't make himself stop. A part of him wanted Bryce, Lyonsford, everyone to know that she was his.

Except she isn't.

He didn't care.

One of his hands moved from the wall to roam the outline of

her waist before moving up the front of her bodice. His thumb dipped below the low neckline of her dress, the sensitive flesh warm to his touch. How could he possibly continue to hold back?

He couldn't. The discussion about Wellingstone, his leaving, could wait.

"Come to me tonight."

Sara looked at him, her full, perfectly formed lips open in shock. He couldn't resist reaching up and outlining them with his thumb.

"Aye," she murmured simply.

He dropped his hands, looking around as if noticing for the first time they truly were exposed. "Go before we're seen."

After giving him what could only be described as a naughty smile, she disappeared into the bailey. Geoffrey watched her go, feeling a maddening tug-of-war between his mind and his heart. Logically, this was madness.

Every time they were together, Sara risked ruin. A broken betrothal would throw Kenshire into uncertainty and turmoil. The earl would be a powerful ally for Sara—but Lord Lyonsford could just as easily become a dangerous enemy if she were to break the engagement. Sara might even lose her own title and lands to the crown.

Not to mention the fact that Geoffrey was probably going to leave with Bryce.

So why had he asked her back to his chamber?

Because he wanted Sara more than he'd ever wanted anything in his life. If he were honest, his thoughts over the last weeks had been consumed by her.

For as long as he could remember, his first waking thoughts had been for the safety of his family and revenge against those who'd murdered his parents and stolen his home.

This morning, however, he had awoken hard and ready. He'd lain abed, remembering the look on Sara's face as she'd given in to pleasure again and again. He could almost hear her crying out for him.

Everything was on hold for one night. His duty, his brother … all of it would wait. He would leave her a virgin, but he'd make sure their last encounter was a memorable one.

AS WORD OF JOHN'S SENTENCE spread and it became clear Randolf's men were no longer a threat, the castle gradually came back to life. Sara had learned from her father not to harbor regret about thoughtful, informed decisions, but knowing a man who served her family would be put to death by her actions was disturbing nonetheless.

Despite the trauma she'd lived through over the past days, Sara found that her thoughts kept straying ahead to her meeting with Geoffrey.

What would happen in his chamber this eve? Could she really allow him to take the precious gift of her virginity? She'd overheard enough female conversation to know her betrothed need not learn she'd lain with another man, but even if Lord Lyonsford didn't know, *she* would know.

Could she do it?

It was a sin of the worst kind. Her father would be gravely disappointed. And if she were ever caught … Sara couldn't begin to consider it.

But why was it so wrong? Geoffrey was everything she'd hoped her future husband would be. Handsome, strong, thoughtful, and most importantly, he spoke to her as an equal. He'd not only opened up to her about Bristol and Wellingstone; he'd actually asked for her advice.

"What do you think?" he'd asked earlier after explaining the situation.

She'd wanted to tell him he would have the support of the Caiser family, that he wouldn't need Wellingstone or anyone else to secure his claim. But she didn't have the authority to make the offer. It would be her future husband's decision to commit men.

It stung to think of marrying someone else when she was in

love with Geoffrey, but titles and nobility still dictated their society. Sara was less free than some of the people who served at Kenshire. She needed to marry someone with a title. Someone of equal rank.

Once, as a young girl, she'd refused to eat for two days after her father forbade her to wear breeches while he hosted guests. He told her, "You feel you've been wronged, so be it. But to refuse what's freely given while others go hungry without that choice is shameful. I've never been ashamed of you, daughter, and I will not start today."

She could remember every word, even now. It was a lesson she'd do well to remember. She must stop feeling sorry for herself and her position and instead accept her duties.

So be it.

But she would not enter into this marriage without being loved first. She would give herself to Geoffrey and have no regrets. Because this, at least, she could control.

"My lady, tis past time to change for supper."

How long had she been standing there, inside the entrance to the keep, lost in thought? When she finally followed Faye to her bedchamber, she squealed in delight. The large wooden tub still sat in the center of the room, and it had been filled with steaming water. She threw her arms around the pleasantly plump woman.

"Bless you."

She quickly disposed of her gown with Faye's assistance and then scrubbed her body clean, basking in the warmth of the water. Some time later, Sara reluctantly stood from the warmth of the tub and accepted a drying cloth. Faye helped her dress, and she submitted to her maid's ministrations with new excitement. She was dressing for Geoffrey, and *he* would be the one who unclothed her.

Once ready, she descended the stairs later than expected. She found Geoffrey already seated at the dais with his uncle and brother. She made her way toward them, confident in her bearing and her person.

The ivory dress she was wearing had a gold trim and deep blue surcoat, and her newly washed dark hair cascaded in waves down her back. Sara nodded to those gathered in the hall but refused to glance in Geoffrey's direction, not confident of her ability to remain composed when he looked at her.

The mood in the great hall was lighter than it had been in weeks, and she was glad to see smiles on so many faces.

"DAMN, SHE'S COMELY."

Geoffrey glowered at his brother seated next to him. "Keep your voice down and your opinions to yourself."

Bryce failed to heed the warning.

"I wonder, does the queen look half as regal as Lady Sara?"

"Bryce."

"Just a question, brother."

"Drink your ale and content yourself by staring at all of the wenches looking in your direction."

Indeed, every female in the room seemed to either be looking at the dais or pretending not to. It was a common occurrence whenever Bryce was about, and Geoffrey knew his brother would take full advantage later.

He'd pacified his brother for a time, promising to give his answer on the morrow. But he actually wanted to speak to Sara first and was surprised to realize he planned to ask her opinion on the matter.

For him, there was only one woman whom Geoffrey wanted to get alone. He eyed her greedily as she made her way toward them.

If only he could make her feel every inch of him. What he planned would stop just short of what he wanted, but it would be pleasing for them both. He'd thought of little else all afternoon.

When Sara finally reached the table, she sat in the chair a servant had pulled out for her and turned immediately toward Hugh. Geoffrey inhaled deeply, his cock stirring at the mere sight and scent of his tormentor.

She was nervous. Otherwise she'd have greeted him by now. He picked up a chalice, drinking deeply of the fine Portuguese wine. Every day he felt less out of place at Kenshire, and he had to admit that some of the luxuries here were indeed pleasurable.

His leg brushed Sara's, not accidentally, under the table. With Bryce sitting next to him and his uncle on the other side of his countess, this was hardly an occasion for flirting.

But he couldn't resist.

She finally looked at him. There was no need to be coy. He'd be gone shortly. There wasn't time.

He didn't say a word, letting his eyes tell her what he planned for them. She swallowed hard as he glanced at the delicate skin of her neck. He would taste her there. And everywhere.

"Stop."

It was whispered so softly, he thought for a moment he'd imagined her voice.

"Geoffrey."

He inclined his head as if it were their first greeting of the evening. "My lady." He stared into her eyes, thinking about touching her, tasting her.

"In all my life, I've never seen you so distracted."

Bryce sounded genuinely confused. Only then did Geoffrey register that his brother had called his name several times. Reluctantly turning away from Sara, he nodded to his brother.

"I already gave you my reply, Bryce. You'll have my answer tomorrow."

His brother was proving stubborn as usual, only now he was the one who wished to throw caution to the wind.

"I know you think me a child, Geoffrey, but men my age lead troops, some with a wife and babe waiting for their return."

Geoffrey smirked, giving his brother a sideways glance. "Had I known you were so eager for a wife and child, I'd have spoken to our aunt and uncle about it. I'm sure Simon will have someone in mind for you."

Bryce snorted, "I'm as ready for a wife as you are."

SARA WATCHED AS THE FIRST course was served, though it wasn't enough to distract her from the Waryn brothers' conversation.

"You don't intend to marry, Sir Geoffrey?"

His look was both carnal in intensity and raw with emotion. "The violence along the border won't diminish anytime soon."

Sara tilted her head in thought. "Aye. We're not immune here at Kenshire, so I understand your concerns. But surely you'll want a child?"

Geoffrey knew this was more than a rhetorical question. "I'd like nothing more than to raise a family in safety, but doubt I'll see such a thing in my lifetime."

Oblivious to Bryce, Sara continued to question him. "If your family's safety could be assured?"

Without hesitation, Geoffrey answered, "I would marry the right woman tomorrow."

Sara included Bryce in the conversation, realizing her intimate banter with Geoffrey might appear suspicious. "Do you agree, Sir Bryce?"

The younger but more somber man shook his head. "Nay, my lady, I don't. I'm sorry to say I've no wish to wed."

"Pray tell, why not?" She was genuinely interested.

"Forgive me, my lady, but women tend to get me into more trouble than they're worth. I'll stick to fighting and let my siblings be responsible for furthering our family name."

"That is," Geoffrey added, "if we're successful in restoring the Waryns to their former position. At present, the name is associated with nothing more than poor freemen and reivers."

"Speaking of reiving…" Sara forged ahead even though both men winced. "Geoffrey tells me you live with your aunt and uncle and do not…" She needed to find the right words. "Partake in Hugh and Geoffrey's activities."

So the man *did* laugh. Bryce was fairly shaking with mirth. "Partake in his activities?" he finally said. "Nay. Thanks to my brother, I wither away at my family's small manor, training with the other knights and playing nursemaid to my younger brother and sister."

Sara sensed his resentment over the assignment—and felt indignant on Geoffrey's behalf. "So you'd rather put your life and reputation on the line, no doubt worrying your brother and uncle, rather than protect your siblings from an attack like the one at Bristol?"

Her words were so softly spoken it took both Bryce and Geoffrey a moment to register the depth of her rebuke.

She didn't care if her words angered the young man. It was exactly what her father would have said to her—one of his teachable moments—and it was something the young man needed to hear.

His face much sterner than it had been a moment ago, Bryce bit back, "I wouldn't put it in quite those terms." Giving his full concentration to his ale, he turned away.

Let him think on that a bit.

Geoffrey, however, looked anything but sullen. A wide grin revealed the dimple she so loved, making him look more approachable. Less menacing. And his scar almost disappeared when he smiled.

Lifting his chalice for a toast, he murmured, "Well played, my lady." After taking a sip, he leaned close and whispered, "My thanks."

Sara smiled back and suddenly felt a strange sensation, a tightening of her muscles that almost made her shiver. Anticipation? Nerves?

Knowing she gave Geoffrey too much attention, she turned to speak to Sir Hugh. As content as she'd been in a long while, Sara sipped her spiced wine, happy to see the hall come back to life. She refused to think about what the next day would bring.

The night was still young.

CHAPTER 20

AFTER SUPPER, THE MEN PLAYED a game of dice while Sara made her rounds of the hall, speaking to people she'd neglected these past days. She ensured their healer was well supplied and met with Peter, who animatedly apprised her of the progress with the gatehouse.

All the while, she continued to steal glimpses of Geoffrey seated with his uncle and brother. Once she caught Geoffrey looking at her. The gleam in his eye gave her the same flutter she'd felt at dinner. She closed her eyes, picturing his lips on hers, and nearly burst with anticipation.

Once upstairs, she prepared for bed with Faye's assistance. As was her custom, the maid carefully placed her dress in a large wooden chest to be aired out another day. Sara crawled under the covers of her decadent featherbed—one of the few luxuries she allowed herself—and bid adieu to her maid. Watching the soft glow of the fire's flames on the nearby tapestry, Sara allowed her mind to stray to Geoffrey's banter with his brother. Something told her that Geoffrey would be the kind of husband her father had been to her mother. Although she had never known her mother, everyone spoke of the rare, loving relationship her parents had enjoyed. Her father had spoken so often about her mother, she sometimes forgot the memories were actually only stories. He'd often say, "A strong union meant to bring the Caiser family greater strength, and with it peace, doesn't exclude the possibility of tender feelings."

Perhaps not, but neither did it signify the likelihood of a love match.

And though Geoffrey would never be considered a "strong union" for her, she couldn't help but wonder what it would be like to share a future with her fierce but charming protector.

But it was a future that would never exist, so she forced herself to concentrate instead on the pleasure Geoffrey brought her. He had told her to come to him tonight, and she would.

Swinging her feet out of bed, she smoothed her unruly waves and made her way toward the door. Listening through a crack, she heard nothing to indicate anyone was about. Slowly, Sara made her way into the hallway.

GEOFFREY LAY WITH HIS ARMS crossed behind his head, his heart beating in his chest like he was an untried lad. Knowing it was wrong but beyond caring, he waited anxiously for the door to open—and was startled when it did. Unable to stop smiling, his cock hard with anticipation, Geoffrey moved toward the door and was shocked to see his brother standing in the entranceway.

"What the hell are you doing here?"

He didn't care how rough his voice sounded. Bryce had to go. Now.

"When did you become so churlish?" Bryce closed the door behind him. Geoffrey watched him take in the sparse but richly appointed furniture, large four-poster bed, and roaring fire which cast the only light in the room save a candle on the table adjacent to the bed.

Rather than answer, he walked toward his brother, attempting to stop his progress into the room.

"What do you want?"

Bryce startled. Geoffrey was usually not so short with him.

"Hugh asked if you planned to sleep in the guardhouse with us now that Sara is safe."

As if on cue, the door creaked open once again. Geoffrey's heart fell, panic overriding good sense. He crossed the room in a few long steps, but it was too late to stop her.

Sara edged into the room quickly, only then noticing that she and Geoffrey weren't alone. All three stared at one another for a moment, no one sure what to say.

Bryce found his voice first. "Hugh will kill you."

The admonition spurred Sara into action. Eyes wide, she turned and fled from the room. Geoffrey didn't attempt to stop her, knowing it would make the situation worse.

"Geoffrey, what are you doing?"

"I haven't bedded the lass."

Bryce snorted, an arrogant sound that would have irritated Geoffrey on a good day.

"So she came to talk politics, perhaps? Maybe to engage you in a game of Nine Men's Morris?"

He briefly considered lying to his brother, but he'd never done so before and knew it was unnecessary. "Nay," he replied simply, watching Bryce's face. Geoffrey still found it difficult to see that his younger brother had grown into a man on his watch.

"I was right earlier. You love her."

Geoffrey poured a mug of ale for both of them from the pitcher on the table. It would be a long night.

"It matters not."

Bryce didn't argue. "You're playing with fire."

His amorous brother was the least likely person in the world to offer advice on restraint,

and Geoffrey found it hard to take him seriously.

"I know what I'm doing."

"Do you? The Geoffrey I know exercises restraint. He waits patiently to take revenge, knowing a premature attack could be fatal. He lowers himself to common thievery for the sake of his siblings but refuses to harm innocents. He fights like the devil and scares the hell out of just about everyone, but he is never ever impetuous."

His brother was right. He had no response. Instead, he poured himself another drink and invited Bryce to do the same.

"To talks of politics." He mocked himself with a toast, signaling the end of a discussion he had no wish to continue.

Bryce grinned, having made his point. "And games of Nine Men's Morris."

IN THE BEDCHAMBER ACROSS THE hall, Sara paced the room, panicked by the possible repercussions of her actions. Would Bryce keep their secret? Did he know what they'd intended? What was Geoffrey telling him?

The pacing helped her sort out her thoughts, and eventually her panic abated. She couldn't imagine Bryce would betray his brother. Unfortunately, she had no siblings, but if her friend Gillian were ever in such a spot, she'd keep a secret for her until her dying breath.

Gillian. Her friend would never put herself in such a situation. Though as wild inside as Sara, she was also much more … typical. Always a lady, she'd never once worn breeches or ridden bareback. She certainly had never shown any interest in learning to shoot with a bow and arrow. Such pursuits were left to her older brother. A powerful baron's daughter, she knew her place and would never jeopardize it.

Which was exactly what Sara had very nearly done by entering Geoffrey's chamber. She had put the future of Kenshire, of the Caiser name, at risk. For passion.

Nay, for love.

The distinction hardly mattered. While her heart raced at the sight of him, and only him, they couldn't be together. Sara's eyes welled with tears as she sat on the edge of her bed. She had lost her father and now she was about to lose the only man she'd ever fallen in love with. Their stolen kisses could not continue. By God's bones, she'd been prepared to give him her virginity!

An image of Geoffrey surfaced in her mind. Him cupping her face, his thumb tenderly outlining her lips, eyes filled with emotion. She tried to hold back tears, but they streamed down her face anyway. She let them come, allowed herself to wish for things that couldn't be. For her father to be alive, for Geoffrey to stay. Why couldn't things be different?

But they were not. Geoffrey was lost to her. Had never been hers to begin with. Lying down at the edge of her bed, Sara wiped her face, not bothering to cover herself, and closed her eyes.

THE NEXT MORNING GEOFFREY WOKE with a splitting headache, gathered his few belongings, and walked out of the comfortable guest chamber for the last time. He stood in front of Sara's door for a moment, looking at the carvings that would have taken Bristol's carpenter a month to complete. Though the man had been skilled enough to etch the intricate roses into a piece of wood, he never could have stopped working for long enough to create such a masterpiece. It was yet another sign of the sea of titles and wealth that separated him from Sara.

Was she still abed or already at mass? Did she worry about Bryce's reaction? He would have to find her to reassure her that their assignation would remain private.

The moment Bryce had opened his chamber door, he'd realized it was over. The close call had reminded him of why he and Hugh had been summoned to Kenshire in the first place—to protect Lady Sara. Instead, he'd nearly ruined her. Hugh would remain to ensure Sara's well-being. Geoffrey would go home where he belonged. They would work with Wellingstone, and while it would smart to allow him to reap the profits of their land, at least it would be theirs. The Scottish swine living in his home would meet the same fate as Kenshire's would-be usurper.

Walking down the stairs into the hall, he was shocked at the late hour. The sunlight peeked through the splayed windows on the second floor, and it appeared the castle inhabitants had already broken their fast. He made his way to the kitchen.

"There she is, the woman of my dreams."

Cook turned and made a distinctly unladylike sound as the kitchen maids turned to stare. "Saucy boy."

Geoffrey raised his eyebrows, delighting in their banter. "Only in the presence of a mistress such as yourself," he said. Then, knowing how best to charm her, he added, "What was that third course?"

Cook lifted her head. "Roast sparrow and baked quinces with spiced apples, sir."

He bowed elegantly. "It was exquisite. Many thanks for such a fine meal." He didn't lie. The five-course meal that had been served as a small feast to celebrate the end of a battle that had never happened was one of the best he had ever eaten.

One of the maids tittered, and her friend joined her.

"Ye'll be wantin' something. Tell me what it is so they can get back to work."

Her words were harsher than her expression, and Geoffrey knew Cook was beginning to thaw.

"It seems I missed the morning meal."

Cook looked down at the bag in his hand. "Leavin', are you?"

Soon enough. "Nay, not yet. A bite to eat, if you please?"

Cook had already walked away. She returned with two large slices of freshly baked white bread, a luxury he could easily get used to, and an assortment of cheese. He swooped down to deliver a kiss on her cheek, gladly accepting the food.

Geoffrey caught the smile he knew was normally reserved for the lady of the manor.

Walking from the kitchen, he made his way to the gatehouse, acknowledging acquaintances along the way. He tried not to consider how pleasant it would be to live among these people.

He had just stepped into the sleeping quarters of the guardroom when a deep voice sounded behind him. "I can understand why you were reluctant to leave your quarters. We need to talk."

For a moment, Geoffrey wondered if his uncle somehow knew about last evening, but quickly dismissed the thought. His brother wouldn't betray him that way.

"Bryce must return to Elmhurst, and Lord Wellingstone requires an answer."

Relieved, Geoffrey sat on the bed, the straw mattress a far cry from the more luxurious one he had been enjoying in the castle guest room, but also much more comfortable than the hard ground on which he usually slept.

"Where is Bryce? He should be here."

The subject of their discussion filled the entranceway. "Thank you, brother."

Sara was right. Bryce was no longer a boy. His surprising words of caution the previous night had convinced Geoffrey of that.

"As you're fond of saying, you're now a man and deserve to be a part of any decisions made here today."

"Our decisions have already been made. It's you who hesitates, brother."

He opened his mouth to give his answer, but something stopped him.

The answer to his prayers was waiting for him at his aunt and uncle's home. Lord Wellingstone's men, along with the pledges of support he and Hugh had gathered these past five years, would be enough to take back his home. His title.

But he hated the thought of bending his knee to a man who cared naught for the home he loved. Was there no other way? He'd never ask Lyonsford for support; pride would forbid it. And the ailing king would be of no help. So what then? This was their best chance.

And yet it felt wrong.

Two expectant faces waited for his answer.

He imagined leaving, Sara welcoming her future husband. Walking out of Kenshire's small chapel as Lyonsford's wife.

Nay, he could not leave. Not yet.

"I'm staying."

Both men started talking at once, Bryce louder than their uncle.

"Do you know what that means? We'll lose Lord Wellingstone's support. Goddammit, Geoffrey! You're a damn fool."

He didn't answer because he knew Bryce was right. He was a damn fool—and yet he would not change his answer.

"There'll be another chance," Geoffrey said.

His uncle, at least, didn't look like he wanted to murder him.

"I've no desire to watch Wellingstone take our profits and Lord knows what else. Prince Edward will return and turn his eyes to the border. We'll find another way."

Bryce paced back and forth in the small room before finally turning to look straight at him. "I know why you're doing this."

If he kept talking, Geoffrey would kill him.

"You're my brother, the man I've admired since I first practiced in the training yard with a wooden sword you showed me how to wield. But I don't agree with you on this."

Geoffrey ignored the unwelcome tingle in his cheek and grasped his younger brother by both shoulders. "I know you don't, Bryce. But I'm asking you to trust me. I don't deserve your trust. I'm a thief by trade, no longer lord of anything. But I'm asking for it nonetheless."

Bryce didn't move or even blink.

"You are the same man I admired before the raid," Bryce finally said. "Lord … reiver. It matters naught, Geoffrey. Only to you." Then he looked back and forth between Geoffrey and Hugh. "I trust you both," he added. "With my life."

With that, he turned toward his meager belongings, packing them up in defeat. Geoffrey watched him, wondering what the hell he'd just done.

SARA LOOKED UP FROM THE ledger in front of her, panicking when she saw Bryce standing at the entrance of the solar with his travel bag. He was leaving? Was Geoffrey leaving with him? "Have you seen Geoffrey?" she blurted out.

Geoffrey would never leave without saying goodbye. Would he?

For a moment, she thought Bryce hadn't heard her.

"I believe my brother planned to train this morning."

She released her breath. So he wasn't accepting Wellingstone's offer? She had been so focused on what had happened last eve that she'd nearly forgotten that it was mid-morning by the time she realize Geoffrey may be leaving. Today. She tried to take her mind off the matter by burying herself in reports.

But if Bryce was leaving now and Geoffrey was in the training yard … had he decided to stay?

"I hope your stay was fruitful?" Sara said, pressing him a little.

"Unfortunately it was not," Bryce said. "But thank you for your hospitality." Graciously, he made no mention of the incident in Geoffrey's room. "Good day, Lady Sara," he said. "I hope we have occasion to meet in the future."

"As do I," Sara replied sincerely. After all, he was Geoffrey's brother and therefore always welcome at Kenshire.

Calling to Faye, who stood at the door, she asked the maid to have Cook prepare a basket of food for Sir Bryce.

Then, with a bow and a wink, he was gone.

The gesture reminded her of another dark-haired man with light blue eyes. One, she was quite relieved to learn, who would not be leaving her just yet.

Sara kept herself busy for the remainder of the day and did not see Geoffrey until supper. When he walked into the hall, she nearly dropped the cloth she'd used to clean her hands before sitting down to eat. She barely noticed when a servant reached out and took it from her.

Geoffrey's damp hair curled around his temples, and his white shirt was a stark contrast to his jet-black hair. He was magnificent in so many ways. His title might be tied to the land he'd lost, but Geoffrey was as much a noble as any man she'd met.

Unfortunately, his polite courtesies told Sara all she needed to know about where they stood. She concentrated on speaking with Sir Hugh and barely touched her meal.

When she rose from the table after an awkward extended silence, the voice she'd grown to love stopped her.

"Do you play chess?"

"Aye."

He stood, pulled out her chair, and offered his elbow. *So formal.* Geoffrey looked at his uncle.

"By all means," Hugh responded to Geoffrey's silent question.

As she stepped away from the dais, a signal that the meal was over, servants began to clear the tables. Geoffrey led her to a table in the corner where a chessboard was always set, waiting for players. He pulled out a large wooden chair, an elaborate carving of the Caiser family crest on its back, a favorite feature of her father's, and she sank into the deep red cushion.

A servant filled both of their goblets with wine.

"I thought you prefer ale."

"I'm getting used to some of the refinements offered at Kenshire."

Sara looked down at her simple but elegantly cut green dress. Though she wore no overcoat or jewels, the material obviously marked her as a noble. She hardly noticed such things before. Knowing the hardships Geoffrey endured, it now seemed there was excess everywhere she looked.

"We must seem extravagant to you." She meant it not as a slight but as an honest statement of fact.

"Aye." He moved pieces about the chessboard automatically.

"Tell me about what you do." She was hoping he wouldn't brush off the inquiry as he'd done in the past. These next days might be their last together, and she wished to know him, truly know him.

Glancing up from the board, his eyes found hers. How could anyone think Bryce was the more handsome brother? She'd heard the servants talking. Of course Bryce's reticence lent his good looks an air of mystery. But in her mind, the two couldn't be compared.

"We run with the same group of men, a mixture of farmers, blacksmiths, nobility..."

"Nobility?" She hadn't meant to ask the question so loudly.

"Aye, minor barons mostly. The lawlessness of the border draws men from every walk of life ... with the exception of the clergy, of course."

Geoffrey had to stop talking to consider his countermove. She remained quiet, allowing him to concentrate.

"It's a simple life, most meals cooked on an open fire. But we do have our share of enjoyment on raids as well."

"Do tell." Though she tried to keep her tone neutral, she was afraid she failed miserably.

"There are few, if any, women on raids," he said, meeting her eyes. "I meant the pipes that my uncle plays. And games like this."

She could feel her cheeks turning pink.

"Naughty wench."

He made it sound like an endearment.

"Most of the men stay together during high season. Hugh and I return to Elmhurst Manor as much as possible to check on Bryce and the others."

"There hardly seems to be a need to *check* on Bryce." Against her better judgment, she probed the subject. "Does he stay to protect the others or because you want to protect him?"

Geoffrey glanced up from the chessboard.

"Both. My uncle Simon is getting older, aye, but he would protect Neill and Emma with his life. Hugh and I wish to shield Bryce from a life of raiding and running. Elmhurst is no great castle, but my brothers and sister are comfortable enough there."

The topic was obviously an uncomfortable one for him.

"Most of the men are just trying to survive in a place abandoned by England and Scotland. My own family's history is proof of the harshness of life on the border."

As they continued to play, he told her of their struggles to secure men and of his worry about his siblings' future.

"Sara." His tone told her that their comfortable discussion was coming to an end. "I've moved my things to the gatehouse guardroom."

She concentrated on her next move. What was there to say?

"I'm aware." *But you stayed.*

"It's for the best," he continued.

She moved a pawn, positioning it to capture one of his own, and looked up.

"When Bryce entered my chamber last eve," he said, staring into her eyes, "I realized the significance of what I could have taken from you.""You cannot take what's freely given." *And am afraid I would offer myself to you again, despite the vow I made to myself. To Kenshire.*

He was saved from responding when Peter broke the spell, calling to them from across the hall.

"Lady Sara!" Out of breath, he rushed toward them, frantically waving his hands. "There's been an accident. Come quickly."

She followed Peter, noting Geoffrey's comfortable presence behind her as she made her way toward the latest crisis.

CHAPTER 21

TWO DAYS AFTER THE SMALL fire that had thrown her people into a panic, Sara was at her wit's end. Although he had stayed at the castle, she'd seen little of Geoffrey since he helped to save the carpenter's home. Both of them had kept their distance. It seemed the easiest thing to do for the helpless situation they found themselves in.

The day before, he'd gone on an impromptu hunting party with some of the men from Kenshire. She'd longed to join them, wanting to show Geoffrey her skill with the bow and arrow. Which was precisely why she had forced herself to stay behind.

"Milady, you should have seen him. I've never seen a horse so fast or a man so skilled with the bow. He took down two deer with such ease, all the men are talkin' about it." A young squire named Reginald had told the tale to anyone who would listen. "No disrespect, milady," he'd added. "He's maybe even better than you!"

"It sounds as if Geoffrey left quite an impression," she'd teased.

"Aye, milady," the squire had said, taking her quite seriously. "It was a most impressive sight!" Moving on, the young lad had continued to sing Geoffrey's praises to everyone present.

Now, seated in her solar, Sara wished she'd participated yesterday. She needed to get out. The air felt stifling on this unusually warm autumn day. Luckily, she wore soft cotton breeches and a shirt made especially for her.

Vowing once again that today would be the final time she donned breeches before Lord Lyonsford's arrival, Sara decided she ought to take full advantage. Leaving behind records and ciphers that would await her return, she gathered her long, unruly waves together in a makeshift braid and then made her way to the stables.

Once outside, she was ambushed by her well-meaning maid. "Do ye need assistance, my lady?"

Sara didn't break her stride. "Nay, thank you," she called back, determined to exercise her neglected mare. Guinevere was saddled quickly. Luckily, the stable hand said nothing of an escort.

Sara took a wide path to St. Oswald's Gate, the original entrance to Kenshire Castle's inner bailey. The main gate housed Geoffrey and his uncle, and the men there were as loyal to them as they were to her. While she was glad the Waryn men had gained the loyalty of her own, she wanted no complications at the moment—and no company.

As it turned out, the guard did question Sara's lack of an escort.

In her most authoritative voice, she called out quite firmly, "I need no escort for a short ride."

Looking skeptical, he turned to consult with the other guards and yelled down, "Eddard will have my hide for this." Yet he opened the gate as she'd asked.

She gave the young knight a brilliant smile as she charged past the gate into the open field, circling north away from the village and toward her destination.

The niggling feeling of doubt that rode with her from the castle faded away as she rode into the dense forest, dissipating entirely when the lake appeared before her. Even though the hidden spot was one she'd visited since childhood, Sara felt awed by its beauty every time.

She dismounted, tied off Guinevere, and walked toward the lake. Looking around to assure herself of privacy, Sara decided an impromptu swim was in order. After all, it was likely one of the last times she could be this uninhibited. An earl's wife simply did not ride unescorted, in breeches no less, for an afternoon swim.

Her father would strangle her.

Sara's mouth turned up in a secret smile. She suddenly felt deliciously daring.

WHEN GEOFFREY SAW WHAT SHE intended, his breath caught in his throat. Dear Lord, please don't let her do it.

He'd have to speak to Sara about her blatant disregard for safety, not to mention her alarming ignorance of his presence. Granted, Geoffrey was known to be as stealthy as any tracker. He'd followed her to this place, keeping a distance close enough for easy discovery. Though apparently not for his countess.

The reckless woman actually meant to disrobe and swim in the small lake.

No good would come of this. He stood rooted to the spot, staring as Sara unlaced her shirt, which looked very much like his own, though was cut for a smaller wearer. He reminded himself to ask Faye who in God's name had stitched it for her.

As she pulled it over her head, Geoffrey let out his breath. Luckily another shirt, nay, a short chemise, lay underneath. As she began to take that off as well, Geoffrey knew he couldn't watch without breaking the vow he'd made to himself—and her—after the night Bryce had caught them.

He was here to protect her. Nothing more.

"Stop!" he shouted into the clearing.

Sara spun wildly around, clearly shocked to have been caught unaware.

Good, let her be afraid. She could have gotten herself killed.

Angered by his carelessness and his own reaction to her, he strode out of his place in the brush.

"What the hell could you possibly be thinking?" he shouted.

"Me?" Sara shouted right back. "I'm not the one who just snuck up on someone and scared them half to death!"

Her brown eyes flashed, narrow slits glaring at him.

She'd not turn this on him. "The fact that I *could* sneak up on you should enlighten you to the danger you put yourself in."

"I don't appear to be in any danger, Sir Geoffrey. Your presence is timely, as usual."

"You're upset with me for saving you from a potential disaster?" Incredulous, Geoffrey allowed himself his full range of volume, which he normally tempered in front of the sheltered countess.

Instead of backing down, Sara ignored the warnings and pressed him further.

"To which potential disaster do you refer, *Sir* Geoffrey? Shall I thank you for saving me from the last enjoyable experience I'm likely to have before my future husband descends on Kenshire to take my land and my people? And *me*, lest we forget that small detail. Pray excuse my behavior. How could I have possibly wished for the freedom to cool off on a beautiful, warm day in a place I've visited since childhood? What *could* I have been thinking?"

She deliberately misunderstood. As angry as he was, Geoffrey knew Sara was sending him a message, and he would do the same. Grabbing her arm, he pulled her toward him—and into the most demanding kiss they'd shared yet. Forcing her mouth open, he plunged his tongue inside to taste what he'd been missing the past few days.

Groaning with pleasure and feeling himself instantly harden, he pulled off her short chemise without thinking and carelessly discarded it. "Is that what you were about to do?"

He didn't get an answer, not that he'd expected one. Cupping both breasts, he rubbed his thumbs over the hardening nubs as he took her mouth even deeper into his own.

There was no stopping now, and they both knew it.

"Touch me," she demanded.

He gladly accommodated her. He caressed her bare back, flawless and smooth. Yanking off his own shirt and pulling her close, he relished in the feel of their bare skin touching one another.

He wanted, nay, *needed* more.

Untying her breeches and reminding himself to tell her never to wear them again—they were much too provocative—he pulled them down in one motion. He knelt below her, kissing her stomach, her hips, and the insides of her bare thighs. Relishing the sight before him, he stood, less frantic and more fully aware. Her sigh, a siren's song, lulled him into a spell he was powerless to withstand.

He grasped Sara's face with both hands. "I want to make love to you with everything that I am."

She never answered him, but rather placed her hands over his, closed her eyes, and took a deep breath. Opening her eyes, she smiled. Slowly. Sensually.

He struggled to keep his composure, quickly disrobing. She was looking at him with such awe and wonder, he had to look away. Bedding a virgin would be a new experience, but he anticipated it with great pleasure because it was her. Because she would be his.

"Sara," he said, giving her another chance to turn away, for both of them to choose sanity, "your first time should not be in the woods tumbled by a man with so little honor that he'd deflower you rather than protect you."

Naked and ready to explode at any moment, he needed to be sure this was what she wanted. She deserved no less.

"Geoffrey." His name was a sweet, intimate caress on her lips. "'Tis fitting my first time should be in a place I hold dear with a man so honorable I'd call him husband if I could."

Scooping her in his arms, Geoffrey carried her to a bed of soft grass below an unusually low overhang of a willow. Its soft buds teased her naked body as he walked with her, and he could feel her shiver beneath his hands.

He placed her on the ground, lying beside her. His fingers trailed a path from Sara's leg to the apex of her womanhood, and he was pleased when she opened her legs wider for him. She gazed at him with a look somewhere between delight and trepidation.

"Relax, love." He leaned down, and this time his kiss was less demanding than before. Coaxing her lips apart, he traced their outline with his tongue, simultaneously filling her with his finger. He teased her small nub with his thumb, slowly increasing the pressure.

Moving his lips to her ear, he whispered, "Feel, don't think."

Faster and faster, he moved his hand, watching the woman beside him as her full lips parted with pleasure and she arched her back, pushing herself closer to him. It was the single most exquisite sight of his life—and he knew he'd never witness anything as erotically beautiful as long as he lived. He'd brought her pleasure before, but this time was different. Her release would only be the beginning. Leaning on one elbow, he moved his hand inside her.

Expertly bringing her to climax, he captured her sounds of pleasure with his mouth, and when her breathing returned to normal, he shifted on top of her.

Though he knew there would be hell to pay, he guided the tip of his hardness into her wet sheath, inch by inch, allowing her to become accustomed to him, watching her expression every second.

"You're sweating," she said softly, wiping beads of perspiration from his forehead.

He was going to explode.

GEOFFREY WAS CLEARLY WORKING HARD to restrain himself. As Sara became accustomed to the strange sensation of him entering her, she allowed herself a quiet exploration of Geoffrey's backside, marveling in the way every muscle tensed beneath her fingers.

Suddenly he stopped.

"Are you sure, Sara? There'll be no turning back." His voice was strained, as if he was physically in pain. The fullness was like nothing she'd experienced. Surely he could never fit entirely inside her. And now his hardness was pressed against the barrier that marked her as a virgin and a suitable wife. If she asked him to withdraw, he would.

"Aye, I'm sure."

Without warning, he thrust hard, and she attempted to pull

back.

"That is the only pain you'll ever feel from me. I promise."

Even as he spoke, the sharp stab began to subside. It was replaced with a feeling she couldn't compare to any other.

And then he began to move.

Slowly, he leaned down to take her hardened nipple into his mouth as he pushed and withdrew, pushed and withdrew. Sara moaned, not sure which sensation to concentrate on. Catching on to the rhythm, faster and faster, she tensed every muscle in her body. His mouth moved to her neck, nibbling and tasting as he continued to move on top of her. Her wildly beating heart would surely explode out of her chest.

Panting, matching him thrust for thrust, she couldn't hold a thought.

"Please." She begged for something. *What?*

Geoffrey accommodated her, grinding his hips and continuing to thrust until he delivered on his promise. No pain. Only complete and total pleasure.

Unlike the other spasms, this one made her buttocks squeeze and her hands clench against Geoffrey's back. She didn't recognize the sounds coming from her, which Geoffrey matched with his own satisfied groan.

Sweating and still pulsating, Sara couldn't catch her breath. She swallowed, wrapped her arms around Geoffrey's broad back, and reveled in the most incredible experience of her life.

H*OLY HELL. WHAT WAS THAT?*

Geoffrey had bedded his share of women, but he'd never come quite so hard.

Sara had matched his passion with her own—and he told her so. "Who knew the countess would be such a minx in bed?"

Sara, never one to back down, said, "Bed? I see nothing but willow trees and grass."

Rolling off and gathering her to him, Geoffrey pushed her long dark locks to the side. "If I recall, you once told me this was your favorite place in the world. Far be it from me to shatter that illusion with something so ordinary as a bed."

"And," he added, "unless you'd like a repeat of what we just did, you may want to stop wriggling against my leg."

She giggled—a sound he was pretty sure he'd never expected to hear from Sara—but her words immediately diverted his attention.

"I wouldn't mind."

Propping himself on an elbow, he leaned over and kissed her gently, running his hand down the valley between her breasts.

"You'd get no argument from me." Then, placing a soft caress on her dark curls down below, he amended, "but you wouldn't be able to mount Guinevere if we were to repeat that performance."

"Interesting," she said, showing her innocence.

Her statement prompted him to question her further. "So how does a sheltered maid give such pleasure on her maiden voyage?"

A light flush crept up her cheeks. "Mayhap she had the guidance of an expert captain."

"I'll not argue with you there, my love."

It came out before he could stop it. They fell silent, the endearment a reminder of everything that lay between them.

Although she would never be his, he did love her. If there had been any question, their lovemaking had confirmed what his brother had not so gently accused him of.

But he couldn't say the words since they wouldn't change anything. Instead, he closed his eyes, allowing himself a moment of peace before reality intruded on their perfect afternoon.

CHAPTER 22

THE RIDE BACK TO THE castle was subdued, with sounds of their slow canter punctuated by intimate conversation. Geoffrey couldn't remember feeling more connected to another human being in his life. Sara's sensual allure, while undeniable, extended beyond her perfectly shaped body and full, tantalizing lips.

Their rash act could not be repeated. He'd not put her in that kind of danger. Having to cover the loss of her virginity was one thing. Increasing his chances of an unexpected pregnancy would be quite another.

Would that be so terrible? How could he *not* have her again?

She had belonged to no other man before him.

The knowledge that he'd taken her virginity made him feel something beyond simple lust. Not guilt … he'd never felt guilty for his actions once committed to them. Nay, a feeling of possession, primal satisfaction that she was indeed his.

Except that she was not.

"Sara," he said after a stretch of silence. "We need to talk about what happened."

Up until this point they'd been discussing anything but—her father and his parents, John and Randolf.

"If we must." Obviously disgruntled, she frowned, a crease of worry shaping her forehead.

"You're worried about the repercussions?" he guessed.

"In a sense, though I don't regret it." Sara looked at him defiantly, as if expecting him to argue. He would not. "I believe I can convince my betrothed I come to him a virgin." Geoffrey could tell she wasn't convinced at all, but she had something else to say, and he would let her say it. "But I am worried," she continued

"About?"

She hesitated.

"Sara?" She'd piqued his curiosity.

She looked at him as they slowly trotted along. Finally, she said, "I'm worried he'll never be good enough."

She didn't have to explain, and he couldn't comfort her. What would he say? *You're right. Lyonsford would never be good enough for you.* Whatever it was between them would be impossible to replicate.

But she wasn't finished. He could tell she was embarrassed, so he smiled to put her at ease.

"I asked once before, but I'm curious. Is that … normal?"

He laughed—an outburst he immediately regretted. She'd asked the question in earnest and looked anything but amused.

"Nay, 'twas not for me," he said.

"And you have much experience to compare it to?"

Geoffrey knew his answer might anger her, but he'd not be dishonest. "Yes, I have some experience in this area."

Unfortunately, she didn't let it drop there.

"A lot of experience?"

"Sara, do you really want me to answer that question?"

She considered for a moment before nodding. "Yes, 'tis strange to me that men are so much more—familiar—in this area than noblewomen. I mean, it's not as if a woman can't enjoy the act as well."

It was his opportunity to change topics. They should enjoy each other, not think of the fact that this thing between them would need to end. "Really now? You enjoy lovemaking, lass?" he teased. "Tell me, fair lady, about this enjoyment you speak of. Which part did you find most enjoyable?"

She refused to be more specific. "All of it, I suppose."

He couldn't resist. "Did you enjoy when I slid inside you and then retreated … over and over again?"

He liked to think she slowed her mare because she was having a hard time concentrating.

"Perhaps you most enjoyed it when I slid my hand between us to touch you as my cock…"

"Enough!"

He trotted alongside her, grabbed the reins of her horse, and stopped them both. Dismounting quickly, he held up his hand for her to do the same. In moments, he secured both horses to a nearby tree. Sara neither attempted to help nor stopped him.

He would show her how right she was about their passion being unmatched.

Crushing her to him, he ploughed her mouth with his own and gently bit her lower lip, eliciting a throaty moan, which had become his favorite sound of late.

He moved his mouth to her neck, tilting her head back for better access. A sheltered countess? Not any longer. His lady matched his passion with her own.

His?

Nay, not yours. She can never be yours.

"You know this cannot be," he said, his breath hitching.

"Why?"

He pulled his head up. Was she serious?

"Why? There are so many reasons I can hardly think where to start."

"You stayed."

A simple statement that nearly knocked him to the ground.

"You're not thinking straight. Listen to me." He held her in his arms, marveling how perfectly she fit there—as if they were made for each other. He tightened his embrace. The warmth of the afternoon had begun to wane, the crisp autumn air hinting at the harsh winter soon to follow.

"We're both fighting for what is ours. You deserve to keep Kenshire. And I wish you could do it on your own. But that's just not the way of the world."

"Fighting for what's ours…" When her voice trailed away, he

lifted her chin, kissing her softly, tenderly before releasing her.

He walked away to untie the horses. He had to stop touching her. When she was in his arms, he forgot the harsh realities of the world—something a reiver ought never to do.

STILL TENDER FROM THEIR LOVEMAKING, Sara stared at Geoffrey's back as he rode in front of her. She'd never imagined he could arouse the same passion in her so soon. Yet if he hadn't stopped back there, she'd have gladly allowed their kissing to turn into something more. As she watched him ride ahead, admiring his silhouette, it occurred to her that her father would have rather liked him. Geoffrey was strong, protective, thoughtful, and unwielding—qualities her father had admired.

And it was not by chance … it was the reason Geoffrey was at Kenshire in the first place. Her father had trusted Geoffrey's uncle to protect her, and by extension, his nephew.

"Geoffrey?"

As the village came into sight he slowed, turning to her.

"Do you suppose my father knew of you?"

His brow furrowed, and even from this distance, she could see the telltale tic, which meant he was either annoyed or deep in thought.

"I supposed he did. Why do you ask?"

She wasn't sure, but it felt important somehow.

"I'm just curious. I'll have to speak to your uncle about it."

"You'll have the chance sooner than you think. Here he comes."

He pointed off in the distance, where a lone rider had come into view.

"How do you know 'tis your uncle?"

Without answering her question, Geoffrey turned to look at her, worry etched on his handsome face.

"Something is amiss," he guessed. As they drew closer, Hugh's expression confirmed the truth of his words.

"Lady Sara, nephew." Hugh reined in his horse, stopping

before he reached them.

Guinevere bucked, which was extremely unusual for her. She sensed Sara's sudden unease.

"What is it, Sir Hugh?" Sara was proud that her voice did not quaver.

He looked at Sara, clearly wanting to question their whereabouts but not having the authority to do so, at least where she was concerned. She was ashamed of nothing; she would explain nothing.

"Messengers from Lord Lyonsford have arrived."

Without thinking, Sara glanced at Geoffrey, who had the good sense to keep his gaze leveled at his uncle. She quickly looked away and spurred Guinevere into action.

"Then let's receive them," she said, leaving both men behind as she sped toward the castle.

Heart hammering, Sara rode on the outskirts of the village. She would need to enter from the south to avoid seeing the messengers. Otherwise, they would most certainly relay her wayward appearance—breeches and all—to her betrothed. She expertly navigated her prized mare through the gate and into the stables.

When Geoffrey and Hugh caught up to her, she couldn't look at them, afraid Hugh would sense her desperation. Her despair.

"Farewell, gentlemen," she said in parting.

The moment she dreaded had finally arrived.

GEOFFREY WATCHED HER LEAVE, MAKING himself appear casual, waiting for the questions he knew his uncle would ask.

He wasn't disappointed.

His uncle turned on him as soon as he handed the reins of his horse off to a stable hand. "What were you doing with Sara? Why didn't she have an escort?"

"I was her escort. Lady Sara convinced the guards at St. Oswald's she would be perfectly safe alone."

Hugh shook his head. "Richard didn't exaggerate."

"What do you mean?"

"He often complained that Lady Sara acted like no other young maiden. I could tell he was secretly enamored with her wild ways, but no doubt they fought many battles over the meaning of 'proper' behavior for a female."

"Yet she carries herself like a queen when necessary."

Hugh stopped and grabbed Geoffrey's arm.

"If you've done anything to jeopardize her future…"

Geoffrey wished he could reassure his uncle without deception, but he was no saint.

"Uncle, you've nothing to worry over." His gaze didn't waver.

"By God, son, I hope you mean it. 'Tis obvious you have feelings for the lady, but no good will come of it."

"I know my place."

At least he thought he did.

His place was as Baron of Bristol. His grandfather had fought for the title, his mother and father had died because of it. Bloody though it was, it was his birthright.

"We'll appeal to Lyonsford as you planned," he said, though the words felt like ash in his mouth.

His uncle gave him a grim nod. Geoffrey hated the thought of asking Sara's husband … her *husband,* for God's sake … for anything. But they were running out of options. The mercenaries who had pledged them their support were not enough to take back Bristol Manor. He tried to convince himself otherwise, but Kenshire's well-trained army reminded him that the mercenaries they'd gathered were not as disciplined. Only the addition of well-trained knights would do the job.

Servants hustled through the dusty inner bailey. One chased a loose chicken, her well-worn but sturdy dress hiked up as she ran after the wayward fowl. Since Randolf's death, mundane, everyday tasks had replaced preparations for siege. His home had never been as grand, but he sorely missed listening to the village healer complain about her patients or watching his sister playing prisoner's chase with the other children.

He couldn't bring back his sister's childhood, but he could damn well give her a home.

A familiar figure bustled toward them, snapping him out of his reverie. With her hair covered, it was hard to determine Faye's exact age, but the lines on her smiling face put her close to his uncle's year of birth. Her dress imitated her lady's in style if not fabric or embellishments.

"Faye," he called to her, "your lady is in need of you."

When she answered, she looked at Hugh instead of him.

Well, that's interesting.

"I'm heading to her now, sir. So the crusader has finally returned home?"

"So it would seem," Hugh said. "Though he couldn't have been long overseas when he

received word of the betrothal. I'm surprised and pleased he's come so quickly."

"Aye, though the prospect of an alliance with the Caiser family would turn most men back toward the shores of England." Then, after giving them both a quick smile that lingered longer on Hugh, she made haste for the castle.

"Your breeches and balls be blessed."

"Boy." Hugh was not amused. "Keep your ribald thoughts to yourself."

Laughing, he left his uncle for the training yard. He intended to keep himself far away from the main keep and its unwelcome messenger.

LORD LYONSFORD'S MEN HAD BEEN given sustenance and a chalice of the finest wine at Kenshire. Now they waited in Sara's solar while she stood outside the door with Peter, not wanting to enter.

She had no choice.

She followed her steward inside, her eyes moving from her two well-dressed guests to the wooden chandelier hanging from the ceiling. A few years back, she had walked past the open door of the candlemaker's shop and stopped to watch him work. When she'd asked to help, the man had worried the earl would not want his daughter doing the work of a common man. After numerous reassurances, he'd finally relented. And while the four unlit candles in the chandelier weren't the ones they'd made that day, the memory reminded her why she needed to marry Lord Lyonsford. Kenshire must be protected from the possibility it could be taken from her forever. At least she knew Lyonsford was a good man. An honorable man. One who would take care of his people.

Jumping from their seats, the men stood and knelt before Sara. She bid them stand, only half listening to Peter's introductions. She sat, willing patience, and waited for the dreaded news.

"Thank you, my lady, for making us most welcome at Kenshire."

"It is our pleasure, sir." The badge on his surcoat stared back at her. Lyonsford's gold and red crest. She knew he served the earl, but seeing the evidence before her was unsettling.

"If it pleases my lady, I've a message from my lord, who wishes to convey his progress toward Kenshire."

The solar suddenly felt like a dungeon. The book-lined walls she normally loved made the space feel small, confining.

I can't do this.

"Is he close?" she said, her voice remarkably composed.

Oh God, please say no.

"Lord Lyonsford is no more than three days ride away, barring ill weather. We were held up briefly by a blocked road, but with any luck, there'll be no more delays."

"And—" the bearded man stood as straight as a poleax, "—he wishes to convey his heartfelt joy for the upcoming nuptials."

"Does Lord Lyonsford wish to return to Archbald for the wedding?"

Already shaking his head, the messenger confirmed her suspicions. "Nay, my lady, he travels with a full household, prepared to wed without haste here at Kenshire."

It was just as she'd expected. Dreaded. He wanted to secure

her hand in marriage immediately.

Everyone else would be pleased. Peter, Eddard, Faye ... all who worried over her safety these past months would only have to wait three days until her safety was secured. Hugh and Geoffrey would be free to resume their quest for Bristol.

Geoffrey would be leaving.

She needed to be alone.

"Thank you for conveying my lord's greetings. Do the two of you travel alone, sir?"

"Nay, my lady. With a small retinue of four other men. They've been well-provided for."

She nodded. "Very good. Then I bid you a good day. I must prepare for your lord's arrival."

Dismissed, he nodded once again, and he and his companion turned to leave the solar. Only she and Peter remained.

He looked at her with such an expression of happiness, Sara could not bear to look at him.

"Peter, please see to the men. I'd like to be alone."

Peter had known her since she was a babe. He was likely not fooled by her casual dismissal. Nevertheless, he nodded his assent and retired from the room, closing the heavy wooden door behind him.

Sara had no doubt her wish for privacy would be conveyed. When the door creaked shut, she allowed tears to flow freely.

She was an impostor, pretending to rule Kenshire with the easy grace and firm hand of her father. He'd said she was as strong as he, but he'd clearly lied. She had never felt more lost or powerless than she did right now.

When the door opened, she lashed out, embarrassed at having been caught in so vulnerable a position. "Give me leave!"

Geoffrey entered the solar, closing the door behind him and walking into the room as if he belonged there. Though she hated herself for putting on such a sorrowful display, she reached out for him as if it were the most natural thing in the world. She could no more help crying on Geoffrey's hard chest than she could stop her impending marriage to a man she did not know.

HE HAD THOUGHT GETTING PAST Peter, who was standing sentry in front of the solar, would be the hard part, but he'd never seen her like this before. He sent the steward away with assurances Sara wanted to see him despite her request for solitude.

His countess looked so defeated. So undone. His arms tightened around Sara, her distinctly floral scent filling his eyes with tears.

Tears?

He'd felt pain plenty of times. When he learned his parents had both been killed. When his face was nearly hacked to pieces by a rival family of reivers. But he knew his mother and father would be avenged someday, and the man who'd come close to ending his life had not lived to regret his actions.

He could neither say nor do anything to console Sara. Their situation remained unchanged. But damned if he wouldn't try anyway.

"Shhh," he said. "No one can take away the day we spent together."

It was cold comfort, and he knew it. The thought of Lyonsford's hands on Sara made his fingers itch to strike someone. He'd made his way to the training yard to do just that before he'd changed his mind and decided to see to his lady.

He'd made the right decision. Now … how to comfort her when he wanted nothing more than to send Lyonsford's men back to the south of England where they belonged?

As she quieted, he attempted to defuse the situation the only way he knew how.

"Do you remember the first kiss we shared on the beach?"

Sara leaned back to look at him. "Of course."

"And the first time I cupped these beautiful breasts," he asked, running his hand over the rich fabric of her dress, dipping his thumb into the exposed flesh at the front of the gown.

Her face streaked with dried tears, Sara nodded.

"Do you recall," he whispered, inches from her ear, "when I showed you what it meant to find release?" He followed it by kissing the sensitive skin behind her neck. Sara's indrawn breath was evidence of his successful distraction.

"My embarrassing display is over," she said.

What does that mean?

She must have seen the question on his face because she added, "My father would never have shown such weakness."

He didn't dare disagree. Instead he offered his honest opinion.

"You're stronger than you think."

"Sheltered was the word I think you used when we first met." Sara shook her head.

The look she gave him was filled with despair … and something more.

"So we wait for Lyonsford, an executioner whose axe is his wedding vow?" she asked.

"Aye, we've no other choice."

"And if we did?" She paused. "If Lyonsford and I weren't betrothed. What then?"

"I assume you'd be married to some other great lord whose title was worthy of the Countess of Kenshire."

"If I were free to choose my own husband?"

He should lie. He should tell her he'd never think of marrying her. It was a fantasy that would never be, so why cherish it? Why share it?

"I will never marry," he stated.

Sara's brown eyes flashed, sorrow replaced by anger.

"In that case, 'tis just as well Lyonsford is on his way."

He silently agreed. Lady Sara could never be his. The future that awaited him was filled with vengeance and turmoil. There would be no place for her. No place for tender feelings of any sort.

Without another word, Sara wrenched free, turned away, and left him standing alone in the lord's solar. If Lyonsford was on his way, it was better they distance themselves. In a few short days, they would part, likely forever.

The thought made him ill, but it was high time to concentrate on Bristol. He'd promised his uncle they would speak to Lyonsford—the thought made him physically ill—and that meant he would need to stay here until the man arrived. He would need to watch as preparations were made for Sara's wedding to another man.

He'd lived as an outlaw for five years; surely he could survive three days.

CHAPTER 23

IT WAS THE LONGEST THREE days of his life.

The first night, Sara paid him no attention, and he spent the evening getting good and drunk. Watching her interact with the guests, the tantalizing cleavage he'd so recently caressed a feast for the newcomers' eyes, Geoffrey's biggest challenge was to refrain from knocking out the brutish knight, one of Lyonsford's men, who kept glancing at her during the evening meal.

The untouchable countess had returned without any sign of the vulnerabilities he'd witnessed in the solar. Now Sara was playing the perfect hostess, making her way through the hall with the ease of one who had been raised to do so. What a fool he had been for considering a future with her.

Yet, despite what he'd told her in the solar, that's exactly what he'd done.

Lying next to her after their lovemaking, he'd let himself imagine what it would be like to have Sara as his wife. He'd imagined introducing her to his sister. The two would get on well, both wild to the point of recklessness.

The next day he paid for his overindulgence with drink. Again his cool countess paid him no heed for most of the day, which was just as well. He worked out his frustrations in the training yard.

As usual, a crowd had gathered around the yard. No one seemed disappointed when Geoffrey held his sword to the throat of a man lying on the ground who had been taunting his abilities moments before. Helping the young but able knight to his feet,

Geoffrey offered a word of advice.

"Work on your shoulder blocking," he suggested, "and your attitude."

Spying a young boy out of the corner of his eye, he walked toward him. He'd seen the lad before at the training yard, always carrying a small shield and sword. A squire.

"What's your name, lad?"

His eyes round, the boy looked behind him.

"You, young squire, what's your name?"

"Uh … Reginald, my lord."

"Sir Geoffrey," he corrected. "I lost my right to that title. Next time," he said, "answer with conviction. No question will be easier for you than that one."

The blond-haired squire straightened and tried again. "My name is Reginald, Sir Geoffrey."

"Better," Geoffrey said. "And a squire, correct?" He pointed to the small sword at his side.

"In a way, my … Sir Geoffrey. My da sent me to Kenshire near seven years ago as a page to Lord Richard, but…"

"No need to explain, Master Reginald. You must be looking forward to having a new lord."

Reginald stared at his feet and shuffled them around in the dirt.

"Look a man in the eye when you speak."

The boy immediately heeded him, impressing him with his willingness to learn.

"'Tis an honor to be here, Sir Geoffrey," he finally replied, not answering his question.

He's looking forward to Lyonsford's arrival as much as I am. "Would you like to train with me in the meantime?"

The look on the boy's face told Geoffrey his instincts had guided him well. It was nothing short of reverence. If only poor Reginald had better judgment, he'd have chosen elsewhere to worship. But in the meantime, Geoffrey needed a distraction as much as this squire needed guidance. The other men scattered as he began instructing the new charge.

He pointed to Reginald's sword. A fine weapon, clearly marking his station as a noble's son. "That's a good-looking weapon."

The boy's smile told him it was likely a gift from his father.

"When I was your age, our blacksmith forged a miniature version of this." He showed him the hilt of his own sword. It was the only tangible reminder of his parents.

"My father knighted me himself and gave this to me. But I once had a smaller one just like it."

The boy looked at the inscription on the blade.

"*In nomine domini.*"

"Aye." He sheathed his sword and gestured for Reginald to hold up his weapon. "Show me how to block with your shoulder." He made a quick adjustment. "Now turn your body to the left as you step back. There you are! Turn to the right as I come at you. Good."

WATCHING FROM AN ALLURE ATOP the wall—a vantage point she'd discovered as a girl—Sara could tell the moment Geoffrey entered the training yard. His presence commanded attention. Though he had no right to claim the loyalty of her people, he had earned it. They considered him their equal, reiver or not. After he won his match—of course he did—he turned his attention to Reginald, who'd been watching him worshipfully for days. How gentle he was with the lad, how patient. It was hard to believe this was the same fierce protector who had ended Randolf's life.

A sleepless night and tormented day had left Sara weary and unsure. She had nearly confided everything to Faye that morning before good sense had stopped her. Upon reflection, she shouldn't have been angry at his response. It was no business of hers if he planned to marry or not. And since they could not marry each other, what claim did she have on him?

Then he looked up.

She stood rooted to the spot, unable to look away from his eyes. Nay, she did have a claim on him. He was the man she had given her virginity to. And if she were being honest, the one she'd give herself to this very moment if she could.

Her weakness was appalling. The only option was to avoid him. To do otherwise courted danger. Turning away, she lifted her long skirts beneath her, already missing the freedom of her breeches, which now sat at the bottom of a clothes' trunk.

For the remainder of the day Sara kept herself busy, not a difficult task given how much needed to be prepared for the party of twenty that Lyonsford's messengers had told them to expect. Her duties brought her to the kitchen, and she inhaled deeply when she stepped inside, savoring the scents of baking bread and drying herbs. Smiling, she startled Cook from behind and laughed when the portly woman gave her a fierce scowl.

"It smells divine in here," she remarked, ignoring the sour face of the very important household servant.

"What do you be needing, milady?"

They discussed the guests, and Cook voiced her need for additional male servants for the heavy lifting.

"Enough of that." Cook wiped her hands on the front of her white linen apron. "Call me impertinent—" She pursed her lips. "Your father did many days. But I've known ya since you were a wee youngin', my lady."

"I know it." Sara forced a smile.

"I'd ask what makes my lady sad, but I already know. I also know you're trying to protect Kenshire by doing what you're meant to do, but—" Cook lowered her voice, "—yer father would want your happiness above all. I know that in my bones."

Sara stared at the woman who had been serving Kenshire's food her whole life. *What could she possibly mean by that?*

"I'm not blind, and neither are you," Cook said bluntly. "I wouldn't be tellin' ya what to do, but some things are worth fightin' for."Sara was sure Cook spoke of Geoffrey. How could she could possibly know about her feelings for him? Cook spent as many days in the kitchen as there was light in the sky.

"I … are you saying…?"

"Aye, I'm sayin' yer thinking you have to marry Lord Lyonsford, and maybe you do, for all this old lady knows. But I do have a few years on ya."

The greying hair peeking out from Cook's head covering confirmed the truth of her words.

"But maybe ya don't."

Then, as abruptly as she had begun the strange conversation, Cook patted her on the behind to move.

"The impertinence!" It occurred to her that Lyonsford would likely not want her to speak with the servants as if they were friends. It felt like a stab into an open wound. "I can tell when I'm not wanted."

Cook, who had already resumed her kitchen ministrations, corrected, "Always wanted, but not needed at the moment. I know well enough how to prepare for a few knights and their lord."

She gave Cook a quick kiss and left the kitchen.

Rather than spend time brooding over Cook's words, she set about her duties for the afternoon. But when she rode to Kenshire's small village, intent on visiting Mary and bringing her a basket of food, the blacksmith's daughter, she finally had time to reflect on Cook's advice.

Of course she must marry Lord Lyonsford. The marriage was approved by the king, or at least his council, and set in motion before her father's death. Uniting their houses would protect her, the people of Kenshire, and her family's other holdings.

Besides, even if she was inclined to walk away from everything her father and his father before him had built as their legacy—which she was not—Geoffrey wouldn't have her anyway. He'd said he would never marry. She should take him at his word.

Alice, the blacksmith's wife, welcomed her at the door of the humble, thatched-roof cruck house.

"Good day, milady," she said, leading her into the small but well-kept home. "Thank you for the extra provisions, Lady Sara."

"You're welcome, Alice. Ahh, there she is. Good day, Mary." The shy young woman stood from her chair, and the straw on the floor crunched under her feet as she approached.

"I've heard your babe grows fine and strong. May I hold him?"

Before she finished speaking, Mary handed her the boy, a tiny perfect bundle wrapped in linen strips.

The precious sleeping infant lay content in her arms. She looked from the babe to the contents of the small cottage. There was only one room to eat and sleep.

Could she do it?

Could she leave her home and all of its luxuries to live like Mary and her parents?

Likely she would not have to even if Kenshire was taken from her. But if everything was taken. *Then what?* She honestly didn't know. Her cumbersome dresses were one thing, Cook's fine food another. Could she live this way if it meant being with Geoffrey? Sara closed her eyes, imagining herself holding a baby of her own.

Geoffrey's baby.

"Is everything al'right, milady?"

"Aye. Quite all right, thank you. Your son is perfect."

She handed the babe back to his beaming mother.

"I wish you well, Mary." She turned to Alice. "Please give Harold my best."

She left the home, glad for the well-being of its occupants. As she headed back on Guinevere, she thought about her last visit to the blacksmith's home. She'd held on to Geoffrey, exhausted and relieved, never imagining they would share intimacies that very night. She wished he was riding with her now.

You will have to get used to missing him.

A quick glance at the sun told her it was time to prepare for supper. Anticipation fluttered in her chest. Even though they'd avoided each other most of the day, they would have to see each other at the evening meal.

A short time later, Sara emerged from the stables. She was preparing to cross the inner bailey when Sir Hugh approached her from behind.

"Sir Hugh." She turned, pleasantly surprised to see him. "How can I possibly thank you for the work you've done here?"

A smile reached the corner of his eyes, making him appear younger. Though certainly not as serious as Sir Bryce, Geoffrey's uncle clearly took much of his family's burden. It was nice to see the man relax a bit.

Before he could respond, she said, "You resemble your nephew when you smile." While it was a forward remark, Sara felt comfortable with Geoffrey's uncle. It was as if her father's own long acquaintance with him had passed on to her.

"You'd have said the same about Geoffrey's father." Hugh accompanied her toward the hall.

"Tell me of him."

He pursed his lips as if he were concentrating on a difficult problem. "Well, there's much to tell. You're likely not surprised to learn he had a bit of the devil in him."

She wasn't surprised at all.

"Emma, Geoffrey's sister, reminds me of his wildness. Geoffrey and Bryce, his thoughtful intelligence."

She wanted to ask more but was worried how he'd interpret her questions. She inquired instead after the state of affairs at Bristol.

"Geoffrey told me of Lord Wellingstone. I hope it would not be too forward of me to ask how it stands."

Hugh looked surprised.

"He told you of Wellingstone's offer?"

Immediately contrite, she was quick to answer. "I apologize if…"

"No need to apologize," he cut in. "I'm just surprised. Geoffrey typically keeps his own counsel. Although—" he paused and glanced at her, "—I shouldn't be."

She knew better than to ask for clarification.

"I fear Bryce almost put us in a difficult spot," Geoffrey added. "Aligning with Wellingstone wasn't in our best interest."

She didn't know the man, so she couldn't say. "I got the impression that Geoffrey would rather not be beholden to him."

"You could say that." Hugh extended an arm to indicate Sara

should precede him into the great hall. The large wooden door of the keep had been opened for her.

Sara knew Bryce had pushed for Wellingstone's support. If they'd decided to spurn his family's overlord, the matter would have to be dealt with delicately.

"It doesn't really matter now. Bryce returned to decline Wellingstone's offer."

Walking arm in arm with Sir Hugh, Sara could almost forget about her guests and impending marriage. There was certainly something about the Waryn men that put her at ease.

"I'm surprised. Getting Bristol back means everything to Geoffrey."

"The decision was his, not mine. He would have needed to leave immediately if he'd decided to accept Wellingstone's help. But I'm glad he chose to stay."

She heard herself saying, "I'm safe, Sir Hugh. Lyonsford will be arriving in just a few days." The words seemed to stick in her mouth.

As he'd done once before, Hugh turned to her and reached for both of her hands, which she gave to him freely.

"I promised your father to see you safe, and I'll do just that. We'll remain until you're wed, my lady. There'll be plenty of time to deal with our own troubles. And perhaps..." he hesitated.

"If Lyonsford doesn't choose to help, I will remind him of who kept me safe. Who saved my life. I will do everything I can to convince him if you wish it."

Hugh said nothing, but he looked as if he wanted to throw his arms around her. She meant every word.

"I want to thank you, Sir Hugh. My father chose his friends wisely."

Spotting Faye out of the corner of her eye, Sara called her name. When Hugh dropped her hands and turned toward her lady's maid, Sara noticed the long, lingering look they shared.

"Excuse me while I change for supper." She hustled to her chamber, asking a young servant to accompany her. But later that evening, her excitement turned to disappointment.

Geoffrey never came.

A long, tedious evening entertaining their new guests. Every time she glanced at the crest on the surcoat of Lyonsford's men, she struggled to remain unaffected.

Now that the prospect of battle had abated, more visitors had come to the keep, including Lady Maude and her aged husband, who'd returned as they passed through the area. Geoffrey had mentioned the conversation he witnessed between Lady Maude and John. Sara had to convince him the poor lady had no involvement in the plot against her.

Where is Geoffrey?

GEOFFREY SAUNTERED INTO THE KITCHEN, knowing most of the evening meal had already been served.

"Does my favorite woman in the world have anything to offer her humble servant?"

"I just sat down after spending the better part of my day cookin' the meal yer missin'. If ye'd not be eatin' with the rest of them, ye not be eatin'."

If Cook thought she could intimidate him, it was because she'd never met Bristol's healer. It was thanks to Evelyn he'd perfected the smile he gave Cook now.

"What are you after, sneakin' in here when ye' should be out there?" Cook gestured toward the hall, the closest building to the kitchen.

"A wee lad took most of my attention this afternoon, and I only just realized the lateness of the hour." His training session with the squire was common knowledge, mostly because Reginald told everyone and anyone who would listen that he was now squiring for Sir Geoffrey. Which was not exactly true, but Geoffrey didn't have the heart to tell the boy it was a temporary arrangement.

"Och, that be a fine excuse.""You're breaking my heart, Cook." He cocked his head to the side and gave her his most despondent look.

"It's not your heart I worry over."

He glanced at the gaggle of kitchen maids huddled together and shrugged his shoulders. "Can I help it if they adore me?"

"I'm not talkin' about those ninnies either," Cook rebuked. "It's her ladyship who you've ruined."

He straightened, no longer amused.

"Ruined?"

"Aye, ruined. I have eyes in me head to know Sara be in love with ya', and if I hit my mark, ya feel the same way."

How much did she know?

"I told her as much this afternoon. I know she feels a duty to her father and her people, but she's got one to herself too. With any luck, she's thinking 'bout my advice."

He was almost afraid to ask.

"And what were these words of wisdom you shared with her?"

"To consider every possibility is all. Cook knows somethin' or two about lost love, and it ain't from talkin' about it."

"I'm sorry to hear that, but I think you're wrong in this case."

"Maybe so. In the meantime—" She got to her feet, sighing all the while, and filled a trencher with food. "Off you go, beggar," she said, handing it to him. "The kitchen is closed."

Indeed.

He walked to the same empty staircase entrance where he'd stolen a kiss from Sara few days earlier.

Before the raid on his home, he'd thought more of himself than he should have. His father had called him arrogant. Growing up, he'd reaped praise from everyone—his mother, father, uncles and aunts, the ladies, his siblings. Bryce had followed him around like a puppy for as long as he could remember.

And then he had lost it all. Fleeing for his life and building a new one with nothing more than the clothes on his back and the sword his father had given him, he'd learned humility quickly.

When Kenshire's cook said she knew of lost love, he didn't doubt her. But he knew this situation between him and Sara had only one outcome.

He had nothing to offer the daughter of an earl with manors scattered through the country, whose holdings rivaled some of the greatest estates in England. He was a man whose birthright had been stolen, who lived among outlaws and could barely support his own siblings. A man like him stood no chance with the Countess of Kenshire, nor should he.

He should retire to his rooms before being tempted into the hall. He knew avoiding Sara was necessary, but it was one of the hardest things he'd ever done in his life. The image of her naked and splayed out before him surfaced in his head. His body reacted in an instant.

The sea gate. A cold ocean swim was just what he needed.

Changing course at the last moment, he nearly ran into someone. People were exiting the great hall now, moving through the private entrance and down the steep slope below the outer curtain wall.

The sound of breaking waves assaulted his senses. The sun had dipped low, the early evening sky light enough to make out the shoreline, but dark enough to hide much beyond the beach from him.

Closing his eyes, Geoffrey allowed the rhythmic sounds to lull him into a more peaceful place. He, too, had grown up along the coast, though Bristol was not as close to the sandy shores of the North Sea as Kenshire, so he understood Sara's obsession with the sea. There was nothing quite like the calm which accompanied wave after wave crashing on the shore.

There was a small movement on the sand dune between him and the path. Someone was here. He reached for his sword.

CHAPTER 24

AS SARA MADE HER WAY through the dunes, she looked back at the castle. From this vantage point, she could see only the top of the tower and King's Hall, the oldest building and the foundation of the sprawling estate that was her home. The closest structure, the Constable Tower, was the one her father had commissioned when she'd refused to stop using the sea gate to leave Kenshire's grounds unattended.

Smiling, she remembered the day workers began construction. She had asked her father about the project he'd commissioned.

"It seems I've been outwitted by a determined daughter. A new watch tower will allow her worried father a bit of peace."

The tower was one of her favorite structures at Kenshire. It had been built for her safety. She'd spent plenty of days running up its stairs to spy on the guards as they scanned the beach. She knew all the spots that were impossible to see because of the tall grass, like the one where Geoffrey had first given her a hint of pleasures to come.

Turning back toward the sound that had drawn her to this spot, she made her way through the dunes, thinking about the man she'd never see again in a few short days.

The one standing directly in front of her.

He was dressed casually in a loose tunic with rolled sleeves. It struck her with absolute certainty that she'd never be as attracted to another man in her whole life. Geoffrey Waryn, once the son of a baron, now an outlaw, was beyond compare.

When his uncle had informed her at dinner that Geoffrey

wouldn't be joining them, she'd attempted to hide her disappointment by acting the gracious hostess. Faye had sensed her true mood, however, and she hadn't argued with Sara's suggestion that they retire early. But she'd slipped out of the hall and headed toward the sea gate instead.

The reason she couldn't reconcile her marriage, the life her father had so thoughtfully planned out for her, was standing in front of her now. He was clearly surprised to see her. As he gazed at her from head to toe, his look turned sensual, and a flush crept up her face as she imagined him naked, his muscular body lifted above hers. Shivering, she remembered the sound he made as he climaxed, primal and distinctly male.

"That is precisely why I didn't dine in the hall this eve."

She knew exactly what he meant. How could she maintain her composure after what had happened between them? How could she pretend they were nothing to each other?

"If you continue to look at me thus, there's a good chance it will happen again."

Sara remained rooted in her spot, not daring to move any closer, but she said, "And that would be so bad?"

He groaned. "Aye, it would. Think of the consequences."

"I find myself caring less and less. In fact—" She was now in dangerous territory. "I'm beginning to wonder if I care at all."

His jaw set so tightly a tic formed in his lower cheek. She knew Geoffrey was at war with himself. Good, let him experience the turmoil she'd suffered these past days.

"You have no choice *but* to care."

"About Kenshire, you mean?"

"What are you implying?"

She thought of Cook's advice, of the despair she'd felt at dinner, of the feeling Geoffrey gave her every time he was near.

"I could go with you."

Saying the words sent a shiver down her back. *If Lyonsford refused to allow her out of the betrothal or the king decided to punish her, could she really forsake everything her father had built?*

"Nay, you could not."

"Why?"

"You have to ask?" Becoming more animated, Geoffrey let her know exactly what he thought of her plan.

"You would give up all of this?" He gestured to the castle above them. "The people you love, your father's legacy, Cook's hot meals, your warm, feather-stuffed bed, the *security* of a fortress such as Kenshire? For what? To be tied to a man who calls his home a bed of grass, who runs from the law, rival families, and clans of thieving Scots. You'd leave Guinevere, who wouldn't make it three days in the hills where we travel? Faye, who's like a mother to you? The families whose eyes light up when you visit them?"

While that struck a chord, she refused to back down. Once the idea had formed in her mind, it refused to budge. Of course she'd miss those things. But she wanted Geoffrey in her future—whatever form that took. It was more important to have love in her life. Passion. The ability to be herself and be valued for it.

"At best you'll be miserable. At worst, dead. Nay, Sara, it won't work," he said, shaking his head.

She would not back down. "Are you finished?"

No answer.

"You're right."

His shoulders relaxed.

"I do love these people as if they are part of my own family. A life without Harold and Alice's smiling faces or Cook's curt greetings would be bleak indeed." She reached for Geoffrey's hands, his fingers automatically winding around her own.

"But my betrothed is to a southern earl with holdings of his own. Life as I've known it, sheltered at Kenshire, is over. Most likely I'll be shuffled off to one of his other castles, lucky to visit Kenshire, which will have a new lord after some vassal to Lyonsford receives an appointment to control *my* home."

Geoffrey's relaxed stance tensed, though he didn't let go of her hands.

"Fancy dresses, fine wine … the luxuries of my station are undeniable. I'll also keep company with the knowledge of lost love, the empty feeling I had at supper when you did not come will follow me everywhere I go, intruding whether it's wanted or not."

Not sure where the words were coming from, she felt as comfortable with her speech as she did with its implications. But she wasn't finished.

"When you first walked into the hall at Kenshire Castle, I wanted nothing to do with you or your unneeded protection. I was wrong. Wrong about the kind of man you were, wrong about needing you, and wrong to despair over how little control I had over the course of my life.

"Geoffrey, I love you and want to be with you. Forever."

THEY STOOD CLOSE ENOUGH THAT Geoffrey could lean down and feel Sara's soft lips beneath his own. Her pale blue dress reflected the moonlight prettily, yet her impassioned speech reminded him of how she'd doled out a death sentence to Kenshire's traitor. Fierce and resolute, she was spectacular. He had thought her confident on the day they'd met. But this woman, the one glaring at him now, was so much more than that. She understood her own strength.

Love?

He wanted nothing more than to lean down and show her just how much her words meant. To throw her on the back of his horse, say goodbye to Kenshire, and take her with him. But if she didn't completely understand the life she'd so willingly embraced, he most certainly did. He would not ask this noble woman to ride off with him into, possibly, an unknown future.

He could tell her that. Insist he could never risk her life and explain exactly what the wife of a reiver could expect. But Geoffrey knew Sara, and she'd not accept such a practical explanation. She would insist it didn't matter when he knew it did. For her own protection, he must convince Sara to marry Lyonsford.

"I told you before, Sara. I've no wish to marry." Letting her hands go, he stepped back and waited for her reaction.

Surprisingly, she was unaffected by his admission.

"I know you think to protect me, but Geoffrey..."

Cutting her off, he changed tactics. "Nay, you mistake me, Sara. I've no wish to marry *you*."

Knowing why he did it made it no less difficult. The look she gave him very nearly changed his mind. But too much was at stake.

"You mistake desire for something more." Schooling his face into a mask of indifference, Geoffrey added, "Marry your southern lord, Lady Sara. He's the only husband for you. I'm nothing more than a failed protector who allowed his desire to interfere with a mission."

Her eyes widened. "A mission?"

"Aye, I told you that when we met. Nothing more, nothing less. One that shall be over within the next few days. And then we move on."

"I don't believe you."

He couldn't relent. Not now.

"You asked if our lovemaking was normal?"

She was backing away now, and the look in her eyes told him she was finally starting to question her convictions.

"I said it was not, but I lied. It's an act I've performed more times than I can count, and while never with such an esteemed lady such as yourself..."

"Stop!" she cried, turning from him.

He wouldn't. Her life was at stake.

"My only regret is that you mistook it for something more."

Her back was to him, but though he couldn't see her face, Geoffrey could tell by the slump in her shoulders his point was well made. When she began to run away, he stood rooted to the spot.

He and his uncle would be residing at Kenshire until her future husband arrived, but she was already out of his life forever. First he'd lost his parents, and now the only woman he'd ever loved.

Geoffrey turned toward the ocean to take that swim. At least the ice-cold water wouldn't affect him. He was already numb.

CHAPTER 25

SHE WOULD NOT MOPE. TOO proud to allow thoughts of the blackguard who'd trampled on her heart, Sara instead threw herself into the necessary preparations. She'd accepted this betrothal for her father's sake, but now she would also accept it for herself. There was no other choice.

Poor Faye didn't know what to make of her renewed energy. The next morning after mass Sara marched from chamber to chamber, giving orders to prepare not only for visitors but for a husband. The blue wedding dress her father had commissioned for her before his death was brought out to air. He had insisted on moving forward with wedding details, but Sara's heart had not been in the planning, especially as his illness progressed. Flowers were gathered and placed in every crevice of the great hall.

"Peter, do we know when the trouveres will arrive?"

Peter was clearly taken aback by the ferocity of her renewed interest in the upcoming nuptials.

"Aye, they're in the village as we speak, telling tales and entertaining as they make their way to the castle. They've been joined by Lord Edmund's own minstrel, making it quite the rowdy group."

Sara groaned. Of course Lord Edmund had sent for his personal musicians. They'd asked to stay for the wedding ceremony, and of course she'd agreed. She quite liked the man but was unsure his wife felt the same way. Of course, if she'd been forced to marry a man her father's age, she would likely feel the same.

At least Lord Lyonsford wasn't *that* old.

"Good, then they'll be here in time for the festivities."

She caught the glance between Peter and Faye.

"I would think you'd be happy I'm taking an interest in my own wedding."

Another look.

"We are, my lady, it's just..."

"You're not yourself," Peter finished.

Sara didn't think she'd ever be herself again.

"I am exactly who I need to be. Daughter of Richard Caiser, third Earl of Kenshire, Countess of Kenshire, and soon-to-be Lady Lyonsford. And that last fact is what we must concentrate on. The banns have been posted long enough and Lord Lyonsford's wishes have been conveyed by his messengers. We'll marry without delay upon his arrival."

"And then?"

She wouldn't consider it. "I'm not sure, Faye. We shall see what the new lord desires."

Without a backward glance, she made her way to the entrance, intent on speaking to Eddard about the readiness of Kenshire's stables to receive Lyonsford's party.

Sara had spent hours considering Geoffrey's words, and while part of her still disbelieved he could be so cruel, she also knew it mattered naught. She was as sheltered as he'd accused her of being, and a fool for thinking he shared her feelings. Her new lord would arrive any day. Realizing how woefully unprepared they were to receive him, Sara had decided to put the mule-headed reiver out of her thoughts for the day.

"Milady?" a small voice asked as she walked toward the stables.

Doing her best to smile, Sara stopped and greeted the young boy.

"Good day, Reginald."

He shifted from side to side. "May I ask you a question, Lady Sara?"

"Why, of course! What is it?" She could tell he was nervous and sought to reassure him. Coddling, her father would have called it. He'd done it oft enough himself to know.

"Well, I just wondered, milady, when the new lord arrives. You see, Sir Geoffrey..."

The poor boy couldn't string his thoughts together. She smiled reassuringly, though the mention of Geoffrey felt like a barb.

"Well, I didn't ask him yet, but if he agrees, that is, Sir Geoffrey..."

Sara guessed at his meaning and decided to put the squire out of his misery. "Reginald, I don't believe your father would approve of you squiring for Sir Geoffrey." She tried to let him down gently. "You'd make a fine squire to him, and Sir Geoffrey would be lucky to have you, it's just..." She stopped, seeing the disappointment on the boy's face. So young and innocent. How could she explain the complications of the world to him?

"What my lady is trying to say..." A familiar voice from behind her cut in. "Is that if your father would allow it, I'd be delighted to train you."

Oh God, no ... not so soon.

She lifted her chin, taking a deep breath.

Spinning, she glared at the man who'd trampled on her heart. "You raise his hopes, Sir Geoffrey."

Shrugging his shoulders, seemingly unconcerned, he walked closer to the wide-eyed knight in training.

"Sir Reginald, I hoped to speak with you today as I'll be leaving shortly."

No! The thought came from deep within her, deeper than all of her anger.

"If, in the future, I am in a position to have a squire as the lord of Bristol Manor, I will send for you. But," he quickly amended, "in the meantime, you must stay here and do as your new lord tells you. You've great promise with the sword," he continued, "and I'm honored to have had the opportunity to train you these past few days."

Beaming now, Reginald thanked Geoffrey profusely, bowed more than once to Sara, and nearly bounced away with pleasure.

That was the Geoffrey she knew. She could hardly reconcile it with the man who had set her aside so cruelly the previous evening. The one who had so casually disregarded her declaration of love.

They stood immobile for what seemed like an eternity. And while Geoffrey looked like he wanted to say something, he never got the chance. A bell rang loudly in the distance, heralding the arrival of someone important.

A flurry of activity confirmed the new Lord of Kenshire had arrived.

EVERYTHING SEEMED TO HAPPEN AT once. The last look Geoffrey gave Sara haunted her. Was that regret she'd seen in his eyes? But having been shuffled back into the hall and to her chamber, she hadn't been given the chance to consider anything beyond Faye's nonstop chatter.

"He wasn't due until tomorrow at the earliest. The blue or yellow? Milady, which dress do you prefer?"

She truly didn't care.

"The yellow," she said flatly, not wishing to deflate her maid's excitement.

"They're saying it's a most impressive party." Faye smoothed the dress with her nimble hands. "Lord Lyonsford at the lead, purple and gold banners fluttering, the lion crest of Lyonsford prominent. Peter said he heard they rode like the wind to get here."

"Faye, you're making me nervous."

"I'm sorry, my lady. But aren't you curious? I wonder if he's as handsome as they say. Do you know how his first wife died?"

"Nay, nor do I believe it will be a topic of conversation, so let's concentrate on something more useful."

"Such as?"

"Such as getting me into that dress so the new lord isn't left waiting."

"Oh aye, my lady. Hurry! They're coming into the hall as we speak."

How she could possibly know that, Sara wasn't sure. But, like Peter, Faye seemed to see and know everything that happened in the castle. With slightly shaking hands, Sara allowed her maid to assist her. It was time to meet her future husband.

ALL EYES WERE ON THE stairs. Lady Sara descended like a queen, her yellow dress with wide sleeves and small train of material at her heels announcing her to be every bit the noble lady that she was. Geoffrey had done the right thing.

He had no desire to be present for her initial meeting with her betrothed, but Hugh had caught him in the courtyard and dragged him into the hall. He could not think of a reason to retreat quick enough that would appease his uncle.

Lyonsford's arrival had sparked an impromptu celebration, and the great hall was bursting to capacity. It seemed as if every man and women currently residing in Kenshire was present. Flowers were everywhere, their scent overpowering all others.

It was an unusual custom to involve the entire household in important events, but from the post-Randolf meal to the arrival of Lord Lyonsford, all were welcome in Kenshire's hall.

Even border reivers.

"Just like her da," he overheard a servant standing directly in front of him say.

"Aye, only much prettier," agreed his companion. They both laughed.

The murmur quieted as Sara walked toward her new lord. Lyonsford was a tall man who looked to be about five and thirty. Though not stocky by any means, he was not as skinny as Geoffrey remembered. His light brown was graying slightly around the temples, and the man carried himself as one might expect from an earl.

Though he was the highest-ranking official in the room, the earl, helm in hand, knelt at Sara's feet on bended knee.

The humble gesture elicited sighs from what seemed like every female in the room.

Geoffrey wanted to kill the man.

It was nearly time for the most celebrated meal of the day, and he assumed Lord Lyonsford and his retinue would make their way to their chambers to refresh. It was a small party consisting of all men, knights who had likely traveled with their lord back from the Crusade, and they appeared battle-hardened but weary. Geoffrey would have admired their show of force under different circumstances.

Smiling broadly next to him, Hugh looked as pleased as he was miserable.

"A right magnificent sight, eh, boy?"

"I suppose."

"And with them, our time at Kenshire is at an end. Come, we need to talk."

Anything to escape the hall. His uncle led him through the crowd, away from the couple. Geoffrey could not stop himself from glancing back at Sara. He could swear she looked his way, but it happened so quickly he couldn't be sure.

"My son." Hugh's use of the endearment spelled trouble. "I've something to confess."

Confess?

"I'd never thought to marry again, and Lord knows I'm not in a position to do so now. But with any luck, we'll manage to take back Bristol before long, and I'll have a home to take her to."

"What in God's name are you talking about?"

"Faye."

It shouldn't have surprised him. He'd noticed how happy his uncle was here, and how he lit up whenever he saw Sara's maid. But how would his uncle support her?"Uncle, I'm happy for you, truly. The woman is a blessing to Sara, but how do you propose to support her, keep her safe until we re-take Bristol?"

Hugh shook his head. "While I haven't worked out all the details, hopefully none of the Waryn men will have the need to reive much longer."

Stunned, Geoffrey tried to take it all in.

"But how could she agree to such uncertainty? Faye is accustomed to luxuries as a lady's maid. Does she understand what life will be like on the manor of a freeman? She'll need to stay at Elmhurst until Bristol is back under our control."

Hugh looked him squarely in the eyes, as if he could see through to his soul.

"Faye is not Sara."

Geoffrey understood.

His uncle knew more than he'd let on. In that simple comment, he'd told Geoffrey not only that he trusted his judgment, but also that he'd made the right choice.

Still, this was about Hugh, not him.

He clasped his uncle on the back, genuinely happy for a man who'd endured so much for their family and asked for so little.

"Congratulations, Uncle. Does Sara know?"

"Nay. Faye planned to tell her last eve..." Lowering his voice, Hugh continued, "but the poor girl was so distraught that she didn't have the heart to break it to her. She won't like it, but I know she'll give her leave to go. She already gave Faye the choice of remaining at Kenshire or traveling south with her."

He imagined Sara leaving Kenshire with her new husband. Leaving her home, the people she loved. It would kill her. And yet it was done all the time.

If only he had something to offer her. Unfortunately, he had nothing to give.

CHAPTER 26

TWO DAYS AFTER THE LORD'S arrival, Sara prepared to become Lady Lyonsford as she stood in her wardrobe, enduring a final fitting of her royal blue wedding gown. As expected, Lord Lyonsford saw no reason for delay. He'd even brought his own priest to perform the wedding ceremony the following day. Since the betrothal had occurred by proxy, and arrangements had already been made for her dowry and inheritance, nothing stood in the way of a hasty end to their planned union.

"My lady," exclaimed Anna, a chamber maid who had just returned from Sara's bedchamber, "that be the most beautiful gown I ever saw!"

Looking down, an action which brought a swift tug from the tailor, Sara had to agree.

"Aye, 'tis lovely, Anna." Lined in soft white fur, the deep blue gown trailed longer than any other she owned. Its sleeves were low-hanging, and jewels were sewn into the silver belt that lay below her hips. It was indeed a garment fit for a queen.

"Done," announced the tailor, a thin, pompous man. He'd arrived with Lord Lyonsford's retinue to put some final touches on the gown Peter had commissioned him at Lord Richard's request. Occupied with Randolf and later Geoffrey, Sara supposed she was grateful her staff had continued to prepare for the wedding, even if she did not.

Stepping out of the gown, assisted by Faye and Anna, Sara changed into a simple brown kirtle, the color a shade lighter than her hair, and made her way into the bedchamber. Sara sat on the bed and ran her hands along the soft fabric of the coverlet, wondering what to take with her on her journey south.

Grateful for the privacy, she thought back over the last two long, miserable days. Her new lord, courteous and pleasing to the eye, was younger than she'd expected and more accommodating than she could have hoped for. After the wedding, they would travel to Archbald, only forty miles outside London. Lyonsford assured her that they'd spend little time in one place—and he'd promised they would visit Kenshire at least once per year.

"I can tell it pleases my lady and, therefore, shall please me as well," he'd said. The day after his arrival they had sat together for nearly two hours, discussing the terms of their marriage, specifics of the betrothal, and plans for their future. With any luck she had hidden her true feelings well. When he'd asked if she was happy with the arrangement, a question many in his position wouldn't have considered, Sara felt compelled to assure him that she was.

"Aye, very pleased."

"That's not much of an answer, if I may be so bold, Lady Sara."

She had to do better. "Though Randolf is no longer a threat, Kenshire is very much at risk from border skirmishes. Your lord's reputation is esteemed, so yes, I look forward to becoming Lady Lyonsford."

Several moments passed without a response, and Sara started to think she'd said something grievously wrong. She was trying to decide whether or not to amend her statements when he finally broke his silence.

"Then we shall join our households two days hence."

He took her hand. Feeling like a traitor, she allowed it. She couldn't help but compare his touch to another—and find it lacking.

"As you know, I was married once. My wife, God rest her soul, died in childbirth."

Sara knew all too well the complications and dangers of birthing.

"A kind, gentle woman, she taught me much about being a

good husband. And I vow to you, Lady Sara, you'll want for nothing as my wife."

Touched, Sara squeezed his hand. "I'll do my best to make you a good wife."

Sara knew love was not required for two people to wed. And for the first time in her life, she was glad for it. She doubted she could ever love again.

She'd not seen Geoffrey since the day Lord Lyonsford arrived, resplendent in his livery. The contrast between the men was evident. One, a great lord with vast lands and an army at his disposal … the other, a deposed baron who lived humbly, forced to fight and plunder for his next meal.

Upon reflection, Sara wasn't convinced Geoffrey had meant those harsh words he'd said to her on the beach. Something told her that he had thought she still needed protecting—this time from him. Faye was engaged to marry his uncle, something that had pleased but not surprised her, and she could not help but reflect on the similarities between uncle and nephew. Both were natural protectors, both put other people before themselves.

It mattered not.

The events set in motion before her father's death had finally come to fruition. A subdued evening meal and final preparations for the wedding feast were all that stood between her and an exchange of vows with her new husband.

A loud, insistent knock on her chamber door interrupted her thoughts.

So much for a moment of privacy.

"Milady, come quick!" The frantic knock brought her stumbling across the room.

Peter wasted no time with pleasantries. "The king's banner has been spied in the village coming this way."

"The king, truly?"

"His banner. It appears to be a royal messenger as there are just two men." With that, Peter hurried toward the spiral staircase, no doubt eager to ensure everything was ready for the unexpected visitors.

Sara's momentary shock gave way to curiosity. Why would King Henry send messengers to Kenshire?

There was no sign of Faye and Anna, and since she did not have time to change without assistance, she took a deep blue overcoat out of the trunk at her bed and pulled it over her kirtle. Smoothing her hair with a few quick strokes of the brush, she pinched her cheeks and left her bedchamber.

She found her maids in the hall, where the trestle tables that had been already set for the meal were being hurriedly put away. Eddard rushed up to Sara as she took her place on the dais. She was about to receive a royal party—while not a new occurrence at Kenshire Castle, it was certainly a rare one.

Luckily the hall and its antechambers had already been prepared for the following day's festivities. Mint-scented rushes, flowers of all varieties, new candles, polished torches, and freshly washed tapestries gave Kenshire's great hall a warm, inviting atmosphere.

Sara breathed in and out deeply, discreetly, looking down at her folded hands. "Where are the new guests now?" she asked Eddard.

"They had already entered the main gate when we received word."

She looked toward the source of the deep voice that had answered her question. Though it had been just two days, it felt like a lifetime.

The look Geoffrey gave her sent chills down her back. It was one of unbridled lust. Mayhap he *had* spoken honestly when he'd claimed to simply desire her. God help her, if he continued to look at her that way, she couldn't bring herself to care.

Looking away, Sara scanned the room. There was no sign of Lord Lyonsford among the crowd, so she inquired to his whereabouts.

"He rides to Kenshire Village, my lady," one of his men said, "inspecting the demesne and its surroundings."

Of course he'd want to see more of the property she brought to the marriage.

"He's been sent for?"

"Yes, my lady," the man replied.

All eyes turned toward the hall entrance as Peter escorted the newcomers into the hall and toward Sara's large, ornate seat on the dais.

"Lady Sara, may I present Walter Gregory de Roquesle and Henry le Galeys, royal messengers from the court of King Henry III of England, Lord of Ireland and Duke of Aquitaine."

Both men fell on one knee in unison, honoring the highest-ranking noble in the room: her.

"The honor is mine," she said. "Please rise."

Lord, please give me my father's strength.

GEOFFREY KNEW SARA WASN'T QUITE as calm as she appeared. The slight lift of her chin meant she was worried.

After two days of avoiding her, two days of hell, Geoffrey had begun to question his decision. Could he truly just walk away, allow her to marry another man, and return to his life before Kenshire Castle? Did he have any other choice?

For five years, Geoffrey had thought about nothing but revenge on the men who had slaughtered his parents and stolen his home. These days, he thought mostly of this woman who was trying so hard to live up to her father's legacy. He watched as she left the hall to speak privately with two royal messengers.

When he'd first learned of their approach, he had felt an alarmingly strong sense of panic. Did they pose some sort of threat to Sara?

"Sir Geoffrey?"

Lady Maude. He'd not seen her since her return to Kenshire. He knew she and her husband, Lord Edmund, often visited Kenshire. Despite the conversation he'd witnessed between Maude and John, Sara had insisted it wasn't possible Maude or her husband were involved in Randolf's plot. Her father had known Lord Edmund as a loyal vassal his entire life.

Still, something was not quite right with the woman.

Bowing slightly, he gestured toward the wall, a slightly more private spot.

"I'd like to speak with you regarding a very delicate matter," the lady said. "I've heard 'twas you who saved Lady Sara's life."

Not wanting to discuss the event in more detail, he asked her directly, "How were *you* involved, Lady Maude?"

The woman looked taken aback. "Involved? In Randolf's plot? Nay, never."

"Then how may I be of service?"

"I wasn't involved, but I did want to speak with you about the incident. You see … I … I was unfaithful to my husband," she blurted out.

What the hell did that have to do with him? Or Sara?

"With Randolf?" It was the only possible explanation that came to mind.

"Nay! Shhhhh." She darted her eyes in either direction.

"What does this have to do with Randolf's plot to inherit Kenshire?"

A flush crept up her cheeks, turning both of her delicate ears red. Her story finally came tumbling out. "John caught me and … you know."

"Your lover?"

She winced, clearly not appreciating his choice of words.

"He caught us in the buttery and attempted to blackmail me with the information. He said, 'All you need to do is flirt with…' Well, you."

He caught on quickly. "When you refused, he threatened to expose your secret, at which point you left Kenshire."

She grabbed his arm, almost frantic. "I thought the servant mayhap had a tender for the lady. Was jealous perhaps? I wanted to tell Lady Sara, but she seemed so preoccupied. I was never able to get her alone."

He was about to ask why she had felt the need to share her story with him, but a commotion demanded their attention. The new lord had returned. As he'd done many times over the past two days, he involuntarily imagined the man in bed with Sara.

Turning back to the young woman, he tried to figure out her purpose. "Why are you sharing this information with me, Lady Maude?"

"I know you're very close with Lady Sara, and I hoped you could relay my story to her. Had I any inkling he was planning harm milady, I'd have come to her immediately, my reputation be damned."

He believed her. The poor woman was nearly in tears.

"But another reason, if I may be so bold."

Geoffrey glared at the retreating back of Lyonsford, who was currently making his way out of the hall. He was barely listening now.

"I tell you because I had no choice but to marry a man more than twice my age."

That got Geoffrey's attention.

"To live without love or passion. Well, I'm sorry to see Lady Sara in such a position."

With that statement, Lady Maude let go of his arm, looking down at it in surprise, as if she didn't remember grabbing ahold of it.

"I fear she's about to make the same mistake."

Cocking his head, considering the woman in a different light, Geoffrey imagined what her marriage must be like for her. Lord Edmund was old enough to be her grandfather. He shuddered at the thought of the elderly man touching her.

And then he realized what the lady was implying.

"Are you saying she has a choice?"

Lifting her immense and impractical gown, bedecked with more jewels than he'd ever seen on Sara, she answered with as much conviction as someone her age could muster. "She's an earl's daughter, is she not?"

Lady Maude took her leave, and he could only stare after her as she walked away. Sara *had* attempted to make a choice. One he didn't necessarily agree with. The thought of Sara near the borderlands terrified him. He couldn't take a chance Lyonsford would simply accept her change of heart or that the king would take kindly to a change in plans. But being without her terrified him even more.

CHAPTER 27

STILL IN SHOCK, SARA WATCHED as her wooden tub was filled with precious hot water that had been heated meticulously over the open fire in the kitchen. Marveling at the number of attendants it took to fill the tub, Sara thanked each one profusely. It was an arduous task, but one she appreciated.

"Ye need not fall at their feet, milady. 'Tis their job to fill a tub for you."

Faye, still tentative around Sara since breaking the news about her engagement to Hugh, scented the water with chamomile and lemon balm, laying out a basin filled with sponges and scented soap.

"Thank you, Faye." Sara stepped out of her chemise and into the tub.

"Yer obviously not listening to me." Making her way to the tub, Faye bent down to assist her lady.

"Nay, I can manage. I'd like to be alone, please."

Faye pulled a small stool to the side of the tub, placing the wash basin beside it.

"Very well. I'll be along to prepare you for bed then."

Sara reached for the soap. "For the remainder of the evening, Faye. I've much to consider."

Faye made a sound which relayed her displeasure. The way she threw the kindling into the fire left little doubt she was upset. "In that case, I leave you to your bath, my lady. Shall I send for it to be retrieved?"

"Nay, leave it. I've no wish to be disturbed. And Faye?" Looking into the eyes of the woman she loved like a mother, Sara added, "I'm just overwhelmed."

Her maid's lips turned up slightly, and Sara knew she'd done her job.

"I'll ensure his lordship and our guests have settled for the night and see you in the morn. Tomorrow is a big day!"

"Good eve, Faye. And thank you."

Smiling more broadly, Faye straightened her shoulders and walked toward the door.

"'Tis my job, milady."

She wasn't surprised Faye had managed to get the final word. She was good at making her point in any way possible. A quality Sara would sorely need.

LOWERING HERSELF IN THE BLESSED warmth of the tub, Sara breathed deeply. After relaying their message, the royal attendants had agreed to stay the night. The message they bore had been a note from the king congratulating her and Lord Lyonsford on their coming nuptials. Seeing that note had made it real—and that had changed everything.

Not surprisingly, Geoffrey had been absent for the evening meal, a good thing under the circumstances. Sara had spent most of the evening speaking with her betrothed.

Even now, hours later, she could hardly believe what had transpired after her brief meeting with the king's messengers. Shivering despite the water's heat, Sara was reaching for the sponge Faye had left for her when a loud noise startled her from behind. Shattering the quiet of her chamber, the door swung open and closed just as swiftly.

What the devil?

"What are you doing here?"

Striding toward her as if he belonged in her chamber at this late hour, Geoffrey lifted the basin and sat on the stool beside her.

Instead of answering, he held out his hand for the sponge she was currently dangling in mid-air.

Handing it to him, she asked again, "What are you doing in my chamber?"

No answer. "Sit up." Geoffrey commanded.

Sara did as he asked, exposing her back to him. She jumped at the first touch of the sponge on her back.

Finally, the deep voice she'd craved to hear these past days answered. "I came to bathe you, of course."

Does he know? Nay, it's not possible.

"How did you get past the guards?"

The sponge moved across her body, dipping into the scented water periodically.

Glad that she was not looking at his face—she couldn't resist him if she did that—she finally remembered why they hadn't spoken since Lyonsford's arrival.

"You've made it clear what you want from me, *Sir* Geoffrey. Under the circumstances, I'm afraid I'm unavailable to be at your beck and call when your *need* arises."

His hand moved to her lower back, deep beneath the water, moving in a slow, circular motion.

"Furthermore, it was you who insisted this could not happen again."

Dropping the sponge, he splayed his hand across her hip, inching it between her legs.

"You mean *this*?"

His fingers plunged inside her, and God help her, she allowed it. They dipped in and out as she lifted her hips to meet them.

"Aye, precisely."

Forgetting her anger, she closed her eyes and dropped her head back onto the rim of the large tub. His fingers moved expertly against her with increasing speed.

She opened her eyes to find Geoffrey staring at her, his ice-blue eyes hooded with desire. He wanted, nay, needed her as much as she needed him. Of that there was no doubt.

Leaning over the tub, Geoffrey took her lips, not giving her any time to adjust. His tongue plunged in and out of his mouth with the same rhythm as his fingers. Water splashed around them. Sara was unaware of anything other than the building of sensations until she pushed against his hand and felt the shattering sensation of release. His fingers were squeezed beneath hers as she groaned.

"Yes…" he whispered. His mouth moved to her ear and his tongue nipped the sensitive skin there.

Her eyes nearly popped out of her head when Geoffrey stood and began to disrobe.

"What are you doing?"

"What does it look like?"

If she weren't worried about someone barging in on them at any moment, Sara could almost appreciate the irony of the situation, given the current state of affairs.

"It looks like you're disrobing, which doesn't make sense since I'm extremely angry with you. Someone could come along at any minute and, oh, that's right … I'm supposed to be married tomorrow."

Just as before, Geoffrey did not see fit to answer her. Instead he stripped off his shirt, revealing the broad, tanned shoulders beneath.

Then came the breeches. He stood completely naked before her, his imposing manhood on full display.

And then he actually climbed into the tub with her.

"You can't be serious!"

As if to prove otherwise, Geoffrey positioned his knees on either side of her beneath the still warm water and leaned forward, grasping the edges of the tub with each hand.

"I'm deadly serious, Sara. So listen carefully."

Her heart would surely stop beating.

"I'm going to make love to you. And afterward, we're going to get out, dry off, and lay in your bed to discuss exactly what that means. But for now, please try to forget about everything except the feel of my cock sliding deep inside you."

This time, Sara's response was to lean forward and take his mouth with hers. She'd never wanted anything more in her life.

THE MOMENT HE OPENED THE door to her chamber and saw her in the tub, Geoffrey's intentions for coming to Sara that eve had been completely forgotten. Hardening immediately, he'd thought of nothing other than being inside of her. The accusing look she'd given him had made him reconsider—mayhap it would be best to start from the beginning, explaining his presence and begging for forgiveness. But the sight of her warm, wet body was too alluring.

Their talk could wait.

Poised above her in the tub, he guided his tip to her opening, teasing his way inside. Sara reached behind him, grasped his buttocks with both hands, and closed her fingers around him.

He filled her with one thrust, and Sara pulled him closer still. Letting out a groan of pleasure, he relished the feeling a moment longer before moving.

Thrusting with increasing speed, his knuckles turning white as they grasped the side of the tub, Geoffrey vaguely heard the sound of water splashing on the floor.

"Sara." His voice was thick with desire.

Sara met his every thrust with one of her own, her hips pushing toward him.

"Please, Geoffrey," she begged. Sara had clearly forgotten, at least for the moment, that she was thoroughly vexed with him.

Relishing the sound of his name on her lips, he gave her what she asked for. Reaching below the water with one hand, his knees supporting his weight, Geoffrey found the nub and pressed and circled it with his thumb.

Getting closer to his peak, he pulled out almost completely, leaving only the tip inside her, and ever so slowly re-entered her tight sheath.

A low groan told him to repeat the gentle teasing, and he did. This time he pressed harder with his thumb, and when her hands squeezed tightly around his buttocks, pulling him closer still, Geoffrey knew she was near her release. He removed his hand to plunge deep into her.

Sara's hands squeezed tighter around his buttocks as she began to pulse around him. The sensations were too much. Geoffrey spilled his seed deep inside her.

"Ahh God." He held still then, both he and Sara continuing to throb as they remained joined. Shuddering, he lowered his mouth, brushing his lips to hers.

"How do you feel?"

Closing her eyes, she released him and laid her head against the back of the tub. "Well-pleasured."

"That makes two of us."

Standing, the awkward position becoming hard on his knees, Geoffrey looked down at the noblewoman beneath him.

How could he have ever imagined he'd let her go?

Climbing out of the tub, he grabbed the nearby drying cloth. "Do you mind?"

"Kind of you to ask at least." Finally, blessedly, she smiled. "Nay, I don't mind."

He dried quickly, then reached out a hand to Sara and pulled her up next to him. Giving into temptation under the guise of drying her off, Geoffrey used the cloth to touch every inch of her body.

Once they were both thoroughly dry, Geoffrey lifted Sara up in one swift movement, carried her to the bed, and pulled back the covers with his free hand. After laying her down in the middle of the bed, Geoffrey stretched out beside her and covered them both with the blankets. Although the fire in the hearth warmed the large chamber considerably, the crisp autumn air made its way inside nonetheless.

Unaccustomed to intimacy beyond the sex act, he positioned a pillow behind him and lay with his face just inches from her breasts. Lord help him, it was a tempting sight.

Propping herself on one elbow, Sara got straight to the point. "What was that?"

"Well, my lady, some call it breeding, others lovemaking, and still others, though much cruder..."

"You can stop there. What exactly are you doing in my chamber, seducing me in my bath after telling me ... let me get this right. 'My only regret is that you mistook it for something more.'"

Wincing at the sound of his harsh words, which he'd regretted almost since the instant he'd uttered them, he gestured around the large chamber. "A four-poster bed with feathered pillows, rich tapestries, a hot bath, for God's sake." But he'd come here to ask a question, and ask he would. "You'd really risk giving all this up?"

Sara sat up then, her barely toweled hair still damp and curling in waves around her, and looked him squarely in the eyes.

He knew before she answered.

Or thought he did, for the answer she gave him was so unexpected Geoffrey could only stare, dumbfounded.

CHAPTER 28

"I DON'T NEED TO."

She'd changed her mind? Of course, how could he have been foolish enough to think otherwise? Good sense had prevailed.

Pushing back the coverlet, he began to rise when Sara pulled him back.

"Nay, you misunderstand."

It was his turn to play the indignant, spurned lover. "What exactly do I misunderstand? That you hinted you might consider giving up your life as a countess to be my wife? What is it that I misunderstand, Sara?"

Clenching his jaw, looking back at the beautiful, proud earl's daughter, he cursed himself for a fool.

She calmly replied, her hand still on his arm. "I don't need to choose between you and Kenshire. There'll be no wedding tomorrow."

That got his attention.

"When the king's messenger arrived with his congratulations on my marriage to Lyonsford, it finally became real."

"It?"

"The wedding, the marriage. I mean, I wore my wedding dress for a fitting. Of course I knew the wedding was real. It's just … I don't know. Something about the missive jolted me. It was so final."

"As most weddings tend to be."

"And I should have been terrified at the thought of angering the king's council. After all, the marriage was sanctioned."

"Was?"

"Was." Her beautiful face stared straight at him. "I sent a return message, thanking King Henry for his well wishes, but informing him I would not be marrying the Earl of Archbald."

He knew what she was saying but had a hard time grasping it. Could this be true?

"I spoke with the earl, who is already on his way home. And none too happy, if truth be told."

"The ramifications, Sara..."

"I know them well. But Lyonsford was placated slightly when he realized he'd be adding Caiser's only southern holding to his own."

"You gave him Lincoln."

"I did. And relinquished two other properties back to the crown to appease the king over my broken betrothal. My father's holdings are sizably smaller this evening."

She was looking at him with such apprehension that he suddenly remembered his original purpose.

"I'm sorry, Sara."

"For what?"

"For everything. For not trusting you to make your own decisions. For pushing you away."

He reached across the bed to hold her hands.

"I came here tonight to tell you that I could never allow you to marry Lyonsford, or any man, consequences be damned. You're mine." He lifted a hand to his lips, kissed it, and turned it around to kiss her palm. Her wrist.

"You've been mine since the day you walked down the stairs, more beautiful and proud than any woman I'd ever met. I just didn't know it then." He smiled. "But it's good to know I don't have to steal you tonight."

"*Steal* me?"

He had never heard Sara shriek before.

"There was no way you were getting married to Lyonsford tomorrow. I love you, Sara. The only husband you'll be taking is this border reiver, for better or worse."

Sara blessedly threw her arms around him.

"I love you, Geoffrey. And I take back what I said. You *are* a reiver."

"Not for long." He was having a hard time thinking straight with Sara's naked body pressed against his own.

"To me, always. You most definitely stole my heart."

Before he gave into temptation, he wanted to be sure she understood.

"Sara. Will you be my wife?"

"I thought you had an aversion to getting married."

"I thought so too, before I met you."

"Well then, my answer is yes."

"In that case," he grinned wickedly, "let's seal it with a kiss."

To which his saucy future bride responded, "Let's seal it with something more than that."

Geoffrey made love to the woman who would be his wife, secure with the knowledge their adventures were just beginning.

EPILOGUE

WITH THE WEDDING BEHIND THEM, and Geoffrey's siblings and extended family permanently residing at Kenshire, Sara sat with her new brother-in-law at the chess table after supper one evening.

"I understand you've had some good news today."

"Aye." Bryce considered his next move, serious as ever. "We've been granted permission from the crown to attack."

Sara frowned, unable to muster much enthusiasm at that news.

"Geoffrey said as much at dinner. I'm happy for you, of course, but..." Trailing off, Sara couldn't quite finish the thought.

Since the wedding preparations had already been underway for her marriage to Lyonsford and Geoffrey couldn't keep his hands off his future wife, they'd posted the banns and married without delay. Her people, it seemed, were as happy as she was, from Faye and Hugh, who would no longer need to leave Kenshire, to the squire Reginald, who followed Geoffrey everywhere he went.

Though pleased with his new squire, Geoffrey had refused to bring the lad to Bristol. Which meant it would be as dangerous a mission as she suspected.

"I don't suppose you'll listen to reason, Bryce. Are you sure 'tis necessary to wage a war to take back a home which will be all but impossible to keep?"

She'd had the same argument countless times with her husband. *Her husband.* The thought made her smile as she watched

Geoffrey across the hall with his sister. When she caught his gaze, he winked at her, the glint in his eye evident even from this distance. Her body tingled in anticipation.

"'Tis our home and Geoffrey's birthright. Or mine now," Bryce amended. Geoffrey planned to fight alongside his sibling, Kenshire's men, and the men whom William, steward of Camburg, had committed to the battle. But when Bristol was won, Bryce would be the new lord of the manor.

She understood, almost having lost her own home more than once, but she was also terrified for Geoffrey's safety.

Though serious to a fault, Bryce was free with praise for his brother."Try not to worry, my lady. No man is as cunning or as skilled as Geoffrey."

She knew it well, having seen him in action. But it was kind of Bryce to attempt to allay her fears. She'd gotten to know Geoffrey's siblings well over the past weeks, and she'd discovered a strange soft spot for the reticent second son.

Attempting to distract herself from the thought of Geoffrey in battle, Sara switched topics. "Has Geoffrey given up on his attempt as matchmaker?"

Bryce's fierce scowl deepened, if such a thing was possible. "I know he means well, but my thirst for revenge is still what keeps me awake at night. I've no need for a wife."

Smiling, Sara considered his words. The brothers were more similar than they realized. "It seems I've heard that argument before." She watched as her reformed reiver made his way toward them. Her pulse began to race.

"Some things are sweeter than revenge."

Looking doubtful, Bryce stood, pausing their game for now.

"I'll take your word for it."

Sara watched him go. Mayhap he could someday find the happiness she had with his brother.

Geoffrey reached down to pull his new bride toward him. "I find I'm in need of attention, wife." He kissed her thoroughly, and Sara melted against the man who had stolen her heart.

"As always, husband," she teased, setting aside thoughts of her in-laws' future to enjoy the present.

For their stories were just beginning.

ACKNOWLEDGMENTS

I'd like to thank my husband for his endless patience and support. From starting the tub while I sneak in a few chapters or entertaining the loves of my life while I escape to Starbucks to edit, he is my real-life knight in shining armor.

Thank you to my mother and siblings who are not allowed to read *The Thief's Countess* due to graphic content. With any luck someone will tell them I've acknowledged them in this book.

Twenty years ago when research was conducted in the library instead of the internet, I began writing this book and am grateful for so many people that helped turn a dream into reality. Madeline Martin, Emma Prince and Keira Montclair came into my life at the time I needed each most. Thank you to my amazing editor, Angela Polidoro, whose input has been invaluable. I'd also like to thank Kim Killion for designing the best version of a book cover imaginable.

And to all those who have lent support and continue to do so including business partner, my Diva girls and all of my family and friends who have endured years of listening to me talk of knights and castles . . . thank you.

Last but not least, thank you Border Ambassadors and readers for enjoying *The Thief's Countess* and spreading the word about the Border Series. I look forward to sharing more stories that allow you to step back in time just as my favorite authors have allowed me to do for so many years.

ABOUT THE AUTHOR

Cecelia Mecca is the author of medieval romance and has loved all things medieval England and the romance genre for as long as she can remember.

Though her actual home is in Northeast Pennsylvania where she lives with her husband and two children, her online home is at **www.CeceliaMecca.com**.

You can also connect with Cecelia on Twitter **@CeceliaMecca**, on Facebook at **www.facebook.com/ceceliamecca** or via email at **info@ceceliamecca.com**.

She would love to hear from you.

Made in the USA
Middletown, DE
05 March 2017